Zaharo
Clark
Nonna
Cedric

Jeffrey
Bernard
Victoria
Characters

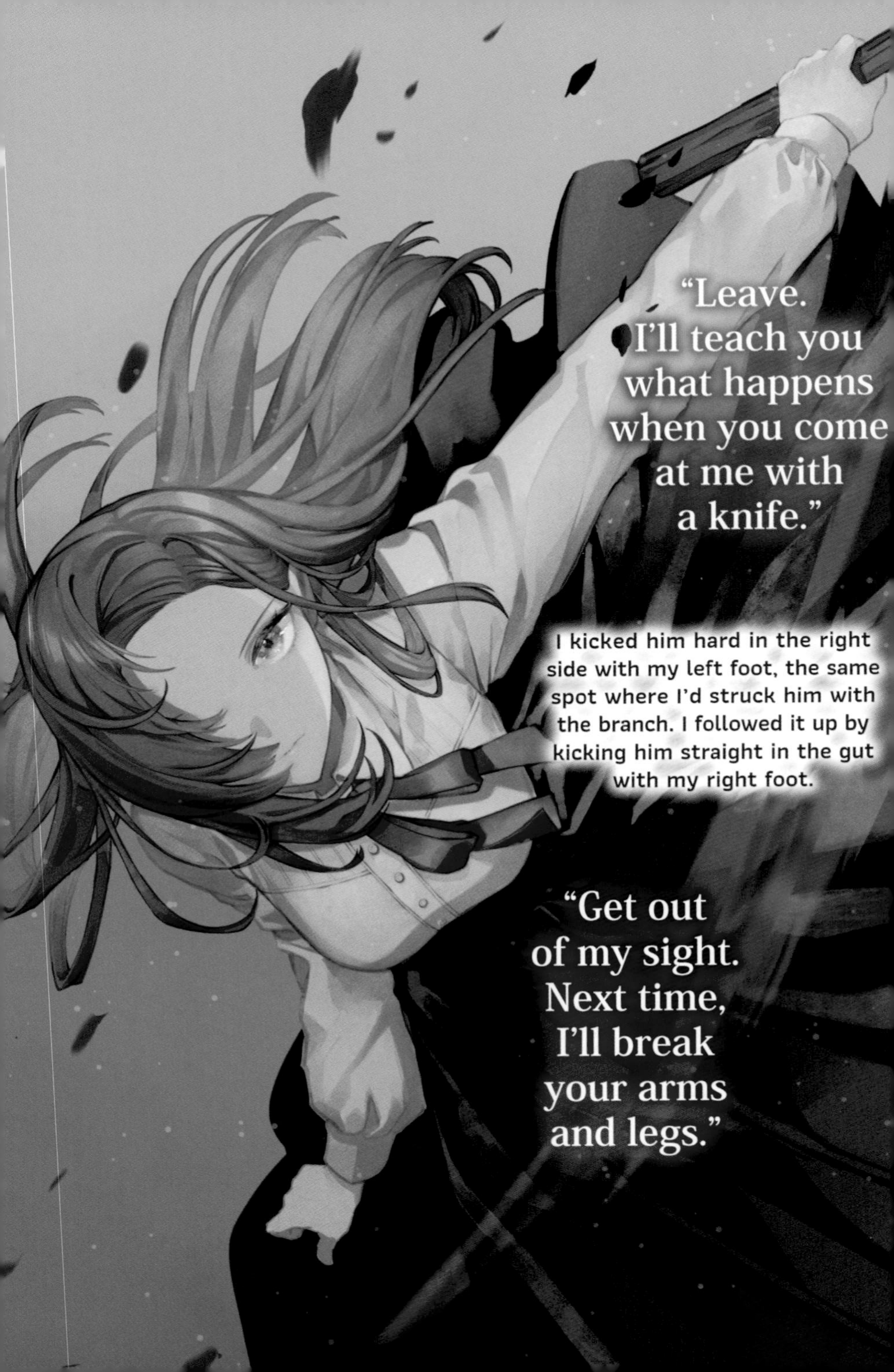
"Leave.
I'll teach you
what happens
when you come
at me with
a knife."
I kicked him hard in the right side with my left foot, the same spot where I'd struck him with the branch. I followed it up by kicking him straight in the gut with my right foot.
"Get out
of my sight.
Next time,
I'll break
your arms
and legs."

01

Syuu

Illustration by

Nanna Fujimi

New York

Syuu

Translation by Andria McKnight
Cover art by Nanna Fujimi

Yen On
150 West 30th Street, 19th Floor
New York, NY 10001

Visit us at yenpress.com
facebook.com/yenpress • twitter.com/yenpress
yenpress.tumblr.com • instagram.com/yenpress

First Yen On Edition: September 2024
Edited by Yen On Editorial: Maya Deutsch, Rachel Mimms
Designed by Yen Press Design: Liliana Checo, Wendy Chan

Yen On is an imprint of Yen Press, LLC.
The Yen On name and logo are trademarks of Yen Press, LLC.

The publisher is not responsible for websites (or their content) that are not owned by the publisher.

Library of Congress Cataloging-in-Publication Data is available.

ISBNs: 978-1-9753-9074-7 (paperback)
978-1-9753-9075-4 (ebook)

10 9 8 7 6 5 4 3 2 1

LSC-C

Printed in the United States of America

World Map
Royal Capital
Kingdom of Subartu
Kingdom of Ashbury
Kingdom of Randall
Kingdom of Hagl
Western Forest
Royal Capital
Farm
Duchy
Fishing Village
Haydn
Cadiz

Victoria of Many Faces 01

CONTENTS

Presented by Syuu

Prologue

Carefully Laid Plans

Chloe, covert agent of the kingdom of Hagl. That was how I was known within the organization.

I was at my favorite place, the edge of a cliff facing the sea. I spread my picnic blanket on the ground and placed a rock on each corner to prevent it from blowing away in the wind. I opened the picnic basket. Just then, the old farmer who always passed by here this time of day called out to me from his wagon.

I waved to him. Surely, he would remember my presence here now.

I nibbled off a piece of my sandwich, poured some tea in my cup, and set it down on the blanket. After confirming there was no one around to see, I lay face down on the edge of the cliff, reached out my arm, and tangled the string from my hat around the branch of a pine tree that'd grown just below.

I kicked off my sandals and tossed them at the rocky shore at the bottom of the cliff. Then I removed my cherished pendant, refastened the clasp, and hurled it with all my might toward the same place as my sandals.

"That should do it."

There was no reason to stay here any longer. I took my boots out from my bag and put them on before turning from the cliff and walking to the mountain on the other side of the road. I wouldn't come back here again.

I was leaving behind both my favorite place in the world, and my life as a spy.

That same night, the central control room of the kingdom of Hagl's Special Operations Force was buzzing.

"Dan, can you go to the Matool cliffs? And investigate the shore below once morning comes. Jacob, check with the security force to see if there's any new information."

Chief Lancome watched the two men hurry out of the room, then pressed a hand against his temple as he let out a sigh.

"Chloe goes to the Matool cliffs a lot, doesn't she, Lancome?"

"That she does, Mary. Despite the many times I've told her not to, since there isn't any fencing."

Mary covered her mouth. "I wonder what happened to her?"

"She's fine. She's gotta be. I'm sending them to check on her, just in case."

"She was quite shocked when she heard you and I got married, you know."

"Knock it off. That's not true. Plus, we still don't know if anything's happened to Chloe."

"Yes, but it's late, and she hasn't come back yet."

It was almost eight o'clock at night. The cliffs would be pitch-dark by now.

"Don't worry," Lancome said. "There has to be some kind of mistake. Chloe's strong."

He slid his arm behind Mary's back and gently patted it to comfort her—the Chloe he knew was a resilient woman who never showed a hint of weakness.

I changed carriages several times to avoid being followed, took a detour, and boarded a long-distance private omnibus.

I hid my chestnut-colored hair beneath a gaudy red wig, caked on my makeup, and padded my blouse to the brim. Then I drew a mole next to my mouth for good measure. With that, my sexy, good-time-gal disguise was complete.

There were five passengers in the omnibus, including me. All the other riders were men. My every expression and gesture oozed sex appeal, and I caught them frequently stealing glances at me. One of them, a middle-aged man, had the courage to speak up.

"Where are you headin', miss? Must be somewhere important if you're on a long-distance omnibus this early in the morn'."

"Yes, quite. My mother's ill, and I'm going to visit her. She lives alone; I'm ever so worried."

"Hmm, that's a shame."

Now all the men were listening intently.

"Honestly, I'm very concerned, but there's no use in fretting over it. I'm just trying not to think negatively." I pulled a silver hip flask out of my bag.

"Hey, that's a nice flask ya got there. What's in it, liquor?"

"Right you are. I know it's first thing in the morning, but we're in for a long trip. You boys care for any?" My matte silver flask was filled with a special spirit even stronger than ordinary calvados. "Go ahead and help yourselves," I said and, much to the men's delight, passed the flask around for them to take sips. When it was my turn, I touched the opening with my lips and only pretended to drink.

Before long, some of the passengers were cheerfully muttering to themselves, while others were dead silent because they'd fallen fast asleep. This would ensure that they would only have the briefest recollection of our encounter.

When they'd try to think back on it, all they'd remember was my thick makeup, beauty mark, and red hair. Oh, and my ample bosom, I'm sure.

* * *

Late that night, I got off at Thurston and started to walk. I would travel from here and enter the neighboring kingdom of Randall.

I was able to pass through the border checkpoint thanks to the fake identification papers I'd forged. According to the documents, I was a redheaded woman named Maria. The name was an alias, of course.

The moment I entered Randall, I sneaked away from any prying eyes and took off my wig. I used makeup-remover liquid to quickly wipe away my thick cosmetics and the beauty mark by my mouth, then removed the padding from my blouse and stowed it away in my bag.

I gave myself a quick check using my compact mirror. Once I stepped out from the shadows, the sexy redheaded bombshell Maria was gone, replaced by a woman in the same outfit with chestnut-brown hair.

After arriving safely in Randall, I boarded the first of many carriages I would be taking. Since the carriages didn't travel overnight, I had to spend the evening in a hotel. All in all, it took me twenty days to cross Randall like this and enter the neighboring kingdom of Ashbury.

I crossed the border using a different set of identification papers, which were for a woman named Victoria Sellars.

Victoria Sellars was a real person who lived in the kingdom of Randall, but she had gone missing. She was the same age as me, and we shared a physical resemblance, but she had no other special characteristics. She'd been missing for ten years now, and her family was scattered all over.

When I first saw her missing person report, I'd thought, *I could use her someday*, but I'd never imagined at the time that this was how I would do so. On paper, it would look like Victoria Sellars had left the country.

Chloe the spy no longer existed in this world. I had every intention of living my life as Victoria from now on. On her identification papers,

I had filled in my own details in the physical characteristics column: brown hair, brown eyes, age twenty-seven, height 165 centimeters.

The real Victoria was slightly shorter than me. Of course, I was in a different kingdom now, so no one could tell that my identification papers from Randall were anything but legitimate.

And so I, Victoria Sellars, left the border and went straight into a restaurant.

"Good morning. What can I get you?"

"Coffee, pancakes, two sausages, and fried eggs, please. Oh, that'll be two eggs over easy."

"Got it. Take a seat wherever you'd like."

After I finished ordering, I chose a corner table and sat with my back facing the wall, then let out a sigh. By this time, everyone at my old job probably thought I'd either fallen off the cliff or jumped.

"Sorry for the wait."

The waitress set down a cup of fresh, steaming hot coffee, sizzling sausages with a nice bit of char on them, and a stack of steamy pancakes with a wad of butter in the center that was already starting to melt. The eggs were over easy. My order also came with a tiny glass pitcher that was filled to the brim with maple syrup.

I poured the entire pitcher over my pancakes, picked up my knife and fork, and began greedily devouring my breakfast. It had been a year since I first started preparing to leave the organization, and eight months since I'd started restricting my food intake.

"*Haah*, absolutely delicious. Now I can eat whatever I want."

The reason I'd kept to such a strict diet was because I needed to play the part of a heartbroken, jilted woman. I'd been absolutely starving the entire time. At one point, Lancome was so worried about me, he made me take medicine that would stimulate my appetite. The hunger pangs had been extreme, but I hung in there. I dropped eight kilograms in eight months.

But now I could finally eat as much as I pleased.

I took my time and savored every morsel of my meal, which was large enough to satisfy even a man's appetite, then walked through the capital city and headed for a hotel. I needed to regain my muscle tone as quickly as possible.

Finally, I entered a large hotel on a main street and went up to the counter.

"Hello, I sent a letter about making a reservation. The name's Victoria Sellars."

"Ah, yes. We've been waiting for you, Ms. Sellars. Your room is on the third floor—a corner suite, just as you requested."

I would use this hotel as my base of operations for the time being to prepare for my new life. I had many cards I could play here, so I was going to take it slowly. I threw myself on the bed with a *plop*.

I wondered if Chief Lancome would continue looking for me. I'd crossed two whole kingdoms to get here to Ashbury; would he really extend the search this far? Or would he give up straight away?

"Knock it off. Sitting here worrying about it is just a waste of time."

From now on, I wanted to live my life freely, without being tied down by anyone.

By all accounts, the royal family here in Ashbury was excellent; they'd gone many generations without engaging in an offensive war, using their military strictly for defense. Trade was healthy, and the population was diverse. No one would bat an eye if a stranger suddenly came to town and settled there. That was why I'd chosen to live in this kingdom.

"What should I do for a living…?"

Lancome had taken me in as a young man, when I was eight years old. I'd performed my first mission at age fifteen and worked nonstop thereafter until twenty-seven. During that time, Lancome rose the ranks to chief.

Every month, I would buy small items for my family and ask Lancome to send them off with some money. He'd check to make sure there were no letters in the packages, then forward them to my parents' house.

One of the rules was that I mustn't contact my family, you see.

The thought of my parents' and my younger sister Emily's joy at receiving the packages was what kept me going while I worked. Even though I couldn't contact them, Lancome would at least tell me if they died. I made sure of that several times.

"I can't believe they're all dead..."

I adored Lancome like an older brother and respected him as my boss. And yet he'd hidden my family's death from me for two whole years.

I'd found out about it a year ago.

After finishing a mission, for the first time in eighteen years, I'd decided to visit the town where I grew up. I wanted to at least catch a glimpse of my family home—no, of my family—from afar. I put on a disguise and went to look at their house, but all I saw there was a deserted lot.

I was shocked. After some investigating, I discovered the house had burned down in a fire two years ago. The district official should have immediately contacted the noble who was my employer on paper. Then that noble, in turn, would've contacted the organization and informed them of my family's death. Those were the rules, so it was impossible that Lancome didn't know. I'd witnessed other spies learn of their family members' deaths before.

I see. So that's how it is.

He knew how much my family meant to me. I'd told him that time and again over my eighteen long years of working for him.

After that, I continued working as if nothing had happened, giving Lancome packages after my payday to send to my parents' house, just as I always did. Then one evening, I followed him after work. He didn't take the package to the post office in the capital.

He didn't notice me tailing him. Honestly, I was disappointed at how much his skills had deteriorated.

Eventually, he entered a high-class apartment complex with guards in fancy uniforms posted outside; this wasn't the dormitory where high-ranking officials lived. I next saw curtains being pulled back and a window opening on the third floor. Lancome was letting in some fresh air.

There he is.

I waited for him to come out of the building. Under the cover of night, I climbed up to the third floor from a second-floor terrace, using small protrusions in the wall as my footholds. First, I sneaked into a separate apartment that had no lights on, then headed into his apartment.

I used my tools to pick the lock and get inside. There, sitting in the corner of the room, was a pile of the twenty-five packages I'd given him.

The moment I saw the packages, my emotions threatened to explode, but I quickly managed to get ahold of them.

I opened up all the packages and confiscated the money I'd stashed inside them without leaving even a single coin behind. I even stole the silver cutlery from the kitchen and the golden candlesticks. I wanted Lancome to think this was the work of a thief. On the way home, I threw anything belonging to him in the river.

I was wrong about him. He's exactly the kind of person to climb the ranks of the spy organization.

From that day forward, I continued business as usual.

Every month, I would ask Lancome to send a package home to my family the day after I got paid. I lived as I always had, but my heart had changed. My family was no longer in this world, and I no longer trusted Lancome.

In between missions, I began investigating him and discovered that he was going to marry one of my colleagues. I made sure to use that information to my advantage.

"My ideal man is someone like the chief."

I wasn't romantically interested in Lancome even one bit, but I began dropping hints here and there to my other colleagues that I had fallen for him. At some point, he would have to go public about his marriage. All this was part of my long con to make people think I'd be so shocked at the revelation that I'd take my own life.

I began restricting my food intake the day Lancome and Mary announced their marriage. Two months later, people were already noticing how haggard I looked.

When anyone would ask why, I'd contort my face in sadness and bite my lip, then say, "It's nothing..." with my eyes full of tears. Everyone would give me looks of pity. The sole exception was Mary, who had to try very hard to conceal the triumphant expression on her face.

So why had I gone to such lengths to defect from the organization?

Because I was excellent at what I did.

For many years, I'd been the top spy in Hagl. If I actually expressed a desire to quit, it was obvious that no one would roll over and say, "Fine, go ahead."

I'd had my future planned out already. I wouldn't marry. I would work in my current position until I was in my forties, then spend the rest of my life training the next generation. Lancome himself had recommended that path for me.

But now that I'd lost my parents and Emily, I had neither the desire nor obligation to devote my life to the organization. I no longer cared about gaining Lancome's approval.

However, the entire time I'd been planning my disappearance, part of me was waiting for Lancome to say, "I've been meaning to tell you this, Chloe, but..." up until the very last morning.

But he never did let me know that my family had died. And now it had been three years since the fire. He'd had plenty of opportunities to admit the truth and never did.

Lancome saw me as neither a younger sister nor or a cherished employee. I was nothing but a pawn for him to use as he pleased. This whole time, the person I thought he'd been was merely a figment of my imagination, so laughable now that I could hardly stand it.

Chapter One

When I Met the Girl

"Well, I suppose I'll wander around town for a bit now."

Deciding to wear something inconspicuous, I put on a long navy-blue skirt that would be easy to walk in and an ivory blouse, then left my hotel room.

"Have a nice day," the person at the front desk called out after me cheerfully.

I exited the hotel and headed downtown where the shops were.

The capital of Ashbury was roughly divided into north, south, east, and west quarters with a castle at its center. My hotel was in the southern quarter, and the neighborhood was bustling with many shops, markets, and offices. According to my research, this area had the largest immigrant population.

The restaurants and food stalls here sold dishes from many countries. All sorts of delicious smells wafted from here and there as I walked down the street. Even though I'd eaten a late and filling breakfast, I felt my stomach growl a little. I bought a fresh pastry from a bakery and munched on it as I looked around town.

"Hmm?"

Just then, I spotted a little girl who looked quite upset sitting on a bench in the plaza. I wondered if she was waiting for someone, so I watched her from afar for a while, but it didn't seem like anyone was coming for her.

What if some bad guy tries to kidnap her?

She wasn't crying—just sitting there, staring off into space. Something didn't feel right about this. I couldn't simply gawk and do nothing, so I walked over to her.

"What's wrong? Are you lost?"

"I'm not lost."

"What's your name?"

"Nonna."

"Where is your family, Nonna?"

"Mom told me to wait right here."

"Do you know how long ago that was?"

"Right before the bell chimed ten times."

It was now past two in the afternoon. If the little girl had been waiting here for her mother for more than four hours, I wondered if she'd been abandoned. Her hair was a bit unkempt, and her skin and dress were slightly dirty.

"Are you hungry? I can buy you something to eat. Then I'll wait for your mother with you."

The girl nodded, so I took her hand and pulled her up, then we both walked over to the food stalls. Nonna seemed very thirsty, so I bought her some water infused with orange juice called "fruit water," and she drank it all in one gulp.

I bought her another one, then got us two sandwiches stuffed with grilled meat and cucumbers. We walked back over to the bench.

Just as Nonna opened her mouth to dig in, her eyes widened, as though she was remembering something. "Thank you," she said, before she began devouring her food.

I wonder what happened.

Her mother hadn't shown up yet. Nonna seemed rather polite, so she must've been raised with some level of care. Maybe her mother went broke or got a new boyfriend who didn't want anything to do with Nonna.

I asked about Nonna's father, but she didn't seem to have one.

"Try to eat a little slower so you don't choke, okay?"

"Okay."

"I have another bottle of water for you. Drink that while you eat."

"Okay."

"How old are you, Nonna?"

"Six."

I had only been eight years old when my father's business went bankrupt. I'd been about to be sent to work as a live-in servant when Lancome found me and took me in.

Though, I suppose it would be more accurate to say that my parents had sold me off to him. But they'd had no other choice, so I never held it against them. In fact, I was glad that I'd been of some help to my family.

Once Nonna was finished eating her sandwich, she began nodding off.

"Poor thing. You've been waiting here for a long time."

She was fast asleep with her head in my lap. Although a bit dirty, she was clearly a very pretty little girl, with blond hair and blue-gray eyes. Precisely the kind of girl someone with nefarious intentions wouldn't hesitate to abduct.

I was so glad I'd found her first.

We stayed there until dusk, but her mother never showed up.

She really has been abandoned.

She was still fast asleep, so I carried her on my back while I searched for a guard post. They would probably send Nonna to an orphanage, where she would have to wait for her mother. As those thoughts went through my mind, I saw a young man running toward me at full speed.

He seems dangerous… I need to steer clear of him.

He was clutching a bag that clearly belonged to a woman. That meant he was a pickpocket. I was carrying Nonna on my back, but I had no other choice. If I were still a spy, I'd avoid him. But now I was just an ordinary citizen with good intentions. Maybe I'd gotten carried away on my first day of freedom and decided to just react without giving it much thought.

I braced myself, and the moment the man passed me, I stuck out my leg, tripping him. He fell with a spectacular *thud!*

"Oww!"

A muscular, silver-haired man who'd been chasing after him caught up with the pickpocket in no time.

"Give it up!" he shouted.

For some reason, the large man was holding a thin rope, which he used to expertly bind the pickpocket's hands. Then he turned to me.

"Thanks for your help, miss."

"Of course. Excuse me, but are you going to hand that man over to the guards? Would I be able to come with you?"

"Hmm? Why?"

"Well, I think this girl might have been abandoned."

The silver-haired man's gaze shifted to Nonna behind me. "Sure, I can take you there."

He didn't say anything else about it. An elderly woman who looked like an aristocrat ran up to him, catching her breath, and he handed the bag back to her. The snowy-haired woman gracefully bowed several times before departing.

The silver-haired man pulled along the pickpocket as he showed me the way to the guard post. He told me his name was Jeffrey Asher. He appeared to be in his early thirties and was in top physical shape, judging by his toned muscles. He was around one hundred and ninety centimeters tall and weighed about eighty kilograms. His clothing looked fairly expensive, and he seemed well-to-do. He had deep-blue eyes, handsome features, and a very nice voice. I had a feeling he was quite popular with the ladies.

The guard post was a two-story building situated in the center of the downtown area. Two guards armed with swords stood at the entrance and immediately straightened their posture when they spotted Mr. Asher.

"I caught a pickpocket."

"Thank you, Captain!"

Captain? If this man was a member of the guard, they'd refer to him as Commander, so he had to be either a captain of the knights or the military. He was in civilian clothes, so this must have been his day off.

"And who's this lady?"

"She found a child who's been abandoned. Would you mind helping her out?"

A member of the guard led me down the path to the left, while Mr. Asher escorted the pickpocket toward the right. I explained how I'd come to find the little girl, presented my identification papers, and signed *Victoria Sellars* on the documents. Once all that was finished, I asked the question that had been nagging at the corner of my mind.

"What will happen to Nonna tonight?"

"She'll have to sleep here. I'll contact the orphanage, but the soonest they'd be able to send someone over would be tomorrow."

After waiting a very long time for her mother to come back to no avail, now she would have to spend the night by herself at the guard post. It reminded me of the day I'd been taken to the spy organization's facilities. I remember crying myself to sleep out of fear and loneliness in that unfamiliar bedroom.

"Do you think it would be possible for me to take her back to my hotel for tonight? I've just arrived in this kingdom, so I have no one to vouch for me, but my heart aches when I think of leaving her after I spent all day waiting with her."

"You don't have anyone to vouch for you? Hmm… If you had someone upstanding to be your guarantor, I could grant you permission. However, without someone to verify you're really a guest at Hotel Fruud like you've written here, our hands are tied."

That made sense. Perhaps it was no use. I was about to give up, when suddenly, I heard a voice from behind me.

"I can confirm whether she's really staying at Hotel Fruud. It's my day off today anyway. The only reason I caught the pickpocket earlier was because she tripped him."

"Is that right? Ms. Sellars, thank you so much for your cooperation! And yes, it would be a big help if you could check out the hotel, Captain."

"It's no problem. I'm just returning the favor for her help with the arrest. Plus, it would pain me to see this little girl have to spend the night alone in such a dirty guard post."

"Please don't call it dirty," the guard said with a rueful chuckle. Regardless, he ended up granting me permission to take Nonna to my room for the night.

"I can carry the girl."

"Thanks, I'd really appreciate that."

Mr. Asher effortlessly picked Nonna up in his arms, and the two of us chatted the entire way there. His voice was deep, with a smooth, velvety timbre I could listen to all day.

He told me he was the captain of the Second Order of the knights, whose duty was to keep the peace in the capital city. They were the superior organization to the guards.

"Where are you from, miss?"

"Randall, the neighboring kingdom."

"How long are you planning on staying here?"

"My whole family passed away in a house fire, so I've come here to make a fresh start."

I told him my cover story without hesitation. There was nothing wrong with making a good impression on the captain of the knights. The key to a good cover story was to answer in a friendly manner with a smile, and to incorporate as much of the truth as possible; that made it easier to remember and reduced your chances of being caught in a lie.

"You speak our language quite well," Mr. Asher said to me.

"Thank you."

We bought a change of clothes for Nonna on the way there, then headed to the hotel.

"Welcome back, Ms. Sellars." The man at the front desk greeted me, and I explained the situation with Nonna to him. Mr. Asher also seemed friendly with the man.

He carried Nonna up to my room and gently placed her on the bed. "Much appreciated," I said, and Mr. Asher straightened his posture.

"Once again, thank you for your assistance with the arrest, and for helping look after the child. Well then, have a good night."

He was all business as he bid me good-bye and excused himself. I watched him go, then locked up my hotel room. I wedged a chair beneath the doorknob just in case and then went to go freshen up.

I felt much better after changing into pajamas and slipping into bed beside Nonna. I was hungry, but I couldn't leave her alone in the room to get something, and ordering room service seemed a bit extreme. So I ignored my hunger and decided to go to sleep.

"Good night, Nonna," I whispered as I lay down. My first day as Victoria Sellars had been very eventful.

The next morning, I awoke to my stomach growling. Nonna was awake beside me, staring me in the face.

"Morning, miss."

"Good morning, Nonna. Shall we take a bath before we eat breakfast?"

"Sure."

We went down to the baths, which were located on the first floor, and I scrubbed Nonna with the complimentary soap. I casually checked her for any signs of abuse, but there were none. That alone filled me with relief.

I carefully dried her off, then helped her change into the simple dress I'd bought her the previous day on the way home.

She hasn't asked me a thing, I thought.

But as we ate breakfast, Nonna suddenly murmured, "Where's my mom?"

"I guess she wasn't able to make it back. What kind of job does your mom have?"

"I don't know."

"What do you do when she leaves you alone?"

"I just stay quiet."

"I see."

I'd thought she was rather taciturn, but perhaps she'd been raised to hide her emotions. I had a feeling that her mother wouldn't be coming home again, and even if she did, I doubted she would properly take care of a girl she'd already abandoned once. At the very least, Nonna wouldn't go hungry in the orphanage.

"And what do you do when you're with your mother?"

"I just stay quiet."

"Does she often tell you to be quiet?"

"Yes."

There are many unfortunate children like her. I shouldn't pry any further. I feel sorry for the girl, but it's not like I can take her in, I told myself.

The hotel breakfast consisted of bread with a side of jam and butter, milk, a bland vegetable soup, fried eggs, and sausage. Nonna ate it quietly. I also ate in silence.

Nonna and I walked hand in hand back to the guard post without exchanging a word. On the way there, I bought her a ribbon that matched her blue-gray eyes at a trinket shop and tied it in her hair for her. I felt like I was assuaging my guilt with material things, but the faint smile on her face afterward made it worth it.

"Thank you, miss," she told me out of the blue in front of the guard post.

I couldn't decide whether I should tell her to be a good girl at the orphanage, because she was clearly trying very hard to be a good girl already. So I just stroked her hair.

Still holding hands, we entered the guard post and saw a middle-aged woman waiting for us.

"Ah, there you are," she said. "I'm the director of the southern quarter's orphanage. I heard you took this girl in for us last night. Thank you for that." The woman grabbed Nonna's hand. "Come on, then. Let's go," she urged, and began walking.

Nonna took a few steps and then turned to look back at me. And those eyes… Those blue-gray eyes…

They wavered with emotion for the first time.

"Wait! Please wait," I called.

"Yes? What is it?"

"Can't I take her instead?"

This definitely wasn't the first time something like this happened, because the director gave her answer smoothly and briskly. "Take her in? I heard you've only just arrived in our kingdom, and you live in a hotel. You don't even have a guarantor, correct? I'm terribly sorry, but I can't possibly let you look after this girl. For all I know, you could pretend to take her in and then turn around and sell her. Oh, but it's nothing personal, of course. Those are just the rules, and I have to abide by them."

The woman's argument made perfect sense. And yet I knew that if I let this girl go, the look in her eyes would haunt me forever.

"She has one! She has a guarantor!" Mr. Asher had headed to the guard post right away after one of the guards sent word to him. "I'll be Victoria Sellars's guarantor."

"I see… I suppose I'll be able to rest easy if you're vouching for her, Captain. Well, Ms. Sellars. Please sign the necessary paperwork, and the girl will be yours."

Once again, I signed *Victoria Sellars* on the documents.

* * *

Nonna circled the pond in the plaza, occasionally dipping her hands into the water. Mr. Asher and I sat on a nearby bench, watching her while we chatted.

"I'm so sorry for calling you here in the middle of work," I said to him.

"Not at all. I have a relatively easy workload today. Plus, I have an obligation to the citizens of Ashbury. Still, why did you decide to take her in? You just met her yesterday."

Nonna turned to look at us. I smiled and waved. Her face remained impassive as she gently waved back.

"I saw something in her eyes that said, 'Help me!' Maybe it was just my imagination. But long ago, there was a little girl with those same eyes, and she reminded me of her. The next thing I knew, I was saying your name. Thank you for coming on such short notice. I really appreciate you agreeing to be my guarantor."

After a short pause, Mr. Asher replied, "To be honest with you, I felt guilty when I went back to my lodgings last night."

"About what?"

"Because I knew you wouldn't leave the girl to go out and get dinner. It was your first night in a new country, and I was worried you would go to bed with an empty stomach. I don't know, but I just had a feeling that you wouldn't order room service, either. I felt guilty over not treating you to some delicious food."

I looked up at him in disbelief. His description was so accurate, it was as if he'd watched me. Like he could read my mind. No wonder he served as the captain of the Second Order of the knights, which was tasked with keeping peace in the capital.

"There's no reason for you to feel guilty, Captain. I knew I shouldn't go out and leave her, and I couldn't bring myself to order room service. You're entirely correct." I smiled at him, trying my best to look friendly.

"I can't help feeling guilty, though. Would you let me treat you to dinner tonight? I'd like to express my gratitude to you for helping to arrest that pickpocket and taking in the abandoned girl."

He was so downright sincere, I had to chuckle despite myself. "Only if Nonna can come along!"

"Nonna, how about we find a place we can rent for the two of us? Somewhere with a kitchen, so I can cook for you."

I was looking forward to hearing what kinds of foods she'd had so far, and what she enjoyed eating.

"Cook for me?"

"That's right. I'm quite good at cooking! Starting today, you and I are family. And I want to make lots of yummy food for you. Oh—and you can call me Victoria from now on. Or Vicky, if you prefer."

"Vicky."

"That's right, Nonna! Let's go look for a place to rent today. Then tonight, we're going to have dinner with the captain."

"Okay." Nonna was impassive, as usual.

Although I could be very expressive when needed at work, in my daily life, I also found it difficult to express my emotions. I had been raised to do the opposite.

"Nonna, let's smile and laugh a lot together."

"Laugh?"

"Yes! Just like this!"

I reached out and tickled Nonna's side. At first, she was surprised, but before I knew it, she was doubled over laughing. For the first time, Nonna truly looked like an ordinary six-year-old girl. It was adorable.

"You're so cute, Nonna. You have to be careful so that bad people don't take you away. I'll have to teach you how to protect yourself."

"Protect myself?"

"That's right. There are things you can do to keep yourself safe called self-defense. If something scary happens, sometimes it's not enough to scream or cry. It'll be good to know how to protect yourself."

"Okay."

"I'll teach you little by little. But first, we need to find a place to live."

"Yeah!"

The more cards you had to play in your arsenal, the better—even for children.

Me and Nonna went around to various letting agents and narrowed it down to two potential locations, then returned to the hotel. Even though I'd told everyone, *"She's very quiet,"* many people turned me down on the basis that I had a child, despite those landlords having been children themselves once upon a time!

I silently cursed those landlords, hoping they'd step in dog poop every time they left the house.

"Nonna, I'm going to look at the two places we chose later tonight, so if you wake up and I'm not here, don't worry and just wait for me to come back, okay?"

"I'll go with you."

"It'll be very late at night, so I won't be able to take a little girl with me."

"......"

Nonna probably didn't want to be left alone at night, but walking around with a six-year-old that late would be asking for trouble.

"Are you sure I can't come?" Nonna asked me.

"There are bad people outside late at night. I can take care of them just fine on my own, but it would be difficult to fend them off if you were with me."

"But I don't want to stay home alone."

Hmm. I suppose that shouldn't be surprising; clearly, she'd been left home alone far too often. She was probably worried sick that I would abandon her as well.

"All right, then. But you must promise me that if I tell you to be quiet, you won't make a sound, no matter what."

"Okay."

"And if I tell you to run, don't worry about me. Just run as fast as you can and hide."

"I can do that."

"And if I tell you to scream, shout at the top of your lungs."

"I can do that, too."

"And if I tell you to stay still, don't move a muscle."

"Okay."

I didn't have the heart to tell Nonna to stay here alone after seeing the desperate look on her face. Plus, I was worried she'd get so anxious that she'd leave the room. Upon reflection, I figured I could deal with practically anything that might happen, even if she was with me. After all, I'd fled and fought while protecting people who were too scared to move before. In the worst-case scenario, I could put Nonna over my shoulder and make a break for it.

Now, I was well aware that ordinary folks didn't often encounter people who wanted to harm them. In fact, I now counted myself among those ordinary folks.

"All right. Let's take a nice, long nap before we go out for dinner with the captain."

"Okay!"

That evening, the two of us got into bed facing each other while I patted Nonna's back. She fell asleep surprisingly quickly. I slipped out of bed and quietly began my training. I'd gotten out of shape from restricting my food intake and exercising less in preparation of leaving the organization.

After I did some muscle work, I took a quick bath to clean off the sweat. I put on some makeup, changed into a dress I'd bought during my travels across Randall, and then woke up Nonna. She got up without a grumble or complaint, which seemed very unlike a child. But on second thought, she'd probably been raised in an environment where she hadn't been allowed to act like a kid.

It took her a few minutes before she was fully awake.

"You look pretty, Vicky."

"Thank you. Let's get you changed, too."

I helped her into the dress we'd bought on the way home from the guard post and combed her hair. Yes, she was adorable. Nonna picked up the blue ribbon. She had folded it up very carefully the previous day and set it on the bureau.

"Would you like to wear this?"

"Yes. I've never had a ribbon before."

"......"

The happiness in her voice made this statement all the more heartbreaking. I wrapped the blue ribbon around her soft blond hair, then tied it into a bow atop her head. She looked like a little doll.

"The captain is a very lucky man to have dinner with such a beauty! What is your favorite food, Nonna?"

"Rolls."

"...Okay. Let's try to find even more foods you like. We can eat all kinds of delicious things together every day. I'll cook for you."

"I want to cook, too."

"Sure! I'll teach you. I'll teach you everything I know, Nonna."

"Thanks."

"You're very welcome. We're going to have a lot of fun living together."

This wasn't bad; having a child was much more enjoyable than I'd thought it would be.

Just then, there was a knock at the door.

"Yes, who is it?"

"It's me, Jeffrey Asher."

"Coming!" I whispered over to Nonna, "Always remember to avoid opening the door right away when someone knocks, even if you're expecting someone. If there's a peephole, use it. If there isn't, ask who's there to make sure you recognize their voice. Don't forget that, okay?"

"Okay."

I opened the door and saw Mr. Asher standing there, wearing a suit in a shade of navy blue so deep that it was almost black. He was a head taller than me. *Yeah, he's definitely popular with the ladies*, I thought once again. I didn't know if he was already married or single, though. But I had Nonna to look after at this point, so I suppose it was no longer my concern.

"Good evening, Captain."

"Well, don't you two look beautiful! I think we're going to have a wonderful dinner together."

I took Nonna by the hand, and the three of us went to a restaurant. Mr. Asher made sure to walk a bit more slowly so we could keep up with him. He was a very attentive man.

Nonna had a spring in her step. I was looking forward to the dinner, too.

Mr. Asher took us to a restaurant called Ivy, and as its name suggested, the outer walls were covered in climbing ivy.

Everyone here knew him as well; clearly, the captain of the knights was respected and adored by the people of the capital. There was one thing that bothered me, though. Both the man showing us inside and a woman who appeared to be the dining-room supervisor gave looks of momentary surprise when they saw he had Nonna and me in tow.

"Everyone knows you at this restaurant, don't they? Are you sure it's okay to bring us here?" I asked Mr. Asher.

"Hmm? There's no problem at all. I'm an easygoing bachelor. I don't mind who sees us out together."

"Oh, I see. That's a relief. If there's anyone sweet on you, I certainly don't want to be the subject of their ire."

"No, there's no one like that."

Oh, there definitely is. A lot of them, I'm sure.

Mr. Asher's tone of voice was casual, but I wondered if he was telling the truth. I couldn't help but notice the mature allure he gave off, with his black dress shirt slightly disheveled.

A man who appeared to be the head waiter came over to take our order. I let Mr. Asher decide for both Nonna and me. After a while, our appetizers came out with some white wine and a glass of fruit water for Nonna, and the three of us toasted. Nonna was so adorable as she gulped down her beverage.

The appetizers included grilled scampi on metal skewers brushed with olive oil, and small canapés made with thinly sliced bread and spread with herb butter, topped with premium ham and chopped herbs.

The scampi was sweet and delicious. Nonna must've liked it, too, because she gobbled it up. As I watched her, I realized that Mr. Asher was staring at me.

"Is something the matter?" I asked.

"No, I was just thinking you seem to really adore children."

"I'm not sure about that. I just really adore her."

Everything Mr. Asher did was polished, from his posture down to the way he ate. He must've had a good upbringing.

"I had to wait to take you to dinner until after work. I hope Nonna's not too sleepy."

"I took a nap," Nonna told him. "After this, we're going to look for a place to live."

Uh-oh, I forgot to warn her not to tell! Just as I expected, Mr. Asher raised an eyebrow.

"You mean, you're looking for a place to rent? After dinner? It's not safe to bring a child out at night."

"I know, but if I sign the contract without checking the place out at night, I might regret it."

"Then let me go with you. It's too dangerous for a woman and child to be walking around so late."

I figured he'd say that. He was the captain of the Second Order of the knights, after all. If he tagged along, however, I wouldn't be able to put my ear to the walls and door of my potential new place and listen to what was happening on the other side.

"I know it might be a nuisance, but please let me escort you. As your guarantor, it's my responsibility to ensure your safety."

"It's not a nuisance at all. It's reassuring," I answered with a friendly smile.

Dinner went smoothly. Nonna didn't know how to eat meat off the bone, so I cut it off and into pieces for her, then wiped the soup from her mouth. It was quite heartwarming, actually.

"What kind of meat is this?" she asked.

"Grilled lamb chop with herbs."

"Hmm."

She seemed to like the lamb. I'd have to make some for her once we moved into our new place.

Once our bellies were full, we left the restaurant and strolled around for a bit. The clock struck nine as we made our way to the first rental option. When we arrived at the building, Mr. Asher looked around to check the surroundings.

"Which one is it?" he asked me.

"The corner apartment on the second floor." I pointed to the window, which was dark.

I was hesitant to share where I would be living with a stranger so easily, but honestly, I didn't know how cautious the average woman was. Regardless, I determined it was very unlikely that Mr. Asher would force his way into our room and kill us—not that he could have, since I was a former spy.

It would be foolish to scrutinize every single behavior of Mr. Asher's. He wasn't an agent or an assassin, and considering how few of those people there were in comparison to the total population, it was a miracle that I'd come across any of them at all.

Come to think of it, the organization's psychologist had once told me with a chuckle, *"Chloe, I think you've only been able to go nineteen years without self-destructing thanks to that boldness of yours."*

I inspected both locations.

At the first place, I stood in front of the door and gracefully listened to check out the state of the neighborhood. A woman on the floor below us was hysterically screaming at somebody, which scared Nonna. I crossed that one off the list.

The second apartment had trash lying all over the stairs and was clearly run-down, so I had to cross that one off the list as well.

"Thank you so much for tonight. Dinner was delicious. I really appreciate you taking us out to eat," I told Mr. Asher.

"I can't recommend either of those rooms to you."

"I agree. I'll have to keep looking."

Nonna was a little tired, so Mr. Asher carried her as he walked. It seemed he intended on escorting us all the way back to the hotel.

"Captain, I can carry her from her and take her home. You treated us to dinner, and you visited the rentals with me. I couldn't possibly impose on you anymore. Thank you so much for everything you did for us today," I said firmly, but Mr. Asher glanced down at me with a look on his face that seemed to say, "You can't be serious," and proceeded to ignore me.

Huh? Right then, he spoke, his face still facing forward.

"You just came here from Randall. I don't know how things are there, but in this kingdom, it's dangerous for a woman with a child to walk around by herself at night. Let me take you home."

I see.

"All right then, if you insist. I appreciate it."

"You're so stuffy."

"Am I?"

"Yes, although I have to compliment you on how well you speak Ashburian."

"I like to study different languages in my free time."

"I hope this doesn't sound like I'm prying, but what sort of work did you do in Randall?"

I gave him a candid smile. "All sorts of things. Perhaps if we meet again, I can tell you more."

"I'm looking forward to it."

"All right, then."

We arrived at the hotel, and Mr. Asher carried Nonna up to my room for me like before. This time, however, I took her from him at the door and said good-bye there.

"I had a lovely night with you, Captain."

"I did, too. Good night."

"Good night."

He turned and walked away, waving as he went. I took Nonna inside and placed her on the bed, changed her into pajamas, and pulled the covers over her.

After that, I got down on the floor and checked for footprints. As was my habit, I'd sprinkled a very thin coating of baby powder over the floors before I left earlier.

There were no footprints. There were no signs that anyone had opened any of the drawers. That was normal, of course.

I hurried down to the first floor and took a bath to wash myself off. I decided I would look for a job the next day. Once I found employment, I could take my time searching for somewhere nearby to rent.

I ran back upstairs and saw that Nonna was still fast asleep.

"I think we'll have a wonderful life together," I said to her quietly. The corners of her mouth curved up slightly in her sleep. I wanted her to have sweet dreams, and I wanted her to have a happy childhood.

My younger sister, Emily, had just been a toddler when I left home. As I took care of Nonna, I found myself wondering if I would've taken care of my sister like this had I stayed with my family.

And if I'd stayed at home instead of leaving at eight years old, would my parents have taken care of me like this? Looking after Nonna almost made me feel like I was regaining the childhood I'd lost out on.

In just two days, I had gotten completely attached to Nonna.

"First thing's first—I need to find a job."

I had enough money to last me for a while without working, but I wanted an income. Ideally, I'd pick up some translation work I could do from home. It would be easier for people to trust me if I was an upstanding citizen who was diligent at my job. I slipped into bed beside Nonna and closed my eyes.

Jeffrey Asher enjoyed a drink as he basked in the afterglow of a wonderful evening. The spacious living room was clean and furnished entirely with antiques made by master craftsmen.

He was at his family's capital residence, which was overseen by his brother, Earl Asher, the head of the household.

While his usual abode was the dormitory reserved for the captain of the knights, he visited his family once a week out of concern for his sickly mother's well-being.

"Oh, you're back?" said Edward, Jeffrey's older brother.

"Yes. Are you still working?"

Edward had silver hair, just like him—both siblings had inherited it from their late father. Edward was forty, eight years Jeffrey's senior, and prone to fussing over his younger brother, which annoyed Jeffrey to no end. No matter how many times Jeffrey told Edward that he was thirty-two years old and didn't need to be taken care of, Edward just wouldn't listen.

"I heard you went out on the town all dressed up," Edward commented. "That's pretty unusual. You were with a girl, weren't you?"

"Did you come all the way in here just so you could ask me that?"

"Aw, don't pout. I'm happy for you. How long has it been since you've been on a date anyway?"

Jeffrey sighed, wondering how many times he would have to repeat himself. "Brother, could you please stop treating me like I'm some kind of tragic victim?"

"All right, all right. I'll drop it." Edward held up both hands in surrender. "So? Was it fun?"

"It was. I had a wonderful dinner with a foreign woman who just came to the kingdom and the six-year-old girl she's taken in."

"……"

"You have an heir, you know. You should worry about him. Don't worry about me. Anyway, I'm going to bed since I need to get up early tomorrow," Jeffrey said, then headed up to his room.

Victoria Sellars was a commoner, but the way she spoke was intelligent, and her mannerisms were elegant. Plus, she was a woman of considerable courage.

Every woman in the capital, whether they knew he was the captain of the knights or not, looked at him flirtatiously the moment they spotted him. It'd been like that ever since he was a young man, so he'd gotten adept at rejecting them with a mere smile.

That was why everything about Victoria felt so refreshing; she didn't insist on relying on him, she didn't look at him like he was a piece of meat, and she'd taken in an abandoned girl on her own right after moving to a new country.

She'd only asked him to be her guarantor because she'd been in a predicament, but even then, she must have been quite reluctant to do so.

He couldn't believe she'd tripped that pickpocket, either.

What if that young man had gotten up and attacked her? She was much too small to take on a grown man, let alone while carrying a sleeping child.

It had struck him as unbelievably reckless.

But when he saw her confidently take on the pickpocket running toward her with Nonna on her back, he realized he'd misjudged her and thought, *Oh, she's quite the fighter.*

And although she was very slender, she had a healthy appetite, which he found far more appealing than the young ladies who put on airs and tried to impress him with their dainty eating habits.

The fact that she'd planned to look at apartments so late at night had also surprised him. When Nonna had let this slip, Victoria seemed perturbed. Although she didn't show it on her face, years of experience working among the townsfolk had given him the ability to tell from her subtle eye movements that she'd been flustered.

He was fascinated by her.

Although it was refreshing to see a woman who was so independent, she also made him worry. He wanted to lend her a hand, at least until she got settled.

But surely, that would be a nuisance to her.

A bitter smile crossed his face as he thought he should abandon the idea of helping her. It was clear she didn't want that. And judging by the hotel where she was staying, she wasn't struggling financially. He resolved to only help her if she asked for it, as her guarantor. This would be the last time he offered his assistance; the situation was already bringing painful memories of the past back to the surface.

The next morning, when he came to the knight's quarters, which were located on the premises of the Asher manor, Jeffrey noticed that everyone was looking at him with a glint in their eyes. *What's going on?* he wondered as he went back to his room. He was greeted by his secretary, a woman in her forties who stared at him the same way her brother had the night before.

"What?"

"It's nothing," she said with a warm look in her eyes. It wasn't until he went down to the cafeteria for lunch that he discovered what that look meant.

"Captain! We saw you! You really enjoyed yourself last night, didn't you?" said Bob, one of the younger knights. Jeffrey wondered if he was the source of all this commotion as he beckoned Bob over.

"You must have a lot of free time on your hands if you're out there gossiping. Come to the training grounds at one o'clock. It's been a while since I gave you some thorough training."

"Whaaat?"

Bob's response was so pitiful that Jeffrey almost laughed, barely maintaining the stern expression on his face.

Three weeks had passed since Jeffrey's dinner with Victoria and Nonna. He'd stuck to his decision and hadn't offered them help, but today, he'd gone to her hotel as her guarantor.

"Is Ms. Victoria Sellars still staying here?" he asked. The woman at the front desk handed him a letter.

His name was written on the envelope in beautiful, feminine script. He quickly opened it.

Captain Jeffrey Asher of the Second Order of the Knights

It's been a while.

Thank you so much for agreeing to be my guarantor so I could take in Nonna. The restaurant where you took us out to dinner was lovely.

I found myself quite lonely when I first moved here, but you gave me so much encouragement. I'm grateful for all you've done for me.

Nonna and I are both doing well. I was able to find a job and a place to rent. Please forgive my rudeness in not letting you know before I moved.

I've heard that in this kingdom, it's required to report to your guarantor each month after taking in an orphan. I'll continue sending you letters each month to the knights' barracks.

Until then,
Victoria Sellars

The letter was written in such a businesslike tone that he had to laugh. But he was glad she was doing well. Victoria had never once seemed lonesome to him, but maybe she was just being polite. He was sure he'd run into her somewhere, and if not, he'd receive another letter from her in a month.

She'd also written her new address on the letter; it was in the eastern quarter of the capital, where the nobility lived. In fact, it wasn't that far from his family's manor. He wondered if she'd found work as live-in staff for an aristocrat.

"I should go check on them sometime," he said, but he was so busy with other things that he just couldn't find the time.

Anyone taking in a child shall report monthly to their guarantor, and their guarantor should then check on the child's new residence to confirm whether the reports are true.

The deadline for that was coming up soon.

Chapter Two

Lady Yolana and the Grumpy Old Historian

Lady Yolana was the wife of the late Earl Haynes.

When her husband died of illness, she'd relinquished her position as head of house to her son and his wife, along with the family manor. She now lived a life of leisure befitting a wealthy dowager countess in the eastern quarter of the capital.

One day, while on her way home from a friend's tea party, she decided to stop by a shop in the southern quarter to pick up some embroidering supplies.

She gave the things she'd bought to her servant, holding only her purse. But after taking just a few steps, a young man ran up to her and snatched the purse out of her hands, putting a great deal of distance between them as he fled. "Thief!" she yelled, and a muscular man in the vicinity immediately began chasing him. Being quite headstrong, Lady Yolana joined the silver-haired man's chase, ignoring her waiting maid's cries to stop.

Up ahead, the man caught up to the pickpocket and restrained him. She was able to safely get her purse back, but on her way home, she realized she'd forgotten to thank him properly. She'd been so flustered that she'd just briefly said thank you before leaving. Feeling terrible about this, she headed to the guard post the next day.

* * *

"I'd love to thank him properly."

"The captain won't accept any money, but I'll relay the message to him."

"Well, would you mind at least telling me where I can find the woman who tripped the pickpocket?"

The guard told Lady Yolana the name of a hotel, so she headed there and asked the man at the front desk if he would call the woman down. A few moments later, a woman smiling softly and a young girl in tow appeared from the stairwell. Lady Yolana told the woman that she wanted to express her gratitude, to which she replied, "Just your thank you is enough," with a smile.

"Would you at least come to my house for tea and refreshments?" Lady Yolana asked somewhat stubbornly, reflecting on her own vulnerability after getting robbed in her old age. Fortunately, the woman accepted her offer with a grin.

A few days later, the woman, whose name was Victoria Sellars, showed up at her house along with the little girl. She introduced herself as a commoner originally from Randall. Despite her status, she didn't seem intimidated to be in the manor of a noble, and Lady Yolana noticed her manners and etiquette during teatime were quite refined. Perhaps Victoria came from a wealthy family.

"And what are you going to do now? Surely, you can't stay at the hotel forever," Yolana said to her.

"I'm planning on renting a place for us somewhere soon."

"Well, in that case, why don't you live here? I have a guest cottage you could live in. It has a kitchen and a bathroom." The next thing Lady Yolana knew, she was inviting the girl to live with her.

Not only had Victoria cooperated in helping apprehend the pickpocket, but she'd also taken in an abandoned child. As a citizen of Ashbury, Lady Yolana wanted to express her heartfelt gratitude to her.

Victoria pondered her offer for a few moments and said, "As long as we'll have a proper lease agreement." She said she would draw up the contract herself, which convinced Lady Yolanda she'd received a proper education.

The agreement Victoria brought the next day was quite reasonable, and her suggested rent was of fair market value. Despite the high rent in the eastern quarter, which was where the aristocrats resided, Victoria didn't seem to want to negotiate for a lower rate.

"Goodness! This is meticulously done. A perfect contract, indeed," Lady Yolana said, before lowering Victoria's suggested monthly rent by half and finalizing the lease. It was a rare instance where the landlady had offered a half-price discount.

And as it turned out, Victoria was an excellent tenant. She never had noisy guests over, and the little girl, whose name was Nonna, was quiet and well-behaved, unlikely to make a mess of the guest cottage. Victoria even paid two months' worth of rent in advance.

Victoria was a pleasant conversation partner when Lady Yolana invited her to tea, and she would often offer her homemade dishes, humbly saying, "Forgive me for imposing; I'm sure you have a wonderful cook." They were not only visually appealing, but they were also positively scrumptious. One such dish she shared was called "chicken and vegetable roulade."

It was made by spreading a layer of vegetables and herbs over pounded chicken breasts, then rolling everything up, searing it, and simmering it in a white wine sauce. The sliced portions were beautifully arranged on the platter. Although chicken was often dry, Victoria's was tender and easy to chew even for a person of Lady Yolana's age. The outer layer was glazed with honey, which was delightfully crispy when seared.

"I'm so glad we met. By the way, is your place of employment nearby?" Lady Yolana asked belatedly, and Victoria informed her she was working as an assistant and housemaid for a famous historian. "It's truly a mystery to me how you manage to do so much, and so well!"

She was impressed for good reason; one breezy day, Lady Yolana was looking at the garden from her second-floor balcony when a gust of wind carried off her hat. The hat floated on the breeze and got caught in the branches of a ginkgo tree.

"My late husband bought that hat for me before he passed, so it's quite special to me, but there's nothing to be done. I just pray it falls from the tree before it rains."

Victoria had just come home from work when she heard Lady Yolana say that. She went into the cottage and changed into pants, then shimmied right up the tree, freed the hat from the branch, and tossed it over to her landlady. The tree was even taller than the roof of Lady Yolana's two-story estate.

Yolana was so surprised, it rendered her speechless. Victoria slid back down the tree and said, "I was a tomboy growing up!" with a laugh.

Not only could this young lady conduct herself just like an aristocrat, but she was also a historian's assistant, a fantastic cook, and even an adept tree-climber!

Suffice it to say, Lady Yolana had grown incredibly fond of Victoria.

Lady Yolana's maid, Susan, was another one of Victoria and Nonna's admirers.

"How could a mother abandon such an adorable girl?" she asked through angry tears. "Your Ladyship, once Nonna gets used to me, do you think she could stay in my room? Then Ms. Sellars would be able to go out at night without any worries. She's still so young, but it doesn't seem like she has any time for courting!" she noted with concern.

Nonna didn't show much emotion, but when Susan talked to her or gave her little snacks, her expression would soften a bit.

"Why, you sound like you're trying to tame a feral kitten!" Yolana cried.

"A kitten! I simply find the girl so adorable that I want to show her a mother's love."

"Unfortunately, the two of us could be nothing more than grandmothers!"

"How gauche, Your Ladyship!"

Lady Yolana was exasperated by Susan's reaction.

Speaking of Victoria, she'd borrowed a large pot from the kitchen to make something for her employer's birthday. A delicious aroma had been wafting in the air ever since this morning, when she began cooking.

"You can use my carriage to transport the food," Lady Yolana offered, much to Victoria's delight.

"Thank you so much! I was wondering how I would carry the food over and considered calling a carriage."

Lady Yolana found Victoria's occasionally absent-minded nature incredibly endearing.

Bernard Fitcher was an elderly historian, and a very cantankerous man. Although he wouldn't do it himself, he insisted on having his tea at a particular time, prepared in a particular way. If any of his items were the slightest bit out of place in his house—even in areas outside the study and living room—he would get irritated.

On top of that, when he was cooped up in his study for too long, even the littlest things would set him off. There weren't many people who lasted very long as his assistants, so he was always having trouble keeping the position filled.

One day, Victoria Sellars saw his job posting at the employment agency and came to have an interview with him. She told him she could speak four languages and was good at cooking and cleaning. This struck him as a bit too convenient, but it turned out to be true.

"Mr. Fitcher, I have the translation of the texts you requested yesterday."

"You got it done in just one night?"

"Yes. Please go ahead and check for any mistakes while I go ahead and finish up the cleaning."

Victoria handed Bernard the papers and then began tidying his desk. She truly had a knack for cleaning. She never put the messy stacks of documents out of order when she organized them; instead, she sorted through the pile of texts and separated them into three piles depending on content, clipping them neatly together and adding a note on the front to make them easier to find.

Because Bernard had weak lungs and lived in this dusty old house, his niece often said he was committing "slow suicide," but once Victoria began working for him, she tidied his whole house. Now there wasn't a speck of dust in sight.

She's the best maid and assistant I've ever had; I'm not letting this one go! Bernard thought several days ago.

At first, when Victoria mentioned she would have to bring a little girl along who wasn't even related to her, he'd thought that was positively out of the question, but Nonna turned out to be a very intelligent child who spent her time quietly reading in the corner of the kitchen. Victoria was teaching her how to read and write.

Bernard had always disliked children, but now he thought perhaps they weren't so bad after all when properly behaved.

When Nonna was helping Victoria clean one day, he mustered up the courage to ask her, "What's your favorite food?" That was the only question he could think of, as he considered speaking to a child at all adventure enough.

The girl pondered his question for a moment, then answered, "Vicky's roast lamb."

Coincidentally, Bernard also loved roast lamb. The next thing he knew, he said to Victoria, "If you don't have any plans tonight, would you make me roast lamb? You two can join me, of course."

"Oh, I'd love to! Thank you for asking," Victoria said with a smile, then quickly went shopping for the ingredients.

Bernard offered to cover the food and give her overtime pay, but she turned him down, saying, "It's a good experience for Nonna to dine with someone other than just me, so I couldn't possibly accept your money." He insisted over and over, but she wouldn't budge.

"You're a stubborn one, aren't you?" he said.

"I get that a lot."

It had been a long time since he'd had such a personable conversation with someone, and he quite enjoyed it.

Victoria skillfully prepared the roast lamb with carrots and green pea pottage, along with creamy mashed potatoes. While she was cooking, Nonna requested some crunchy buttered toast, so she added that as well.

This was the first time he'd eaten such a feast at home since his wife passed eight years ago. And his previous chef had never made something so elaborate. Ever since the chef quit, Bernard had been eating lunch and dinner out at nearby restaurants, choosing the same things off the menu each time and finding everything quite bland.

Both Victoria and Nonna ate the meal heartily and engaged in enjoyable conversation with him. Victoria said she came from Randall, but she also had a wealth of knowledge about this kingdom as well. When Bernard spoke about history, she always listened to him attentively and with great interest.

After Victoria and Nonna cleaned up and went home, the house felt very quiet to Bernard. He had always regarded the presence of others as a nuisance, so he found this change quite bewildering.

"I thought she wouldn't want to indulge me, but I'm glad I wasn't stubborn about it and tried talking to her. I never imagined I would have so much fun at dinner. And the food was absolutely delicious." In the silent room, Bernard spoke to the portrait of his late wife.

From that day on, Victoria and Nonna would occasionally eat dinner with the old historian.

Bernard's niece, Eva, came to check on him once a week. A caring woman in her thirties with reddish-brown hair, Eva was the daughter of Bernard's younger sister.

The moment Eva opened the front door today, her eyes widened, and the more she looked around, the more astonished she grew.

"The house is spotless! Even that dank dungeon you call a study has been completely transformed! Now it finally looks worthy of a scholar. Uncle, what in the world happened? Did you get a nice housemaid?"

"You're always so noisy, Eva. I put out a job posting at the employment agency for an assistant and found someone very capable indeed."

"An assistant? Not a housemaid?"

"My assistant knows four languages and can clean and cook!"

"How much are you paying them, Uncle? Please don't tell me you're only paying them an assistant's salary."

Bernard didn't know much about social graces and could be a bit oblivious when it came to common sense; just as Eva said, he'd only been paying Victoria an assistant's salary.

He began to panic. *Have I been thoughtless?* His late wife had often scolded him for being ignorant of the ways of the world and lacking common sense.

Bernard nervously smoothed down his hair, which was more white than brown, and fell silent.

"Uncle, this capable assistant of yours is clearly doing the work of three people! If you keep paying them such a pittance, someone else will scoop them up right out from under you."

"Absolutely not. I can't have that! I need her."

"Her? They're a woman? Introduce her to me. I simply must thank her and apologize!"

The next morning, Victoria came to work with Nonna in tow and was immediately greeted by Eva. She bowed her head and said, "Please forgive my ignorant uncle for underpaying you," then offered to triple her salary.

"Triple? Oh, I couldn't possibly. That's too much!"

"It isn't. Before you came around, my uncle not only had an assistant but also two other housemaids, and his house was never this clean! And they only lasted three months each. Uncle says you even listen to his stories and have conversations with him. We should pay you four times as much! He has nothing else to spend his money on. Please don't be shy."

Eva became very animated when she spoke, and she was gesturing so wildly that she nearly knocked over a vase on the nearby table. However, Victoria, who was sitting across from her, quickly reached out and caught the vase without so much as blinking. She kept her eyes on Eva the entire time.

"Why, I'd even love to hire you for myself! But I'm sure Uncle wouldn't dream of parting with you now."

Several days had passed since Eva met Victoria.

Eva had told her that Bernard was going to be having a party for his sixty-fifth birthday at his house.

"All our relatives will be there. Though, there's really only four of us—me and my husband, Michael; and my two cousins. I'll pay you overtime if you cook. It doesn't have to be anything elaborate."

"Sure, I'd love to," Victoria agreed with a smile.

Eva was the wife of an earl and had a lot on her plate, so that was music to her ears.

They were also connected in an unexpected way; one of the two cousins Eva had mentioned would be attending was Jeffrey, captain of the Second Order of the knights. However, Victoria wouldn't discover this until the day of the party.

Chapter Three

Our First Picnic

Jeffrey Asher was getting ready to attend his uncle's birthday party. His uncle was his mother's older brother, and a historian.

When he went into the living room, his brother, Edward, addressed him.

"Apparently, Uncle has a new assistant who can do just about anything. Eva wouldn't stop going on about her. Not only is she a polyglot, but she's also skilled at housework. She spared no compliment about the girl and even mentioned that she'd love to hire her for her own household but was suppressing the urge."

"I see."

Honestly, Jeffrey wasn't very fond of his uncle.

He knew that his cousin Eva visited him frequently to check on him, but Jeffrey only saw him a few times a year. His uncle was a typical scholar who'd devoted his life to academia, often arrogant and oblivious to the ways of the world. Jeffrey wasn't surprised about his inability to keep household staff.

And yet when he went to see him this time, Jeffrey was struck at how much his uncle had softened. His uncle's house was beautifully cleaned and warmly furnished, just as it had been when his aunt was still alive.

Napkins were folded and placed neatly on the table along with cutlery. The flower arrangement in the center of the dining room table was so elegant, it looked like it belonged in a restaurant.

Eva, and her husband, Michael; as well as Jeffrey, and Edward all took their sets.

Just then, his uncle's assistant made her first appearance to serve them their soup, and the moment Jeffrey saw her, his mouth fell agape. It was Victoria Sellars, wearing a white maid's apron.

"Ms. Sellars!"

"Goodness! Hello, Captain. It's been a while. I was just thinking about sending you my report for this month."

Edward watched their interaction and then said, "Anyhow, shall we start the party?" Jeffrey toasted with everyone and began to eat his soup. Then his eyes widened even more.

"Jeff, this soup is delicious!" Edward took the words right out of his mouth.

The mushroom pottage had a delightful flavor, with a beautifully swirled pattern of crème fraîche decorating the surface. It was as pleasing to the eyes and palate as any dish from a fancy restaurant.

The appetizer was marinated trout with onions and pickles served atop miniature toasts, and it was so delicious, he thought he could finish off the entire platter. He felt even hungrier after eating them. The pinch of dill and capers garnishing the trout masked any fishiness and enhanced the richness of the dish.

The main course was crown roast of lamb with stuffing—lamb chops arranged into a crown-like shape. The stuffing included roasted pearl onions and finely sliced carrot pieces, which composed the "jewels" of the crown. The juicy lamb was so tender, it practically melted in Jeffrey's mouth. It was seasoned with herbs and a hint of chili pepper, which added a slight punch to the flavor. The meat was coated in a layer of chopped nuts, giving it a crunchy texture and a delightful aroma.

"Victoria, this is different from last time, isn't it?"

"Yes, Mr. Bernard. I coated the lamb chops in nuts this time."

"Well, it's delicious, as always. Won't you and Nonna join us?"

"Oh, we couldn't possibly..."

Eva intervened and said, "Please join us, Victoria. You're the one who brought Uncle back to the world of the living for us. Please."

Victoria smiled and called out to the kitchen. Nonna appeared, carrying a book in her hand. Even though it had only been two months, she looked much healthier and even more adorable since the last time Jeffrey had seen her. If someone told him she was the daughter of a noble, he'd believe them.

Come to think of it, Victoria had put on some weight, and she seemed curvier than before. Her complexion had also improved.

"I had no idea you were working in this place," he said.

"'This place'?! Don't be rude, Jeffrey. Victoria is fluent in four languages, and her housekeeping is perfect," his uncle exclaimed.

"Four languages..."

Edward listened to his uncle and younger brother with amusement and interjected, "How do you two know each other?"

Jeffrey explained how they'd met, prompting a smirk from Edward. He must've put two and two together and realized this was the lady his brother had gotten dressed up to go out to dinner with.

Victoria noticed that Jeffrey had refrained from telling them he was acting as her guarantor, but she said nothing and listened quietly.

Eva looked astonished. "What? She tripped a thief while carrying Nonna on her back? I'm not sure if I should compliment her for being fearless or chide her for being reckless!"

"Looking back on it now, it was certainly reckless," Victoria agreed. "But thanks to that twist of fate, I'm now renting a guest cottage belonging to the woman whose purse the pickpocket stole. She's giving me exceptionally low rent for the eastern quarter."

"Who are you renting from in the eastern quarter, if I may ask?"

"Dowager Countess Yolana Haynes."

"Oh, the widow of the former head of house! I see. She's quite difficult to get along with, isn't she?"

"No, not at all. She's very kind, and she adores Nonna. She's a wonderful landlady."

The Asher brothers exchanged glances with Eva and her husband.

"But she's notoriously exasperating. Although, I suppose if you've tamed Uncle, it makes sense."

"Edward! What do you mean by 'tamed'?! How rude."

Everyone laughed. Nonna looked bewildered. Victoria more or less understood what they meant. But she thought Mr. Bernard and Lady Yolana's fussiness was rather endearing. Besides, the more difficult someone was, the kinder they tended to be to those they let into their inner circle.

"I've met so many wonderful people since coming to this kingdom," said Victoria. "I'm truly grateful."

Eventually, the birthday party came to an end, and Eva and Michael left. Not long after, Edward looked at Jeffrey and suggested they head out as well.

"I'd like to stay and talk with Victoria for a bit first, Brother. You go on home without me."

"Hmm, all right. I'll be going, then."

Earl Edward Asher smirked but said nothing more before climbing into his carriage and leaving for home. Victoria watched him go and stopped cleaning up, then turned to Nonna and asked, "Can you go play for a bit?" Mr. Bernard's afternoon drink must've kicked in, because he was snoozing away blissfully on the sofa.

Now it was just Jeffrey and Victoria standing outside the foyer.

"What did you want to talk to me about?" she asked.

"The dinner we had a few weeks ago was wonderful. I wanted to know if you'd be interested in doing it again sometime."

Victoria felt warm inside. She'd been in romantic relationships several times before to extract information from a target, but that had just been business. She'd never truly fallen in love with someone before.

"If it's not an imposition, of course," Jeffrey added.

"Not at all. It's just...I'm not sure it's a good idea for me to get too close to a nobleman like you."

"I'm the second son. I'm not the heir, so there's no reason to fuss over social status."

"I see..."

Victoria realized Nonna had opened the door ever so slightly and was peering at them with concern. She smiled and told her not to worry. "My main focus right now is raising Nonna properly..."

Nonna rushed over and hugged Victoria, who gently began stroking her hair.

"All right," said Jeffrey. "In that case, how about the three of us have a picnic?"

"Vicky, what's a picnic?" Nonna asked with sparkling eyes.

"Look, now you've gotten her hopes up," Victoria chided Jeffrey lightly, but then she noticed his eyes were shining with anticipation, just like Nonna's. She relented and said, "All right, then," with a chuckle. "We'll have a picnic lunch. By the way...was there a reason why you didn't want your brother to know that you're my guarantor?"

"No, nothing of the sort. I was just afraid that if Uncle or Eva found out, they'd insist on being your guarantor instead. Anyway, I'll contact you later about the date of the picnic. I'll make sure to schedule it for one of your days off," Jeffrey said, then walked home.

As we'd promised on Mr. Bernard's birthday, the captain and I scheduled a picnic for a date when we both had the day off work.

I filled a basket with sandwiches and fruit water, but then hesitated.

I'd gone on picnics alone with men for work when I needed to get closer to them, but I'd never brought a child along. And I didn't know what children did at picnics because I'd never gone on one as a girl.

"I'm sure it'll work out," I said aloud, trying to be positive as Nonna and I waited for the captain to pick us up.

A few moments later, he showed up in a small carriage. After Nonna and I climbed in, he said, "We'll be traveling through the forest, about an hour each way." Nonna could barely sit still.

"Isn't this fun, Nonna?" I said.

"Yeah."

"What should we do when we get there?"

"Climb trees!"

"You love climbing trees, don't you?"

"Yep."

I'd been teaching Nonna all sorts of things. Since I lacked authority or social status here, this sweetness of hers could be a disadvantage if things didn't improve.

As long as she was willing, I would teach her anything, from reading, writing, and arithmetic, to foreign languages, cooking, and martial arts, and so on. I didn't want Nonna to have to depend on a man for money, and I didn't want her to need to sell her own children to get by, like my parents. I wanted to give her the means to become financially independent and the skills to resist those who would try to dominate her by force. I'd lived my whole life seeing women who weren't so fortunate. My own parents had been so desperate for money, they'd handed me over to Lancome when I was eight.

It was better to know how to climb trees than not. You always needed to have more than one escape route in case of an emergency.

At last, we reached the forest, and the captain stopped the carriage in a small clearing.

"You must be tired. Shall we rest for a bit?" he asked.

"Yes, let's."

The two of us sat down, but Nonna had never been to a place like this before, so she was quite excited. She walked around, picked up some pebbles she found on the ground, and threw them at tree trunks in the distance.

Crack!

She kept walking, throwing pebbles one after the other at different tree trunks. The captain was surprised to see that six-year-old Nonna struck her target every time.

"Nonna, you're amazing. It's impressive you're able to throw that far at all, to say nothing of hitting your targets every time!"

"Vicky's better."

"Really? I'd love to see a demonstration, Victoria."

"Ah-ha-ha. Me?"

Should I pretend to be bad at it? But maybe he'd notice I was faking...

"Why don't you show me the basics first, Captain?"

"Sure."

He threw a few rocks, and they all struck the same spot on the tree trunk. *Hmm, I see.* Since he'd tossed them so adeptly, I thought it would be all right if I did the same.

I tossed my rocks, purposely missing the target once, but hitting it the other times.

"You girls are both very impressive," he said.

"I was a tomboy when I was little."

"A tomboy!" Nonna echoed happily. Her blue-gray eyes were sparkling.

I'm glad we came on this picnic, I thought as I gazed at her happy face. Next, she took off her shoes and began to shimmy up a tree in her socks.

"Hey, hey. Now we're climbing trees? Don't fall!" the captain called.

"Vicky's better than me!"

The captain looked at me in surprise. His eyes felt like daggers.

"I was a tomboy who grew up in the country," I said, revising my earlier statement.

I hadn't restricted Nonna from saying anything in particular. I'd assumed that if I wanted her to understand how to keep secrets, then the fewer rules and restrictions she had, the better. However, I'd just learned a very important lesson—excited children will simply blurt out anything unless you remind them not to.

"I'm not demonstrating this time. I'm wearing a skirt."

"I know that." The captain laughed. When he smiled, the corners of his eyes crinkled, making his handsome, stern face look kind and soft. And how I loved his voice. Nonna climbed high in the tree and sat on a branch. She swung her legs back and forth, gazing down at us cheerfully.

"That's dangerous," the captain cautioned as he started walking toward the tree. He wanted to be close enough to catch her if she fell. I knew Nonna's skills, so I wasn't worried, but I accompanied him nonetheless.

"Did you really teach her how to do this? Don't you think it's too dangerous?"

"If I stop her from doing anything unsafe, she'll grow up to be a sheltered woman who can't protect herself."

The captain glanced at me. I wondered if he didn't like my comment.

"I'm sorry, I'm sure you think that's brazen of me," I said.

"No, I was just surprised because I've never heard a woman say that before."

Nonna safely climbed down from the tree. I was expecting the captain to warn her to be careful, but he didn't say anything. After that, we played tag and picked flowers, and then it was time for lunch.

"The dinner you made the other night was delicious, but these sandwiches are wonderful, too," the captain told me.

"Thank you."

I'd prepared three types of sandwiches: chicken and vegetables with hard-boiled eggs, jam and butter, and pulled pork with a generous helping of mustard and chopped onions.

The captain seemed to prefer the chicken and pork sandwiches, which I'd been expecting. The jam-and-butter sandwiches were Nonna's favorite.

"Did you used to be a chef or a scholar or something?" the captain asked me.

"I have worked as a chef before, yes. Languages are just a hobby of mine."

"I see. That's impressive."

"Since you're a nobleman, I'm sure you studied languages ever since you were a child."

"Well, yes. But you're a commoner, aren't you?"

"That's right. I was born into a poor family, so I had to learn how to do everything."

"I see."

There was a fleeting look of sympathy in his eyes that made me feel a little guilty. *Yes, that's right*, I said silently.

Nonna crawled onto my lap as I sat on the picnic blanket and put her arms around my neck. I adored the feeling of her slender arms around me, and I gently caressed them as I spoke to her.

"This is fun, isn't it?" I said to Nonna.

"Yeah."

When we first started living together, Nonna was hesitant of my touch, but she'd grown very affectionate and touchy-feely with me lately.

Since I'd only been eight when I left home, I remembered thinking that my sister, Emily, was adorable, but I didn't have many memories of us spending time together as siblings. But now Nonna was like my little sister and a daughter all in one.

"She's very fond of you," the captain mused.

"Yes. She's just so adorable. I had no idea children could be so precious."

As Nonna listened to our conversation, she pressed her cheek against my hair. She often did this when she was content and wanted to be affectionate.

"Aren't you glad we came on this picnic?" I asked.

"Uh-huh! Do you think so, too, Vicky?"

"I do. It was very fun."

All of a sudden, Nonna let go of me and sprinted off. *Thud! Swish!* She leaped high into the air, bent her upper body forward, and pulled her knees up to her chest, executing a clean somersault before landing gracefully on both feet.

Goodness!

She'd never successfully done a forward somersault before. I wondered why she was able to pull one off now. When children were excited, they had about five times the skill and energy as usual.

The captain's eyes were as big as saucers as he looked over at me. "Did she learn that from you, too?"

I chuckled wryly but didn't answer. He shook his head with disbelief and returned his gaze to Nonna.

We made all kinds of wonderful memories at the picnic. The three of us headed back to the carriage, and the captain put one foot up to climb into the driver's seat, only to pause.

"I thought it would be nice if only the three of us came, but now I'm regretting not bringing a driver," he said.

"If you're tired, I can take over and drive us home."

"I'm not. I just meant that if I'd brought a driver, we could've chatted during the two-hour trip. And you driving... Never mind, it's pointless to ask anymore."

"Haven't you heard the saying *jack-of-all-trades, master of none*?"

"That doesn't apply to you."

The captain reached for my hair, which was tied in a ponytail. He gave it a brief, affectionate caress and then sat in the driver's seat.

If this were a job, I'd put on a happy smile, but right now, I had no idea how my face looked. I was completely flustered. But I did know that when the right person touched you, they could give you chills in the best sense of the word.

Nonna was tired and fell asleep on my lap. I gazed out the window, feeling a pleasant kind of exhaustion on the ride home.

I'd experienced all sorts of trades while working as an operative and had posed as women of all different social classes. I didn't hate the organization or my job. It'd been a means to help my family, and I'd spent a very productive and beneficial nineteen years there.

But to think this whole time, I'd never experienced a real picnic or truly been in love. I must have been lacking in all sorts of areas compared with someone with an ordinary job.

From now on, I could fill in those gaps as much as I wanted. And there was no reason to rush. Plus, I didn't necessarily need to have a perfectly well-rounded life. It would be fun to make up for lost time anyway. And it would be exciting to add more cards to my arsenal.

The next thing I knew, a faint smile was on my lips.

Interlude

Lancome's Recollections

Back in the central control room of Hagl's Special Operations Force, Lancome was deep in thought as he ran his fingers through his light-brown hair.

He'd first encountered Chloe when he was a young operative. One day on his way home from work, he spotted a little girl drawing a picture on the ground with a nail. Her drawing was so detailed that he grew intrigued; the girl seemed intelligent, skilled.

She had brown hair and brown eyes. There was nothing strikingly beautiful or unsightly about her, nothing that would leave a lasting memory.

I think she might be a good candidate, he thought, so he approached her parents and said "I'm a member of a noble family who's in search of a servant. Would you let me take her in?" Her parents turned down the young stranger's request once, but they were struggling financially, so when he offered them money in exchange for her, they accepted right away.

Once Chloe entered the academy, he would chat with her frequently. Learning that she would be handsomely rewarded for missions was all the motivation she needed to buckle down on her studies. She quickly excelled and rose to the top of her class at fifteen, then took on her first assignment.

* * *

One day, Lancome learned that Chloe's family had died. She was in the middle of a very important mission.

He knew Chloe cared deeply about her family. But it would put the organization in a tough spot if she lost her composure now. So he elected not to notify her of their deaths.

However, her skills were needed for one mission after the other, so he never found the opportunity to tell her. Meanwhile, her health started to fail. Once news of Lancome's impending marriage spread, she began to get progressively thinner. A colleague of his told him that according to the rumors, Chloe's poor health was due to a broken heart. But he found that hard to believe because she'd never once looked at him that way.

He made her take some time off. Immediately after resuming work, she disappeared.

The most likely scenario was that she'd fallen off the cliff. They'd found her necklace at the bottom. Lancome had given it to her as a present to commemorate the completion of her first mission.

The waves were rough, and the current was fast, so her body still hadn't been found.

Upper management had concluded that the wind had knocked off her hat, and she'd fallen off the cliff when she went to retrieve it. But Lancome just couldn't accept that Chloe was dead. Not only was she a woman of mental fortitude, but she was also a very cautious person who wouldn't have done something so reckless.

Chapter Four

The Soiree

One day while the captain was in the middle of a shift at work, he dropped by his uncle Bernard's house to see me.

"The royal family is having a soiree at the castle soon, and I was wondering if you might like to come with me."

"A soiree? Thrown by the royal family? Why, I couldn't possibly!" I demurred.

"I'll provide you with a dress and some jewelry. You don't have to dance if you don't want to. All you'd need to do is stay by my side and be friendly to everyone."

"So you're saying I'd be arm candy?" The troubled smile on his face when I said this was so adorable that I couldn't help but smile in return. "I'm sure there's no shortage of women who'd love to accept that job, Captain."

"Those women are only interested in one thing, and it would lead to trouble."

"Ahh, so you want me to come in order to keep other women away from you!"

"That's part of it, but mainly, I want my boss to stop trying to fix me up with someone. I thought you'd fit right in among all the other noblewomen."

I let out a sigh. Though the chances were slim, it was possible that

I could see someone I knew at the castle. Surely, there'd be nobles or other dignitaries who often traveled to other kingdoms. I was adept at pretending to be a noble's daughter, but I didn't want to do it.

I'll just say no, I thought and lifted my face when Lady Eva interjected all of a sudden.

"Oh, won't you go with him, darling? Think of it as an extension of your job. We can pay you for your time and trouble. You spend all day every day dealing with our cantankerous old uncle, and then you have to go home and deal with an equally cantankerous old lady! You poor thing. Seeing you spend all your time with the elderly and children makes my heart ache for you. You're still so young."

"Oh, but I..."

"I'll look after Nonna. You go on ahead and enjoy yourself. Think of it as helping out our poor Jeffrey. Nonna, you'll be fine spending one night away from Victoria, won't you? I'll be with you the whole time, and you can stay at my house with me."

"I'll be okay. Vicky, go to the party with the captain!"

"What?! Nonna..."

In the blink of an eye, all my avenues of escape were cut off.

I had no other choice but to agree, which meant I had to carefully consider all the possible outcomes that might happen on that day. *Prepare for the worst but hope for the best* was ingrained into my bones. All I could do now was pray that I wouldn't run into any acquaintances.

That evening, I went to tell Nonna good night in bed but found her still awake.

"Can't you sleep, Nonna?"

"......"

"Are you scared of me leaving you, after all?"

"I can do it. I just didn't like it when she called you a poor thing."

"Oh, Nonna." I couldn't help but take her little face in my hands. "I love living with you, Nonna. It's not something for anyone to pity at all. Lady Eva didn't mean anything by it. Don't take it to heart, okay?"

"Will you wear a dress, Vicky?"
"Yes."
"And jewels?"
"Maybe."
She smiled a little.
"What is it?"
"I want to see you dressed up like a princess."
"Okay. Nonna, I'm not a poor thing. Don't dwell on it, okay?"
"Okay."
"Good girl. Sweet dreams."
"Good night, Vicky."

Lady Eva insisted on giving me lessons, saying, "I'll give you a crash course on proper etiquette."

I didn't want to make Nonna wait around every day after work, so I told Lady Eva, "I'm the kind of person who can get the hang of something after one or two tries."

"You're amazing. How can you learn so quickly?" she asked in disbelief.

"Honestly, this isn't the first time I've been invited to a party to keep other women away from someone. Though, I am a bit rusty; the last time I did it was quite a while ago."

"Oh, I see! That makes sense."

I told Lady Eva that I used to work for a noble family and had been tasked to play the role of the master's lover to ward off a woman who was trying to get into his pockets by becoming his second wife. That was partly a true story, but my actual task back then had been investigating the ties between the nobleman and someone from another kingdom.

I was prepared for people to think that I was the captain's mistress, and if any of them said, "We can't have a girl like that working for us,"

I was willing to look for another job. But Lady Eva's attitude toward me didn't change after I told her about my past, and Mr. Bernard didn't seem to particularly mind, either.

Ten days after Lady Eva took my measurements, a custom-made, tailored dress from Captain Jeffrey Asher arrived at Lady Yolana's estate instead of my cottage.

The deliveryman must have assumed the lady of the house had ordered it.

The dress was lilac in color and elegant in design, with a tasteful neckline. A pair of matching lilac shoes arrived in a separate box.

The maid delivered the packages to me, accompanied by Lady Yolana.

"So you're still seeing the captain, are you?" she asked.

"I'm not sure I'd say that I'm *seeing* him. He visits Mr. Bernard's mansion occasionally."

"Then what's the meaning of this dress?"

"Well, you see..."

After I explained the situation, Lady Yolana laughed cheerfully. "He's so awkward. He should've just invited you as his date instead of making up silly excuses like that!"

I smiled vaguely, finding it difficult to tell her we'd already gone out to dinner and a picnic. But then Nonna happily exclaimed, "We went on a picnic together!"

"My! Is that so? How wonderful. You and the captain are both single. And nowadays, nobody cares much about differences in status!"

"Oh, but we don't have that sort of relationship..."

"Poppycock! Everyone needs the sparkle of love in their lives. Especially when you're young."

I wasn't really sure how to take Lady Yolana's encouragement. Even though I'd be there to ward off other women, people would surely assume the captain and I were dating. That might lead to more trouble, but I'd already been prepared for that when I accepted.

Never make a promise you can't keep. And never break a promise you make was a conviction I held dear, after all.

I spent the whole day of the soiree getting ready, then waited for the captain to arrive.

He came to pick me up at four o'clock on the dot in his carriage. His eyes widened with surprise the moment he saw me in my formal attire.

"You look like a gorgeous noblewoman. I knew lilac would look wonderful on you. I'm going to be the subject of many envious stares tonight."

"Thank you. You can never give a lady too many compliments, you know." I tipped my chin upward to feign haughtiness, and he laughed.

Nonna had asked if she could stay in the main residence tonight with Susan, the lady's maid, instead.

"We'll keep her until morning, so don't worry about coming home tonight."

"Oh, Lady Yolana! I'll be home tonight. Just what kind of trouble do you want me to get into?"

"Ha-ha! Go on now and enjoy yourselves," she said with a wink. I bowed my head to her and waved to Nonna, then climbed into the carriage. Mr. Asher offered his hand to help me up, and I noticed it was large and calloused, dry but warm.

"Eva told me this isn't the first time you've been asked to keep other ladies away at a party," Mr. Asher said to me.

"That's right. I'm an expert. Also, will you tell me the name of the man who keeps trying to set you up? I want to make sure I know who he is before I meet him."

"Sure. I'll show you once we spot him at the party. He might not turn up, though."

The two of us chatted the whole way to the castle.

The royal palace was aglow with dozens of oil lamps and hanging chandeliers, along with a large bonfire in the garden. The dazzling light from inside only enhanced the darkness of the garden. Guards in navy-blue uniforms stood at attention outside, alongside royal guards who wore gleaming white uniforms with golden embellishments.

The party was overflowing with ladies wearing fancy dresses. It reminded me of a meadow full of blossoming flowers. This was my fourth time attending a soiree at a royal palace, including those in other countries, but it was definitely the most glamorous I had been to yet. The gathering was truly befitting a prosperous kingdom like Ashbury.

The moment we stepped inside the venue, a murmur spread through the crowd, and people turned to look at us in waves. Some glanced at us discreetly, while others brazenly stared. *Just how popular is the captain anyway?* I wondered. The other partygoers' gazes fell upon me as I stood next to him.

Guess it's time to fulfill my duty.

It had been such a long time since I'd been enveloped in this pleasant buzz of nervousness. I straightened my posture and tightened my grip on my companion's arm, glancing up at the silver-haired captain with a smile.

"It looks like you're popular with ladies and gentlemen alike."

"Well, everyone's probably shocked because it's been ten years since I attended a party with a woman."

"What?" This was news to me. This gorgeous man had gone ten years without a date? What in the world did that mean?

"Oh, Captain Asher! Long time no see. I'm surprised to see you here with a lady."

"Hello, Earl Wald. It took me a very long time find someone I wanted to bring."

"May I have your name, miss?"

"I'm Victoria Sellars. I'm from the kingdom of Randall."

"Ah! I thought I hadn't seen your face around here before. So you're from the neighboring kingdom, then."

The story we had agreed to beforehand was that I was the daughter of Lady Eva's cousin, who lived in Randall.

"If we were going to be honest and say you're a commoner, that's all people will talk about. I don't want you to feel uncomfortable, Victoria," Lady Eva had said.

But just to be safe, I'd slipped the identification papers from Randall that I'd forged into my pocket.

As we greeted various guests, a young lady who seemed to be around age twenty or so dragged her date over to us.

Uh-oh, I better be careful with this one, I thought upon seeing the intensity of her stare and nudged Mr. Asher slightly to let him know. He kept his eyes forward and nodded.

"Oh, good evening, Lady Gilmore."

"Captain Asher, how many times must I insist that you call me Florence? Anyway, it seems tonight is quite unusual, isn't it?" As she spoke, she looked me up and down to appraise me. There was nothing I despised more. Not to mention, the expression on her face was so uncouth that I couldn't believe she was a noblewoman. It was full of envy; clearly, she'd forgotten to correct herself. I smiled at her, patiently accepting her rude stare and doing my best to exude a mature confidence.

"Victoria," Mr. Asher began, "this is Florence Gilmore, the daughter of Earl Gilmore. Lady Gilmore, this is Victoria Sellars. She's the daughter of a viscount from a neighboring kingdom."

"My! A neighboring kingdom!" The ill-natured look on Lady Florence's face only grew more twisted once she learned I was of a lower social status than she.

Idiot. How foolish can you be, putting your terrible personality on full display in front of someone you like?

"I'm Victoria Sellars. All the young ladies of Ashbury are just so elegant and refined. I'm impressed."

"Pfft." I heard the captain stifle a laugh. He'd picked up on my sarcasm. "Victoria is very important to me. I hope you'll get along with her well," he said, then slipped his arm around my shoulder and planted a kiss on my hair.

"Wha—?!" Lady Florence froze in shock, her face and neck gradually turning red with fury.

Since the captain hadn't even brought a date out in ten years, his romantic gesture caused quite a stir. Honestly, I was surprised by his display of affection, too, but not terribly so. In our meeting before the party, he'd told me to do my best to play the part of a woman in love.

"Oh, Jeffrey!" I cooed sweetly. I twisted my upper body slightly, allowing everyone to see the pure joy on my face as I gazed at him adoringly.

The captain gave me an even sweeter look in response. *Whoa!* And in the process, he made me very uncharacteristically nervous.

"If you'll excuse us," he said, ushering us away from Lady Florence, who by now looked like she might emit flames from her eyes. The captain took me around the party to greet the other guests, but so far, the man who'd been trying to set him up—his boss—remained elusive.

Before long, the crown prince made an appearance, representing the royal family. He had blond hair and blue eyes, and there was an intimidating quietness about him.

He made a simple speech, then began to dance with a woman I assumed was his princess. Afterward, they both went off to socialize. Since the other guests had started to dance, the captain and I followed suit. Despite his tall, muscular frame, he was a surprisingly elegant dancer. He knew exactly how to lead, which made dancing with him a breeze.

"Eva told me you were a good dancer, Victoria, and she was right. I swear, the more time I spend with you, the more you surprise me."

"Thank you. Now, who's your boss you spoke to me about?"

"The man who was just dancing over there. The crown prince."

"Goodness!"

I gave the captain an impressed smile. *It would make sense if his boss was a member of the royal guard, but Jeffrey is the captain of the Second Order! Don't tell me he's the crown prince's favorite, too!* I thought with surprise. While I was still processing this, a man in the corner caught my eye.

He was wearing a white servant's uniform, but he hadn't been working for a while now. He was holding a silver tray carrying silver glasses filled with alcohol, and he seemed to be looking for someone.

On rare occasions, suspicious individuals could blend into large soirees like this, but not at a royal castle. The government conducted strict background checks on anyone working at the castle, and they wouldn't have a new hire stationed at such an important party.

But I could tell by from this man's movements that he was an amateur. Yet there were only a few reasons why someone of his standing would be here. I briefly considered ignoring him for a moment, but then quickly dismissed that idea. I would have to get the captain to spring into action.

I squeezed his arm, sending him a signal.

"What's the matter?" he asked.

"There's a man behind you who's dressed as a servant but hasn't been working for a while now. I think he may be after the ladies' jewels. Do you think such a thing could happen at the castle?"

The captain casually spun me around to change directions, angling us toward the man. He watched him for a few moments, then nodded. "It seems like he's looking for someone."

As we danced, I watched the man. All of a sudden, he began walking away briskly. He must've found his target. I shifted my gaze ahead, searching for a route he would use to escape.

"I'm sorry, Victoria. I'll be back."

"Go right ahead."

I expected nothing less from the captain. He also noticed that the man had sprung into action. In all likelihood, the man had chosen to commit his crime at such a heavily guarded event because it was the only opportunity he had to get close to his target.

Now that I was alone, I hurried to the terrace as quickly as I could without seeming unnatural. I climbed down over the railing and landed in the garden, then crouched down in the shadow of a tree, keeping my eye on the spot where I expected the man to pass through as he fled. Although the inside of the castle was bright, the trees and brush here were thick, so it was very dark.

Before long, I heard several women scream, and the sound of glass breaking.

That's too bad. Did you let him get away, Captain?

A dark silhouette leaped out from the bright venue. He bounded over the terrace railing and ran, his back hunched. He quickly peeled off his servant's uniform as he came closer to me. I'd predicted he would do that as well—the pure-white uniform would make him stand out way too much otherwise.

Now!

I rose to my feet, lifted the hem of my dress, and delivered a roundhouse kick to the side of the man's head as he attempted to free his arm from his jacket sleeve right in front of me. I grabbed both his shoulders without hesitation and kneed him right in the abdomen. Then I brought my hand down and gave him a swift karate chop on the back of his neck as he pitched forward. The entire sequence lasted about three or four seconds. The man let out a grunt and then fell forward, unconscious.

I ran away from him at full speed. Keeping as low to the ground as I could and glancing back over my shoulder, I saw several men jump down from the terrace. They'd probably apprehend the thief while he was still unconscious.

I took a few deep breaths to steady myself before casually returning to the party. The evening had been ruined as soon as it had begun. I saw the captain looking around anxiously, so I walked over to him discreetly and addressed him in a soft voice.

"I'll take a carriage home."

"Oh, good. There you are. Use my carriage to go back. I can't leave right now, I'm afraid. I'll see you later."

I wondered if I should ask him not to tell anyone I had alerted him

to the man. No, on second thought, that might draw even more suspicion.

One section of the event hall was utter chaos, with scattered glass shards, spilled alcohol, and food all over the floor. I slipped out with the departing guests. Even though the culprit had been caught, the lax security response was very concerning. If I were in charge, the first thing I would do was conduct interviews before letting anyone leave.

I found the Asher family carriage. Just as I was about to climb in, the driver looked at me with concern. "I heard some kind of commotion in the party. Is everything okay?"

"There was an incident, but it's fine now. I'd like to change my clothes before going home; could you stop by a shop in the southern quarter for me?"

"Of course."

I'm sure he was wondering why I needed to change if I was just going home, but he didn't say a word about it, as an earl's servant should.

The coachman stopped in front of an inexpensive clothing shop in the southern quarter.

"I can go home by myself from here."

It looked like he wanted to say something, but I tipped him generously and sent him on his way. It had been a while since I'd done something like I did at the party, so I didn't feel comfortable going straight home to Nonna yet. I had a feeling she'd be very sensitive to that sort of thing.

I bought a plain dark-navy dress at the shop and quickly changed into it. I paid for the dress and said I'd come back the next day to pick up the one I'd worn to the party.

There was a pub on the street behind the clothing shop. I pushed the door open, fortunately finding that it was mostly empty. I took a seat at a table in the back where I'd be inconspicuous in the dim light. A man who appeared to be the owner came over to take my order, but I just asked for him to give me their best liquor.

I felt satisfied, comfortable.

It was the kind of accomplishment you got when you anticipated something would happen and planned ahead for it. I was so full of adrenaline that everything around me seemed to be moving in slow motion. That hadn't happened in quite a while.

The owner set down a stiff drink in front of me, and he'd barely moved to leave before I downed the whole thing in one gulp.

"Give me another," I asked.

The owner, who had short black hair and a beard, turned around and glanced at my empty glass. "You got it," he said.

I thought I was only working for the sake of my family and Lancome, but I guess a part of me really liked my job, I mused.

Of course, I had no intention of going back to the organization after everything that had happened. I had Nonna now, and I wanted to live with her.

I savored my second drink. Once I felt like I had calmed down, I paid my tab and then left the pub. The bearded owner called out, "Come again," in a deep voice as I departed.

As I walked down the street, I reflected on what had transpired tonight.

I had interfered with the man because I didn't want him to kill anyone.

Granted, I had no idea whether his target at the party was good or bad. But I'd had a sinking feeling he was out to murder someone, and if I'd done nothing and found out later that his victim had been a decent, innocent person, not even *my* mental fortitude would've been enough to keep me from feeling regret. And I knew from experience that regret could torment one's heart.

Plus, that man had been an amateur; when people like him wanted someone dead, it was usually out of some kind of personal grudge. Whatever had happened in the past to stoke his grudge could never be undone, even if he succeeded in killing his target. I sincerely doubted anyone who had committed murder ever thought, *Now that I've killed the person I hated, I've completely forgotten how they wronged me!* I knew several people who had taken a life because of their personal grudges, and they all lived very dark lives afterward.

I had stopped the man from getting away for no one but myself.

The wall surrounding the garden was very high, but there was one tree a short distance away from it that was even taller. An agile man could shimmy up that tree and easily hop over the wall to a separate section of the estate. Because of the soiree, there would either be very few people out and about, or no one at all. Though a failed landing could result in both legs being broken, he would have had a slim chance of escaping if he'd stayed cautious.

And that section of the grounds was a dead end, so there weren't any guards stationed there. Amateur though the man was, he'd planned this out carefully.

If the man had escaped, the castle would have investigated the party guests in an attempt to ascertain his identity. That would've been a very inconvenient situation for me, since I was a foreign first-time guest and a commoner who was pretending to be a noble—with forged identification papers, to boot. If I were in charge, I would have investigated myself before anyone else.

But now that the man was captured, the chances of me being investigated once his motive was identified were very slim, since I'd had nothing to do with it.

Those thoughts ran through my head as I walked home. The instant I got back, Lady Yolana began to interrogate me, asking me such questions like "Why did you walk home alone?" and "Why are you back so early?" and "What happened to your gown?"

All in all, it was an eventful night.

Jeffrey was attending an emergency meeting called by the king.

There were eight participants in total: the king; the crown prince, Conrad; the second prince, Cedric; the prime minister; the captain of the royal guard; the chamberlain; Marquess McKenna (the target of the attack); and Jeffrey, the captain of the Second Order of knights.

First, the events of the night were explained in detail. Leading the proceedings was the crown prince.

"Lord McKenna, do you have any idea why someone would try to harm you?"

"Not in the slightest, I'm afraid. The man must've been hired, of course, but I can't think of any reason why someone would hold a grudge against me." Marquess McKenna, a man in his fifties, straightened his imposing figure and responded with a hint of bewilderment. "However, I must apologize for causing such inconvenience at Your Majesty's soiree. If it weren't for the swift arrival of the captain of the Second Order of the knights, I'd likely be..."

"Dead. The knife on the man's person was coated in poison."

Everyone's faces turned grim when they heard the crown prince announce that.

"Jeffrey, when did you notice the assailant?" the crown prince asked.

"Actually, I wasn't the one who noticed him first. It was the lady who accompanied me tonight. We were dancing when she said there was a servant who hadn't moved at all. I looked over and noticed that he was acting suspiciously. That was when he rushed into the crowd, so I chased after him."

The crown prince steepled his hands together, tapping his fingers against each other. "I see. The woman brought it to your attention?"

"Yes."

"That man had been working at the castle for a year. Baron Eld wrote a letter of introduction for him, and we've already sent soldiers to summon him for questioning. The assailant must have bought his claim of relation to the baron."

The chamberlain, a middle-aged man responsible for hiring all castle staff, had failed to recognize this and was currently dabbing at the cold sweat on his brow with a handkerchief. "Additionally, the first guard who ran into the garden after the man has exceptionally keen night vision. When he found the culprit collapsed on the ground, he caught a glimpse of a woman running away."

"A woman?"

"You mean to say a woman knocked out the culprit?"

A buzz of surprise ran through the room.

"He didn't actually see her knock him out, but the guard chased the man from the venue to the terrace and then into the garden. The culprit disappeared from his view for only a few seconds after jumping down to the garden. By the time the guard found him, the culprit was already unconscious. Even a man would have difficulty knocking out someone that fast. It could very well be a mistake on the guard's part. Or perhaps the woman just happened to be out in the garden at that exact time and was startled, then ran away."

"But someone had to have knocked the man out, correct?" asked the king.

"What did the woman look like?" the captain of the royal guard asked.

"She ran away quickly, and since it was dark, the only identifying feature the guard could pick out was that she was wearing a dress," Prince Conrad said with regret.

Victoria's face flashed into Jeffrey's mind as he listened quietly. She was the one who'd first noticed the culprit. He thought back to how she'd tripped that pickpocket while carrying Nonna on her back.

"First, we need to investigate the man's background. Lord McKenna, may we ask you some more questions?"

"Of course," the marquess replied to the captain of the royal guard.

There was no further information, so the meeting was called to a close, and several of the people there hurried out of the room to attend to their duties. The ones who remained were the king, the two princes, the prime minister, and Jeffrey, who had stayed behind at the request of the crown prince.

Prince Conrad spoke first.

"Jeffrey, I just have a feeling the woman spotted in the garden was your date. I didn't share this in front of the others, but the guard who saw the woman confirmed the color of her dress. He said it was either light blue or light purple but wasn't sure which. Your date was wearing a lilac dress, was she not? And you say she noticed the man acting suspiciously before anyone else? Who is this young lady?"

"Her name is Victoria Sellars. I only met her recently."

"And may I ask how you two become acquainted?"

Jeffrey decided it was in Victoria's best interests to be honest, so he apologized to the princes and the king for allowing a commoner to attend under the guise of being a noble.

"That's fine—don't worry about that part. I want to know the details of how the two of you met. Is it possible she approached you with an ulterior motive in mind?"

Jeffrey recounted how his relationship with Victoria had progressed, going through the events one by one.

He started with the story of her tripping the pickpocket while carrying Nonna, then explained how they'd reunited at his uncle's house, and finally told the prince about how he'd invited her to the soiree.

"Hmm." The crown prince nodded. "I see. By all accounts, it appears to have been a chance encounter, then, especially since you were the one who made advances toward her. I don't believe she was targeting you."

"I didn't *make advances*..."

"No matter how you look at it, that's precisely what you did. That's unusual of you. May I ask why?"

"The way she looked at me didn't make me feel uncomfortable. I felt at ease with her. But most of all, despite being a woman, she's lived a very independent life. She had the courage to take in an abandoned child even though she just moved here from another country, and..."

"So you've fallen for her?" the king interjected frankly.

Jeffrey nodded honestly. "...Yes, Your Majesty."

"*Haah...*" The first prince let out a deep sigh as he stared at Jeffrey. "You've rejected every lady I've tried to set you up with, and here you are falling for another handful of a woman, Jeffrey."

"And I'm sorry about that. But I promise you, she's wonderful."

"Brother, I'd like to meet this lady. If she really did knock out that man, she must have incredible skill," Prince Cedric, who was very confident in his swordsmanship and martial arts abilities, piped up.

"Meet her and do what? You've got nothing to do with this," the crown prince said.

"Don't you want to see what she can do, though?"

"Knock it off, Cedric."

"Please stop, Your Highness."

Both the king and Jeffrey intervened.

"Your Majesty, Prince Conrad. It seems you may think Victoria's working for someone, but if that were the case, why would she take in the child? That would just get in the way of her job," Jeffrey said.

"That is true," the king agreed. "Jeffrey, I won't say a word against you getting close with this woman. However, if you notice anything suspicious about her at all, you must come to me right away."

"Yes, Your Majesty."

"If the captain doesn't want to, I'll take on that responsibility."

"No thank you, Prince Cedric. I'll watch over Victoria."

The five of them called the meeting to a close, and Jeffrey excused himself.

As the king returned to his quarters, he turned to the prime minister beside him and said in a quiet voice, "I want you to contact our people in Randall and have them look into this Victoria Sellars."

Interlude

Jeffrey's Regret

"Brother, are you sure we should just let this woman go free?" Cedric asked Conrad.

"According to Jeffrey's account, she's most likely innocent. However, it's unclear why she knocked the man unconscious. Let's surveil her, for Jeffrey's sake. It's partly my fault that he's been struggling for the past ten years. If anyone has to be the bad guy in this situation, let it be me. I don't want you to worry about it."

Although the two princes looked very much alike with their golden hair and blue eyes, their personalities couldn't be any more different.

The crown prince, Conrad, was twenty-five years old. He was thoughtful and gentle. The second prince, Cedric, was twenty years old. He was vivacious and cheerful.

The incident that Conrad had said was partly his fault was the cause of a war that had occurred ten years prior.

A western tribe declared they were going to reclaim sacred land that was rightfully theirs, then launched an attack on the western border of the kingdom of Ashbury. There was a sprawling, thick forest in that region. Long ago, the borders of the neighboring country and Ashbury, which lay beyond the forest, had been ambiguous.

Later on, after negotiations, the border was clearly defined, and the settlers of Ashbury developed the land on this side of the border.

They made it fertile and prosperous. That was when the western nation suddenly turned around claimed, "That forest has been our sacred land since ancient times!"

Ashbury didn't back down, of course, and so war broke out.

That had been the crown prince's first battle. At the time, Jeffrey was a member of the First Order of the knights, and he'd also participated.

In the beginning, it seemed like Ashbury would achieve victory by overwhelming the enemy, but opinions differed when it came to strategy.

There were two proposals. One was that they should launch a surprise attack the night before the enemy could regroup. The other faction thought it would be too dangerous to strike at night if the enemy was familiar with the terrain, so they believed they should wait until sunrise to hit their foe with everything they had.

Both proposals had advantages and disadvantages, so it was difficult to reach a consensus. The battalion commander looked to the crown prince to make the call, even though it was only his first battle.

After some thought, Conrad decided it would be best to attack the enemy at night, before their reinforcements could arrive. But a squadron leader named Kaiser disagreed with his decision.

"Your Highness, if the enemy anticipates a night attack, not only will we suffer severe casualties, but it may also be difficult to distinguish between friend or foe if we stumble during the initial strike, which runs the risk of friendly fire. Please reconsider your decision."

Despite Kaiser's objection, Conrad ultimately chose the night ambush after some careful thought.

Unfortunately, the enemy had expected a night attack, and arrows rained down upon the Ashbury army like a storm from the hilltops. They suffered significant casualties.

Although Conrad survived the battle, Kaiser had shielded him from above and was struck in the back by several arrows.

Despite the assault from enemy archers, Ashbury emerged victorious in a fierce counterattack, saving the settlement.

Squadron leader Kaiser's only surviving family member was his twin sister, Katherine. Shortly before Kaiser's death, their parents had died of illness in short succession, so poor Katherine had lost her entire family in the span of one year.

However, she did not lose her composure when she received the tragic news of her brother's passing and remained calm.

Many people were impressed, saying they expected nothing less from a daughter of a family who'd been knights for generations.

However, amid the aftermath of caring for her ill parents and the stress of losing them one after the other, the tragedy of also losing her twin brother was secretly eating away at eighteen-year-old Katherine's heart.

At the time, she was betrothed to Jeffrey Asher, a twenty-two-year-old member of the First Order of the knights.

He knew that twins had a stronger bond than even a parent and child, so he'd been sincerely worried about his fiancée ever since their triumphant arrival home. Jeffrey had fought close to the crown prince and witnessed Kaiser's final moments firsthand.

The squadron leader had been struck by an arrow, sending blood spurting from his mouth. When he realized he could no longer be saved, he used his body to shield the prince.

Jeffrey thought it would best to let some time pass before telling Katherine about Kaiser's tragic end; that way, she could have some time to stabilize after her parents' passing.

But when Katherine received some visitors, they ended up breaking the news to her by expressing their condolences. To make matters worse, they gave her an inaccurate account.

"The prince was impatient for victory, so he insisted upon that unreasonable night raid."

"Squadron Leader Kaiser was opposed to the prince's strategy from the get-go."

"He covered the prince's body with his own to protect him and died in battle."

Their accounts were a mixture of truth and hearsay, yet Katherine accepted them all as completely factual, unbeknownst to Jeffrey.

About ten days after the funeral, Crown Prince Conrad summoned Katherine and Jeffrey to the castle. He wanted to meet with Kaiser's younger sister and apologize to her directly.

The prince asked everyone else to leave the room and rose from his seat, then bowed to her. "I'm sorry."

Jeffrey was beside himself when he saw that.

Kaiser's death in battle wasn't Conrad's fault, and when the crown prince himself was genuflecting before her, what else could Katherine do but forgive him?

There was no need for Conrad to apologize. I wish we could've waited to talk about this until Katherine had more time to heal, Jeffrey thought. But back then, the prince was only fifteen, so it wasn't surprising that he hadn't taken those factors into consideration. Perhaps the king wasn't even aware of this meeting in the first place.

Katherine quickly got to her feet and said, "Your Highness, please lift your face!" as she approached him. She reached out to him with a serene smile. Jeffrey tried to stop her, as touching the prince without permission was considered rude. Just then, however, he realized she was hiding something in her hand.

He silently jumped on his fiancée and held her down, wrenching her hand open to find a tiny, sharp dagger there. It was a miracle she'd even made it into an audience with the prince without being patted down first.

Jeffrey bumped into a table, sending cups and plates to the floor with a *crash*. Hearing the commotion, guards rushed into the room. Jeffrey quickly concealed the knife and said, "She wasn't feeling well," then took Katherine to the infirmary without a word.

* * *

Jeffrey carried Katherine to the infirmary and set her down on the sofa. She didn't cry, nor did she seem angry. She just sat there quietly, her eyes like marbles staring vacantly at him but not *seeing* him. It was then that he realized she hadn't accepted her twin brother's death, and she most certainly hadn't forgiven the prince.

After Kaiser's death, she'd put on a cheerful smile, remarking over and over again about how her brother had chosen to die in battle to protect the prince. Jeffrey was overcome with regret at having ever believed her.

The only ones who knew Katherine had pointed a knife at a member of the royal family were Jeffrey and the prince, but the four guards who'd rushed into the room might've been suspicious of her. If the truth got out, Katherine would certainly face execution.

Fortunately, the prince decided to keep the incident under wraps, so Jeffrey took Katherine back to her house. He told the servants, "Keep her under close watch and don't allow her to leave the premises. Please call a doctor." Then he took several days off work to stay overnight at her manor with her.

"Kaiser's death wasn't the prince's fault."

He tried to explain the truth several times, but Katherine just stared at him with dead eyes.

The day after Jeffrey went back to work, Katherine took her own life. He could still vividly recall the despair he felt when he heard the news of her suicide. She left a note that only said, *I am going to go be with my family.*

After Katherine's death, Jeffrey went to the captain of the knights and asked to resign for personal reasons, intending to take responsibility for failing to predict her violent behavior.

But the king thought this was in poor judgment, and the crown prince didn't want him to resign; consequently, his request was not granted. Instead, he was assigned to the Second Order of the knights, which was tasked with protecting the city, a post he still occupied to this very day.

Even after ten long years, Jeffrey's regret over not noticing Katherine's suffering and being unable to be someone she could rely on remained a stain on his heart, refusing to fade away.

But then one day, Victoria, a woman who relied on no one but herself, appeared in his life with Nonna on her back.

Chapter Five

The Incident at the Soiree

"Vicky! Vicky!"

"Hmm? Oh, I'm sorry. What is it?"

"What's the matter?"

Nonna stared at my face with concern. I was teaching her how to sew, but my mind had wandered, and I'd abruptly stopped.

"Nothing's the matter. I'm fine."

To be perfectly honest, even though several days had passed since the soiree, I still hadn't been able to shake the emotions of that night.

"Now, I'll show you how to sew two pieces of fabric together."

"Okay…"

Nonna picked up the cloth and needle and resumed sewing, but she still looked sad. *She's really such a sensitive child*, I thought regretfully.

"I'm sorry, Nonna. I just spaced out."

"Vicky, you looked like my mommy. She froze just like that."

"…Hmm? What do you mean by that?"

I had a feeling this was too serious to ignore, so I encouraged Nonna to tell me. She paused and then, with some difficulty, slowly began telling me the story of her mother.

* * *

It took some time to coax everything out of her, but the gist was that Nonna's mother would come home very late at night and sleep until noon. Then she would have a hard time getting up, almost as though she was in pain, which would lead to her being grumpy and going out again. That was how Nonna had been raised.

But one day, her mother spaced out and got lost in her thoughts, like I'd just done. And gradually, those spells grew longer and longer, until she stopped doing any housework. One day, she took Nonna to the plaza and said, "I'm just going to do a bit of shopping. Wait here." And then she never came back.

I couldn't bear it; I hugged Nonna tightly. "I'm sorry. I promise I won't space out like that. And I'll never abandon you somewhere. I swear!"

Nonna shook her head.

"No, Vicky. That's not it!"

"What's not it? I won't make you worry anymore, Nonna."

"Vicky, what were you thinking about? Tell me."

She looked into my eyes. Her gaze was so intent that I knew she'd be able to tell if I lied.

"You want to know, don't you? Well, I have no idea what your mother was thinking about, but I'll share what *I* was thinking about. It might not be a fun story for you. Do you still want me to tell you?"

Nonna nodded, her eyes fixed on me.

"There was a strange man at the party in the castle. It seemed like he was going to try to hurt someone. The captain tried to catch him, but the man ran away. I'd predicted where he was going to run, so I went there beforehand to stop him. And I took him down with a roundhouse kick, and a knee to the gut."

"...Wow. Wow, you're amazing, Vicky!"

Nonna's eyes sparkled with admiration. I'd only ever defeated men for my own purposes, something I found deeply unsettling.

"I've always beat up every bad guy who's come near me, but I'm starting to think maybe I should stop doing that. Maybe instead of fighting, I should run away. Because if I fight, I might put you in danger."

Nonna pondered this. "Can't we just fight the bad guys together?"

"Hmm. Well, I don't want to put you in danger. Protecting you is way more important to me than defeating bad guys."

Nonna fell silent and didn't say anything else. She just stared at the cloth and needle in her hands.

"Nonna? What is it?"

"I don't want you to hold back for me, Vicky. It makes me feel kind of bad for you."

"Nonna, you're the most important thing in the world to me. You don't have to feel bad. I want you to understand that."

"No. I don't want you to hold back!"

I suppose children wanted to be proud of what their parents did.

But I couldn't act like a spy and protect Nonna at the same time, and I had no intention of continuing to apprehend criminals. Right now, I was simply taking the time to process the emotions from that night.

"If you hold back…then you'll disappear, too," Nonna said to me.

"Why? I won't disappear!"

"You should defeat the bad guys! And don't hold back!"

Nonna suddenly burst into tears, as if a dam had broken, sobbing uncontrollably. It was the first time I'd seen her cry since I'd taken her into my care.

I wondered what her mother had been thinking about when she was having those episodes before she abandoned Nonna. I knew that I would choose Nonna without hesitation no matter what, but her mother hadn't done the same. And that wasn't Nonna's fault at all.

I gently rubbed her tiny back. She'd never cried once this whole time. Perhaps she felt like she couldn't cry, thinking she'd been abandoned because she'd forced her mother to hold back somehow.

She was so pitiful that I thought I would cry, too.

When I was eight years old, I was told, *"You're going to go work for a noble family. Do your best,"* and then I was handed over to Lancome. Even though I was a child, I accepted the situation as best I could. Although I'd been lonely, I'd never held a grudge against my parents.

But Nonna's situation was different; she'd been abruptly abandoned. There was no telling how deep her emotional scars went.

I scooped her up and set her on my lap.

As she hiccupped and sobbed in my embrace, it struck me how petite and slender she was. The lightness of her body spoke to how malnourished she'd been during those crucial years of development, and how she'd spent her time quietly inside the house instead of playing outside.

I gently wiped away her tears and embraced her.

"All right. If any bad guys show up, I'll take care of them when I have to. But you're the most important thing to me, Nonna. And that will never, ever change. So if I have to run, I'll run. And I'll never let you go."

I wondered if what I was saying was getting through to her. She seemed exhausted from crying and had a vacant expression on her face. Eventually, her breathing slowed, and she pressed her face against my chest.

"Don't worry, Nonna. Everything's okay," I told her.

Then she suddenly looked up at me. "Hey, Vicky. I have a favor to ask you."

"Hmm? What is it?"

"Show me what you did to take down that bad guy. I wanna see it."

"Here? Right now?"

"Yeah. I wanna see it," she repeated.

"Really...?"

The thought of doing so made me feel painfully embarrassed, but I was too weak to refuse the pretty little girl who'd just finished crying. I relented and demonstrated how I'd taken down the thief in the castle gardens. And I made Nonna promise she'd never tell anyone about it.

"I grabbed him like this, then kicked him like this, and *bam*! That's how I did it!"

If someone was peering in through the windows at me right now, they'd think I was having a fit. That was because Nonna kept clapping her hands in delight, saying, "Again! Do it again!" So I demonstrated how I'd given the man a roundhouse kick, grabbed him by the shoulders, kneed him in the stomach, and finished him off with a karate chop over and over again.

"Nonna, promise me that you'll never, ever use these techniques on someone else unless I give you permission. You're too little for any of these moves to be effective yet, so trying it would be very dangerous for you. Do you understand?"

"Yes, I understand!"

"Promise?"

"I promise!"

Nonna finally seemed to cheer up. The two of us took a bath, ate dinner, and got into bed together. Then she fell asleep in my arms.

Children understood a lot more than adults thought they did. At the very least, I did when I was eight.

From now on, I'll tell Nonna everything, I thought.

That night, I fell asleep feeling Nonna's warm body next to mine.

My main task today was sorting through the books packed in Mr. Bernard's library.

He hadn't been using the books much recently, but occasionally, he'd be unable to find one in particular and raise a huge commotion about it. I told him I was going to organize the books, and when he didn't reply, I tried again, but there was still no answer. When Mr. Bernard was absorbed in something, he couldn't hear anything going on around him.

"Stay back, Nonna. I'm going to take these books off the shelves. I don't want you inhaling this dust."

"I want to help you."

"Hmm… Well, let's get you ready first."

I tied a cloth around Nonna's hair, then another around her face like a mask to cover her nose and mouth. To finish it off, I tied an apron around her waist.

It was a beautiful clear day with no breeze—the perfect day for cleaning out the library.

"Vicky, where should I put this?"

"That goes in the third spot from the right."

"What about this little book?"

"If you stack it on that pile, it'll fall. Put it on the very edge."

There were eight bookcases in the library, and each one was crammed full of books. It took a long time separating them all into categories and setting them in the hallway.

I carefully dusted each volume, then wiped each bookshelf off with a damp rag.

"All right. Time to put away the books," I said. When I stepped out into the hallway, however, I saw Nonna completely absorbed in reading a small book. "Oh, did you find something good?"

"Yes. This one's interesting."

It was a collection of famous fairy tales from this kingdom and the surrounding nations.

"Hmm, there are children's books here, too. Aren't there words you don't know yet in there, though?"

"Well, I just kind of guess as I read."

I remembered doing the same kind of thing when I first started reading at the training facility, simply guessing at the meaning of words. "I'm going to put the books away now, okay?"

"Okay."

First, I placed all the books I'd set out in the hallway back on the shelves. I organized them by author first, then title. By the time I was finished, my arms, back, and hips were aching. Nonna was lost in her book the whole time. Mr. Bernard hadn't emerged from his study, either.

Since it was teatime, I called out to him, and the three of us had tea together.

"Oh, Nonna! You're reading that book, are you?" he said.

"I'm sorry she picked it up without asking first. She found it while we were cleaning the library."

Bernard's eyes widened, and he rose from his seat, then headed to the library. Nonna and I followed him.

He opened the door, walked over to the shelves, and stared at the neatly arranged books.

"I organized the books according to author, but if you'd like me to organize them in a different way, I can redo it," I told him.

"No, this is fine. Perfect, in fact! That must've been an awful lot of trouble, on account of how many books there are."

"Not at all. I actually enjoy doing tasks like this."

Mr. Bernard said, "Hmm, hmm," as he nodded. After he walked around and examined each shelf, we returned to the parlor, and then he spoke to Nonna. "Do you like that book, Nonna?"

"Yes, it's very interesting."

"I see, I see. You're welcome to read any of the books in my library anytime you want."

"Wow! I can read all of them?"

"You certainly can. History books are very interesting. It's like being able to chat with people who lived long ago."

"Hmm..." Nonna sipped her sweetened tea as she earnestly listened to Mr. Bernard.

I was glad that she'd developed such a fondness for books, but I had made it a rule not to buy any. Books were hard to transport, so if an emergency arose, I'd have to leave them all behind. And I hated leaving things behind, so until now I'd just been borrowing books from the book lender and having her read those.

"It's unusual that you have so many children's books, Mr. Bernard," I noted.

"Well, history books for children are unusual in and of themselves. And the content is quite solid. Still, it's wonderful seeing a child read. I don't have any children myself, but I'm sure if I did, I would have grandchildren by now. When I look at Nonna, it's like I'm seeing a glimpse of the life I could've had."

Those words really struck me.

"I feel the same way. I think this is the life I would've wanted if I had children."

Mr. Bernard looked at me like he wanted to say something, but he stayed quiet. I wondered if it was about the captain, but there was no sense in talking about it or him asking me about it, so I was grateful for his restraint.

That night in bed, Nonna turned to me and said, "Vicky, books are fun, aren't they?"

"Yes, they are. I'll take you to the book lender whenever you want to borrow lots of them."

"Okay!"

After she fell asleep, I pulled the comforter back up over her and gazed at her sleeping face. I wondered what my children would be like if I had any.

"To have kids of my own, there would have to be a father first," I murmured with a dry chuckle. Wishing for things I couldn't have would only make me unhappy. I had Nonna, and that should have been enough. Right now, my joy was raising her until she reached adulthood.

The following day, the captain dropped by Mr. Bernard's estate and invited us to eat with him.

"Would you and Nonna like to join me for a meal out?"

"Actually, there's something I needed to discuss with you. Would you mind coming over to my house for dinner instead? It's something I don't want anyone else to hear."

"I see. All right, I'll be there."

The captain arrived dressed in civilian clothes on the appointed day, right on the dot. He must've been fresh out of the bath, because his short silver hair was gleaming like it was made from spun silver threads.

"Come in, come in," I said. "You have to eat it while it's hot!"

"It smells delicious. I've been looking forward to tonight."

Nonna led the captain inside to the dining room, and he took the seat across from mine.

I ladled the steaming white soup into bowls and placed them on the table before taking my seat. There was also a basket of freshly baked bread, along with a dish of butter and pâté as well. The captain took a sip of the soup, then closed his eyes.

"Mm, that hits the spot!"

"Do you like it?"

"Yes, quite. Is this asparagus soup?"

"Yes, the market had some white asparagus. There's so much produce available in this kingdom."

"I'm glad you like it here."

I waited until we were done with our soup, then rose from my seat and put on the oven mitts I'd made to take the dish out of the oven. I'd timed it perfectly. Beneath the bubbling cheese was bacon, carrots, broccoli, and squash.

The captain calmly ate the piping hot food, but I blew on my portion first to avoid burning my mouth. The melted cheese had a crispy crust and a fragrant aroma. The vegetables were tender and sweet, with a rich flavor from the white sauce and cheese. Nonna was blowing on it to cool it down, too.

"So what did you want to talk to me about, Victoria?" the captain asked.

"Well, ever since the night of the party, a man has been sneaking around and following me. It's creepy and frightening, so I'm thinking about notifying the town guard to have him arrested. But I thought I should let you know first."

The captain thought this over as he ate and took a sip of wine, then stared straight at me. "I haven't heard anything about it, but I have a feeling this person may have been hired by the crown prince. I'm surprised you noticed you were being followed."

"It was a complete coincidence I found out. I saw his reflection in the window of a shop I was passing by. After that, I paid more attention and noticed him following me every now and then. But you think the crown prince is behind this? Does he investigate every young woman who comes around, since he dotes on you so?" I asked, even though I doubted that was the case.

"No, I don't think so. Actually…someone knocked out the thief in the garden the night of the party. They suspect it was you. That's probably why the prince is trying to investigate you."

"Me? Knock a man unconscious? Why would they think such a thing?"

At that point, I figured I probably shouldn't let Nonna hear the rest, so I glanced at the captain and then looked over at her. He got the message and also looked at Nonna, who was gobbling up her dinner.

"Nonna, after dinner, let's brush your teeth and get you to bed, okay?" I said.

"Okay."

I wouldn't know what to do if Nonna suddenly demonstrated a roundhouse kick, a knee to the gut, and a karate chop, so I thought it best to get her to bed as soon as possible.

The captain listened to our exchange quietly, his face tense as he took a sip of wine.

Finally, Nonna began yawning at the dinner table. I quickly brushed her teeth and took her up to the bedroom, then changed her into pajamas. I tucked her into bed, then left the room and closed the door behind me.

I got some new glasses and was about to open another bottle of wine for us when the captain took the bottle from me and uncorked it with expert hands, pouring it into glasses for us.

"To be honest, one of the security guards saw a woman running away from the unconscious man in the garden that night. He testified that her dress was either light blue or light purple."

What? But it was so dark there! Apparently, someone else had night vision that rivaled mine. I inwardly chastised myself.

"I was in the corner of the venue. It's quite a nuisance to be followed on account of something I didn't do. If the crown prince insists on continuing to have me followed, then..."

The captain interrupted me before I could finish my sentence. "I'll take responsibility and have the prince stop the surveillance. So please don't just up and disappear or anything."

"What do you mean, 'disappear'?" I repeated, and the captain flinched slightly.

"I don't know. I just have this feeling that you'll vanish one day."

"I won't do that. You're overthinking things."

He was an unusually perceptive fellow.

Truth be told, it startled me that he'd said that, because at that exact moment, I'd thought, *If the royal family is taking an interest in me, it might be a good idea to move to another country...*

After that, I brought up several mundane topics. I asked the captain several questions and took over the role of the listener. He made me laugh telling stories of his subordinates' various blunders. The night went on, and then he rose to his feet.

"May I come visit you again?"

"Yes, of course."

As we stood in the foyer, the captain put both his arms around me and hugged me softly. It went on a bit longer than one would expect for a normal farewell hug. I stood still and didn't hug him back. After he released me, I smiled at him and said, "Good night," then saw him off.

I stood at the sink and washed the dishes in warm water, lost in thought.

Ever since I'd started working as an operative at the age of fifteen, I'd trusted only one person. And the sole reason I was here now was because that one person had trampled on my trust.

Trusting someone meant you also had to prepare yourself for their inevitable betrayal. That way, if they really did turn on you, cutting things off with them wouldn't hurt. You could just laugh and say, "I knew it."

That's what I told myself as I fell asleep that night.

The next day, there was no one tailing me.

It seemed like the captain really had spoken to the prince.

A few days later, I had the day off from Mr. Bernard's.

I wanted to go out with Nonna somewhere and clear my head. Worst-case scenario, we could live anywhere. But continuing to be afraid of something I didn't know would happen or not was just wasting energy.

"Nonna, how about we buy you a new ribbon? It's sad that you only have a blue one."

"But I like this one."

"Since you have blond hair, I think a dark-red ribbon would look lovely on you, too. Like the color of wine. And we can buy a pair of shoes the same color."

Lady Yolana made a big fuss and told us we should take her carriage, but I replied with a smile and said I'd like the exercise. And so Nonna and I set off for the southern quarter.

We went in a little shop and looked through ribbons of all different colors and patterns. Nonna wanted another blue ribbon, so I bought her one that was a little darker blue than the one she already had, and a red wine-colored one as well.

"You should get one, too, Vicky."

"Me? Hmm, okay. How about we get matching ribbons, then?"

Nonna looked up at me with a dazzling smile.

Buying a gift for the one you love fills your heart, too, I thought as I held hands with Nonna. Come to think of it, I'd always felt happy when I bought gifts for my family as well.

Tonight, Nonna would be staying with Susan, the lady's maid at the main estate, so I was planning on going to that bar again.

Zaharo was the owner of the little pub called The Black Thrush.

He was a dignified man of forty with black hair, dark eyes, and a beard. He had a sort of bad-boy appeal that was popular with the ladies.

A particular woman had been frequenting his pub as of late. The first time she showed up, she drank two stiff drinks and left right away. The second time, she calmly savored her drink. Tonight was her third visit, and she ordered a new kind of drink. Zaharo was glad she seemed to like the place.

But a young man had been pestering her for a while now. He was a first-time customer. Zaharo didn't want that kind of man to disturb his business or interfere with the relaxation of his female customers.

"Excuse me, but you're bothering the lady here," he told the customer politely; however, the man ignored him and wouldn't back down. He kept stubbornly flirting with the lady. Zaharo was just about ready to throw him out when the lady put her money on the table, stood up, and left the pub. The young man rushed to put down his money and followed her.

This is dangerous, Zaharo thought, quickly leaving the pub. Did they go right or left? He looked around the darkened streets for the two of them and spotted the man running back toward him from the right. It appeared that he'd lost sight of the woman.

Once the man noticed Zaharo, an awkward expression came to his face, and he left.

Good... At least the lady's safe, Zaharo thought with relief. Just as he was about to go back inside, he paused. All of a sudden, he heard a cat screeching from behind.

"A cat fight?"

It wasn't even mating season, but nevertheless, he heard hissing and yowling.

"Wow, somebody's angry."

He realized the noise was coming from above. He looked up at the roof and saw the lady customer standing on the eaves of the neighboring

store! She was crouched down low, with both hands on her knees, trying to conceal herself. Only her eyes were turned toward him.

A black cat was facing the woman and arching its back with its fur on end, its tail so thick that it looked like a feather duster. It hissed at the woman as she tried to calm it down.

"Oh!"

The moment they made eye contact, the woman let out a noise and stood up. She held down her skirt and then lightly jumped down from the rooftop, landing right in front of Zaharo. She pressed a finger against her lips and smiled shyly, turned on her heel, and then ran off into the night.

Zaharo watched her go with his mouth agape. The cat seemed satisfied and walked along the eaves, then disappeared. Apparently, the woman had been trespassing on its territory.

"Ha-ha-ha!" Zaharo chuckled and then went back inside.

The female customer's movements had been so soft and lithe, it was almost as if she were a cat transformed into a human. The sheepish look on her face when she'd been discovered was adorable, like a child who'd been caught playing a prank.

Once inside, Zaharo pondered this.

He didn't know who the young man was, but if he was some sort of street thug, he had to do something about it. He couldn't let this keep up.

The next afternoon, Zaharo went to a pub deep in the backstreets, where respectable folks wouldn't dare venture. He made his way through the crowd of men who were already drinking despite the early hour and headed to the farthest seat in the back. There sat the boss of the local ruffians.

"Hey there, Zaharo. Long time no see."

"Hector, you got a young man with light-blue eyes and curly brown hair working for you? He's got a mole on the right side of his neck."

The man called Hector puffed on his cigarette and thought about it. "Maybe I do, maybe I don't. Who wants to know?"

"He was disturbing one of my top customers. If he continues interfering with my business, I was thinking about taking care of him, but I thought I should give you a heads-up just in case he was one of your guys."

Hector raised a hand to signal the pub owner, who brought over a glass of amber liquid and set it in front of Zaharo.

"This top customer of yours a woman?"

"A top customer is a top customer. Doesn't matter if they're a man or a woman."

"Hmph. I see. Well, don't worry. I won't let anyone disrupt a legitimate enterprise. You and I, we're on the same page, ain't we?"

Zaharo picked up the glass, stood up, and downed it in one gulp.

"Much obliged. Dealing with trash is too much of a hassle. That's all from me."

"You should drop by for a visit every now and then."

"I've already left your group. I paid my price."

Zaharo left the money for his drink and exited the pub. All eyes were on him until he reached the door, but he pretended not to notice. He remained on guard, just in case they were planning on attacking him, but his worries proved to be unfounded.

"She might not come back." And not because of the irritating man, but because Zaharo had seen her up on the roof. He hadn't even had a conversation with her, so the thought of her never coming back made him a bit glum.

A short while later, however, he spotted the lady in the shopping quarter. She had a bag full of vegetables slung over her shoulder and was holding hands with a little girl as they strolled along.

"Miss?" he blurted out. The woman looked at him and seemed to recognize him immediately.

"Oh! You're the owner of the pub. Hello. Are you out shopping?"

"Yes, that's right. You are, too, huh?"

"I sure am."

"I hope you'll come back again soon," he said.

It looked like she didn't know how to answer, so he pointed up ahead. "If you've got time, how about something sweet? It'll be my treat."

"What do you think, Nonna?" she asked the little girl.

"Sure."

"All right, then," the woman said. "That would be nice."

"Oh, by the way—my name is Zaharo." He introduced himself as they walked.

She was slightly behind him to the left. "You can call me Vicky," she said in a friendly voice.

He took them to a quiet little sweets shop that had tables inside. It was one of his favorite places, because he had quite a sweet tooth.

"Everything here is delicious," he said, handing Vicky a menu.

She ordered tea and a cookie, the little girl ordered apple pie and fruit water, and Zaharo ordered chestnut cake dipped in syrup and tea.

"This cookie's so crunchy and delicious," said Vicky.

"Vicky, the apple pie is good, too!"

"Isn't it great? Want to taste a bite of mine?" he asked the little girl.

"Sure! Mm, yummy!"

Vicky smiled as she watched the little girl sample Zaharo's cake. The two didn't look alike enough to be mother and daughter and were too far apart in age to be sisters, but Zaharo tried not to be too nosy about other people's affairs.

The three of them focused on eating their treats for a while. Then Zaharo said, "I don't think that man will come back again."

"Why's that?"

"Just in case, I went to check with the guy who oversees this area, and I found out that man was one of the boss's minions. I told him he'd better not be interfering with my business, or I'd have something to say about it."

"But won't that invite retaliation?"

"No, the boss is an old acquaintance of mine."

"I'm so sorry for the trouble."

"It was no trouble at all. Will you come again?"

"Yes, although I can't stay for very long."

"That's more than enough."

Vicky finished her tea and stared directly at Zaharo. "Aren't you going to ask me anything?"

"Do you want me to?" He dropped the formal, businesslike tone and asked her frankly.

"No."

"I won't ask, then. I'm a pub owner, and you're my valued customer. And that's fine. But more importantly..." The corners of his mouth began to twitch, and he started laughing like he couldn't hold it back anymore. Vicky must have remembered what happened, too, because she flushed a deep shade of pink. "I've never seen a cat get so angry at someone before. It was hissing at you because you were blocking its turf! Ha-ha-ha!"

"W-well, I wasn't expecting that, either! Pfft..."

Vicky started chuckling, too. Since they were inside the café, they both held their stomachs and tried to suppress their laughter, but it was no use, and they ended up in tears. The little girl asked, "What's going on?" which just made the two of them crack up all over again. They took some deep breaths and finally managed to settle down with some difficulty.

"I can't even remember the last time I laughed so hard," Vicky said, rubbing her stomach muscles. It seemed like she'd hurt herself from all the giggling.

After that, they bid each other farewell. And from then on, Vicky became a regular at Zaharo's pub. She'd come about once a week, only staying long enough to down two or three drinks.

That young man never showed up again. Zaharo figured Hector must've given him a stern warning.

I finished translating the documents Mr. Bernard requested and handed them over, then went into the kitchen to make some sandwiches for lunch.

Nonna sat at the table, polishing glasses. She seemed to enjoy repetitive tasks like this. She turned to me and said, "Vicky, are you friends with that man with the beard we saw the other day?"

"Hmm, not exactly. I just met him. You want to make friends, too, don't you?"

"No, I don't need them. I prefer training with you."

"Goodness!" I leaned toward her and lowered my voice. "Shall we practice jumping from high places soon?"

"Yeah!" Nonna suddenly got very excited.

"You're pretty, so you should be strong, too."

"I'm pretty?"

"Yes, you're very pretty. And it's very dangerous for pretty girls to be weak."

"Hmm…"

I'd once gone undercover in a human-trafficking organization. Every single little girl who had been kidnapped and kept locked up underground until they were sold had pretty faces. Human traffickers didn't target nobility because their children were always heavily guarded. The traffickers went after pretty commoner girls.

It was already getting dark outside when we walked home later that day. Nonna and I practiced climbing the stone wall that belonged to a vacant house near ours. It was about as tall as my shoulders. Since it was made of stone and had a bumpy, uneven texture, it was the perfect practice spot.

"Jump up high and put your hands on top of the wall, then push off against it with your arms and the tips of your toes, like this!"

I demonstrated, hopping up on top of the wall. Nonna's eyes widened. I jumped off the wall and made her try it. I held her by the waist to assist her while she was learning.

"No, don't use your arms. Use your stomach muscles."

"Nngh! Oof!"

She got very close, but she just couldn't quite make it to the top of the wall in one leap. Not that I was expecting a beginner to succeed immediately.

"If we practice every day, you'll get the hang of it in no time. And then, you'll be able to scale even taller walls than this! Once you learn this skill, it'll be easy for you to make an escape."

"You're so cool, Vicky."

"Thanks. Isn't it more fun knowing how to do lots of things than not knowing how to do anything?"

"Yeah!"

After we practiced climbing the wall several times, I turned to Nonna and whispered, "Nonna, can you go on home without me? There's a suspicious person over there, so I have to go warn them to stop coming here."

"Is it a bad guy?"

"I'm not sure yet. Run as fast as you can and lock the door behind you. Can you do that?"

Nonna nodded, and I patted her back. She took off in a sprint toward home. She didn't look back even once, just as I'd taught her. Lady Yolana had two very skilled men guarding her estate, so Nonna would be fine once she reached the property.

I turned and called out toward the nearby trees. "What do you want?"

A young man with black hair emerged from the glade. He had a scarf tied around his face beneath his eyes. "Oh, you knew I was there?"

He's not a pro. Someone who's used to killing people gives off a whole different vibe.

I picked up a nearby fallen branch from the ground and climbed to the top of the wall. Keeping my eyes on the man, I broke the branch over my knee and gave it a test swing. *Yeah, it's not that strong, but it'll hold up long enough for one swift hit.*

"Who are you?"

"Who do you think?" I asked.

"I wanna talk to you. Come down here."

"No. Go away. Or else I'll attack you."

"Ooh, I'm quiverin' in my boots! Like I said, I just wanna talk." He raised both his hands in surrender but didn't leave.

"Get out of here."

The man walked over toward me and hopped up on the wall.

I had no obligation to wait until he tried something with me. The moment he landed on the wall, I readied my branch and stepped forward. He quickly backed up and put distance between us. *Hmm, so he has some level of skill.*

"I honestly just came here to talk, but since we're up here, you might as well show me what you've got. I—"

Before he finished his sentence, I swung the branch down at an angle, then quickly swept it back up, aiming for the man's face. He dodged the branch but lost his balance. One needed practice to fight on elevated ground.

"Wha—? Oof!"

I swung the branch forcefully at his right side as he lost his balance. The branch broke; hopefully, I'd managed to crack a rib or two. The man landed deftly on his feet back on the ground, but his face twisted with pain.

I landed beside him and faked a punch to his face, then kicked him hard in the right side with my left foot, the same spot where I'd struck him with the branch. I followed it up by kicking him straight in the gut with my right foot. He staggered backward, groaning with pain. If I really had punched him in the face, he probably would have grabbed my arm. My blows were quick, but the drawback was that they were also light.

"Since you came at me with a knife, you can't complain if I use one against you, too, right?" I said.

I'd noticed he had a knife in his pocket when he faced me on the wall. I took my own folding knife from its hidden spot on my hip, held it sideways, and clicked open the blade.

"Wait! I swear, I don't want trouble. I'm sorry. I had no idea you were this strong! My knife is for protection. I wasn't planning on using it!"

"I don't believe you. I'll teach you what happens when you come at me with a knife."

"I'm sorry! I'm really sorry!"

"Then get out of my sight. Next time, I'll cut your arms and legs all the way down to the bone." I dropped into an offensive stance, still gripping the knife. After hearing my warning, he ran away.

Who in the world is that man?

He wasn't exactly green, but it was clear he wasn't experienced in actual combat.

It was bad news that he knew where I lived. From now on, I would have to keep an eye on Nonna at all times. I needed to go over my belongings once more in case we had to leave the country in a hurry.

That night, I slept on the floor, sitting up against the bed in case of an attack. The sudden incident had rattled my everyday routine and had sent shock waves through my heart, showing me that I'd clearly let down my guard.

The next day, I had the captain come over to Mr. Bernard's estate. During my lunch break, I had Mr. Bernard entertain Nonna with tales of his childhood.

"What did you want to talk to me about, Victoria?"

"A strange man was near my house yesterday. I told him to leave several times, but he ignored me and tried to approach me. He had a fairly large knife hidden on him, but I scared him away with a tree branch. I've trained with a sword a little. I'm still being followed, so I think I'm going to leave the capital. Since you're my guarantor, I thought I should tell you in advance."

His eyes darted around.

"Yesterday, you say? I'm glad you weren't hurt, Victoria. What did the man look like?"

"Black hair, blue eyes, handsome. He was in his twenties, around one hundred and eighty centimeters tall, slender. He had half his face hidden with a scarf."

"He must've been wearing a wig, then..."

"What? Do you know this man?"

"The second prince went out incognito yesterday, without even a single guard. That in and of itself is a huge problem, but he returned with two broken ribs. The First Order of the knights is furious about someone attacking him."

What in the world?

"The prince keeps telling them he fell down."

"I see..."

That man was a prince?

If he had been attacked by anyone but me, he could've been dead and buried without even a question. I was certain he was clueless about how much danger he'd put himself in.

"I'm training Prince Cedric in swordsmanship, and he's rather strong."

The captain stared at me. I stared back at him. He looked away first.

"Are you going to arrest me, Captain?"

Depending on his answer, I would immediately grab Nonna and go into hiding. But that would have to wait, because the captain was sitting right in front of me. He was a skilled, muscular man, and more importantly, he was my guarantor—what was I to do with him?

"I have no intention of arresting you. I'm going to tell the prince never to approach you so violently again. But I'm sure you'll still feel anxious. Would you like to stay at my family estate for a while? There's always plenty of people around no matter what time of day it is, and my brother is in a much better position to protest strongly against the royal family than I am."

"Please let me think about it."

The captain nodded silently, then left.

Despite my response, I had absolutely no intention of going to stay at his family estate. I didn't want to drag his family into my own affairs.

In an emergency situation like this, Mr. Bernard and Lady Yolana sprang to mind. The prospect of leaving the country and having to cut ties with them hurt my heart so much, I could cry. And I would surely feel sad not being able to ever see the captain again.

It dawned on me that at some point, I'd gotten emotionally involved with these people.

On the way home with Nonna, I stopped by the post office in the southern district. A reply from the letter I'd sent the day after the soiree to another country had been delivered for me.

It was from someone I'd used privately when I was an operative; the organization did not know of this person.

At first glance, the letter looked like any other, with the writer discussing the weather as of late, the growth of their child, and so on. But when I used the cipher I'd sneaked into my letter of request, its real contents became clear.

"Woman...still...officially...ash...out...country..."

"The real Victoria is still missing and officially on record as having left the country for Ashbury."

In that case, I don't have to run away yet, right? Hmm, I'll have them look into something else, too. Out of the utmost caution, I decided to request the writer's assistance in another matter. I went back home and wrote another seemingly ordinary letter.

I finished my message and put it in a small box along with the doll I'd sewn the payment into.

Prince Cedric let out a groan as the doctor examined him.

"If you get plenty of rest, the bones will heal on their own. And when I say rest, I mean it." The elderly doctor bowed and then excused himself.

It hurt to breathe, to speak, and even move. This was his first time ever breaking a bone, and now he knew why everyone said it was so painful.

He'd sneaked back to the hospital the day before but unfortunately ran into his older brother. It only took a few moments of conversation before the crown prince caught on to the fact he was injured. He knew he should probably tell the truth, so when he explained how he'd gotten hurt, his brother was furious.

"I promised Jeff!" said Conrad. "I told him I'd let him take care of her, and I would leave her be! So I ordered our man to stop tailing her. But because of what you did, Jeff's going to think I broke my promise to him!"

He was right, so all Cedric could do was bow. "I'm sorry."

"Tell everyone else you got hurt in a fall. And then when the time is right, I want you to go apologize to the lady."

"All right. I'm sorry."

Now that Cedric was alone, he opened his drawer and took out the thin, golden locket and opened it up. The picture of his former fiancée, Beatrice, smiled faintly back at him.

"You're so strong, Your Highness."

Beatrice had always praised his strength. He'd been struck by her beauty and proposed to her, but she fell ill shortly afterward.

According to the doctor, it was stress. Perhaps being engaged to the second prince and a future of being a duchess was too much for her.

"Let me know if anyone is giving you a hard time. I'll protect you."

"No, I'll just brush it off with a smile," she'd said, but he thought perhaps Beatrice was bottling up all her worries inside.

He was fifteen, and she was fourteen at the time. She'd had a persistent high fever, so he went to visit her. His fiancée was struggling to breathe. He clasped her hot hand and gazed at her face for a while.

Her life is being cut short all because I wanted her as my wife.

That night, he scolded himself as his voice trembled and asked his father to break off the engagement.

"Please figure out a way to cancel our marriage so that it doesn't negatively affect her."

A pained expression came over his father's face. "I see," was all he said, but he did as Cedric wished.

After the engagement was broken off, Beatrice was said to have been devastated and spent her days crying, but she gradually regained her health.

This was for the best, Cedric thought, but he still felt like he had a hole inside his heart.

He'd thrown himself into honing his skills with the sword, but there were no signs of war on the horizon for Ashbury. Of course, that was a good thing, but what was his path in life? Eventually, he'd become a subject of the kingdom and assume the title of duke, but then what?

He was struggling to find his place in life, and that was when the incident at the soiree happened. And he'd heard the woman who took down the culprit had incredible skill. He was dying to know what she was made of and sprang into action. And the result of that was his broken ribs.

Her movements had been efficient and surprisingly quick. When she took out her knife, he really thought that she was going to kill him. It was the first time in his whole life that he'd ever been faced with the fear of death.

Looking back on it now, he realized she'd been desperate to save the little girl who was with her. She'd warned him several times to leave, and when he didn't, she turned as hostile as a mother cat protecting her kittens. He was no match for her intensity, not to mention her skill.

I wonder if she'd train me..., he thought, then burst out laughing. Pain raced through Cedric's ribs, and he grimaced.

Chapter Six

Peaceful Days

I hadn't received any word from the royal family, although I'm sure it would be difficult for them to admit the second prince had his rear end handed to him by a commoner woman. The prince had started everything, but I was still glad he was going around telling people that he'd fallen. The most important thing to me right now was peace.

Amid all that, my work as Mr. Bernard's assistant abruptly stopped. One day, he'd been trying to get a book off the very top shelf in the library and fell off the ladder, breaking his right arm. Fortunately, Lady Eva was there at the time, so she was able to get him help right away.

"I'm so sorry, Victoria, but Uncle will be staying at my house until he fully recovers. Until then, why don't you come tutor my son? I'll pay you the same salary my uncle gives you."

Why should I tutor a noble's son? I thought, but then Lady Eva explained:

"My son, Clark, is twelve years old, and he needs some work with his foreign language studies. He has a tutor, of course, but I'm just not seeing any results. Since you know four languages, I'd love to ask for your help. What do you say? My husband's been saying we should get Clark a new tutor. It would only be until Uncle recovers."

"But I'm a commoner, and I'm not a teacher. Plus, I have Nonna to look after."

"My husband says if you're skilled enough to be a historian's assistant, then you're more than capable enough to tutor Clark. And you can just bring Nonna along. Your Ashburian is perfect; you have nothing to worry about."

"May I have some time to think about it?"

"Of course. I'm hoping for good news!"

I decided to ask Nonna first, and she answered right away.

"It's fine with me as long as I can be with you, Vicky."

"But I'm worried about you. You'd be with a little noble boy."

"That's fine."

"Are you sure? Promise you'll tell me if you're ever uncomfortable or scared, okay?"

"Sure."

Since Nonna was all right with it, I went over to Lady Eva's estate to accept.

I went to go say hello to Mr. Bernard first and discovered he was feeling quite down. The pain and the reality of his physical decline from falling off the ladder was taking a toll on him mentally.

"I'm sorry this happened so suddenly, Victoria. Please say you'll come back as my assistant after I recover."

"Of course I will, Mr. Bernard. But first, you need to concentrate on getting better!"

Seeing him so depressed made my heart ache. I'd never known my grandparents, and I would never say it out loud, but Mr. Bernard had become something like a grandfather to me.

Master Clark was a red-haired, freckled boy with a slender build. When Lady Eva told me he was twelve, I'd expected him to be more of a handful, but he was very quiet and well-behaved. His green eyes were full of nervousness as he greeted me and Nonna politely.

"Good afternoon. I'm Clark Anderson."

"Hello there. I'm Victoria Sellars, and this is Nonna. She and I will be coming over often for a while. It's nice to meet you."

"I'm Nonna." Nonna bowed to Master Clark.

When I'd heard he was an only child, I thought he might be difficult, but he seemed very sweet.

"Lady Eva has asked me to work with you on your Haglian and Randallish skills."

"Can you speak both of those languages, Ms. Sellars?"

"Yes, I can. I like to learn languages in my spare time. I have no trouble engaging in everyday conversation in the ones I've studied."

"I'm no good at foreign languages. My father is the minister of foreign affairs, so he says I need to learn Haglian and Randallish, but I just can't get the hang of them. I'm not good at exercising, either. Actually, I'm not good at *anything*."

Evidently, he was quite lacking in self-confidence.

"I'd like to see what your classes were like before this. Would you mind showing me your notes?"

Master Clark took his notes out of his desk and brought them to me. The notebook was filled with very neat handwriting. It was evident that he was a hardworking boy who had practiced his vocabulary in earnest. However, when I looked at the content of his lessons, I heaved an inward sigh.

First of all, his prior instructor had tried to teach him grammar right off the bat. Teaching languages through the use of classic literature while explaining the grammar as you went may have seemed efficient, but this method overlooked each student's struggles. It also left them no room for mistakes. People learned languages much more quickly and enjoyably when they were allowed to try out new grammar without fear of making mistakes. After all, errors could always be corrected.

"Let's start with my way of teaching, shall we? What sorts of things do you enjoy, Master Clark?"

"What do I enjoy?"

"Yes. For example, I enjoy cooking and exercising."

Master Clark pondered this.

Meanwhile, I asked Nonna, “What do you like, Nonna?”

“Books. And training!” she answered.

“Training?” Master Clark asked with a puzzled expression.

“I climb up high walls. And trees. And I spin through the air!” Nonna boasted proudly. I couldn’t help but let out a dry chuckle.

“Wait, really? Could you show me?” Master Clark asked her.

“Sure!”

Nonna looked at me. When I nodded, she leaped off the ground, ran a few steps, and performed her front somersault. Her form was perfect, but it reminded me that I needed to tell her to wear pants instead of a skirt the next time she wanted to show off in front of others.

“Wow, you’re really good for a girl!”

“I’m good *because* I’m a girl! I have to know how to be strong and run away on my own in case a bad grown-up attacks me! Knowing how to do this is useful for a lot of reasons… That’s what my self-defense teacher says.”

“Hmm…” Master Clark’s eyes had been lifeless before, but now they sparked with curiosity. *All right. He’s hooked.*

“Well, what are you interested in, Master Clark?”

“I want to train like Nonna!”

I figured he’d say that. I’d have to be careful that he didn’t get hurt, but learning words while you exercised was actually good for retention.

“Very well. Let’s start with your Randallish. It might be confusing to do two languages at once.”

I was glad that Nonna was here to participate with us.

“First, we’ll begin with basic exercise. I’ll give you instructions in Ashburian, then again in Randallish. You can memorize them by ear. If you learn the spelling of these phrases after training, remembering them will be a cinch.”

“Okay!”

“Lift up your arms.”

<Lift up your arms.>

I followed the instructions in Ashburian with the same phrase in Randallish in this fashion, then lifted up my arms. This was how I had learned languages. I wasn't sure if Master Clark would take to this style of learning, but there was only one way to find out.

Halfway through the lesson, Master Clark lent Nonna a pair of shorts, along with a string to act as a belt.

We lay plenty of cushions on the floor to minimize any injuries. *There's no way I can let the lady of the house see this!* I thought, but thankfully, Lady Eva was a busy woman.

Once Master Clark had learned seven words in this manner, he remembered how to spell them perfectly. And surprisingly, so did Nonna.

Since Nonna was still learning how to read and write Ashburian little by little, I was worried that studying another language so soon would confuse her, but she said she would be fine. Her resilience had been catching me off guard lately.

Master Clark looked like he was having a wonderful time as he wrote in his notebook, wiping the sweat from his brow. Once he memorized all the words we'd covered for the day, his face sparkled with glee.

"Teacher! I've never had this much fun in a language class before!"

"I'm pleased to hear that. Let's work just as hard during our next class. However, I don't want to worry your mother, so let's not have you do somersaults."

"I won't tell my mother! So please let me do them!"

I suppose any child would want to learn how to do a somersault once they saw someone else do them. Plus, I'd be here to support him... Maybe it would be good for the boy to have at least one thing he felt confident in, since he seemed so delicate both emotionally and physically.

That was how my very enjoyable job started.

* * *

We ate dinner at home every night.

Nonna said all the food I made was delicious. I'd heard there were many children who disliked vegetables, but she happily ate all of them.

"Nonna, what's your favorite dish that I cook for you?"

"Roast lamb."

"What's second?"

"The soup with beans and veggies and meat. I like that, too."

"Well, how about we make it together tonight?"

"Sure!"

Being in the kitchen together was fun. I handed Nonna the little apron I'd made for her and tied the ribbons for her. I put on a matching apron made from the same cloth, and we began washing the vegetables. Nonna was very thorough when it came to this kind of work.

I peeled the vegetables with a knife. She chopped them very carefully with another knife.

"Now put the vegetables in the pot."

"Okay. I want lots of beans."

"That's fine. You love beans, don't you?"

Since Nonna loved beans so much, I always had dried beans on hand. I would soak a small portion of them every day to rehydrate them so that I could use them for dinner that night.

I lit the firewood, placed the pot on the stove, and then set a frying pan next to the pot.

"We'll put bacon in the soup tonight."

"I love bacon! I want to cut it."

"Okay."

The serious concentration Nonna displayed while cutting the bacon was adorable. I found myself getting sentimental, wondering if my mother had tried to teach me to cook in this way. Living with Nonna often made me think about how my late mother had felt. When Nonna got hurt, even if it was just a little scratch, I always wished I could've been the one to get hurt instead. When

Nonna was happy and smiled, I found myself wanting her to smile like that again.

Being with Nonna allowed me to vicariously relive my childhood. I'd grown up apart from my mother, so this made me feel like I was with her again. It was an incredibly comforting feeling.

"Why are you smiling, Vicky?"

"Hmm? Because I'm having fun. I always have so much fun when I'm with you, Nonna."

"Oh."

"How about you?"

"I'm having fun, too!"

Oh, I'm so glad I took this girl in, I thought.

A smile was glued to my face as I sautéed the bacon and then cooked the beans in the bacon grease. After that, I drained the excess fat from the pan into a bowl.

"What are you going to do with that?"

"This grease is really delicious when you use it in stir-fry."

"Oh!"

That night, we ate bread along with some soup that was chock-full of ingredients. It was a simple but delicious meal.

The next day, Nonna boasted to Master Clark during a break from his lessons.

"I cooked yesterday. Yummy soup."

"Wow, you made food, Nonna?"

"Yep! Vicky taught me!"

"Can I try your cooking sometime?"

"Sure. Do you like beans?"

"Beans...? Not really..."

"Then you can't have it. I only cook for people who like beans."

"I'll learn to like them! Please let me try it!"

I chuckled at this innocent exchange between the young boy and the little girl. How much longer would their conversations be like this? In just three years, Master Clark would no longer be a boy, but a young man. *I suppose we only have until then*, I thought, feeling a little wistful about it.

It was my first day off since I'd started tutoring Master Clark.

I taught him during the week and got the weekends off. Nonna and I cleaned the house and did the laundry. "Why don't we embroider for a while? I can teach you how," I offered, but then suddenly there was a knock at the door.

"Yes, who is it?"

"It's Clark Anderson."

Surprised, I quickly went to open the door, and sure enough, I saw Master Clark standing there.

"Master Clark! What's the matter?"

"I just wanted to see you today, Ms. Sellars."

"Goodness me. Well, come on in."

He glanced around the room curiously but seemed rather shy.

"Would you like some tea?"

"Yes, please."

Nonna went to get the teacups ready while I boiled the water. I cut some slices off the walnut-and-dried-fig cake I'd made the day before and served one to him. Master Clark fidgeted nervously, but once he took a bite of the cake, his entire face lit up with surprise. "Mmm!" he said.

"Do you like it?" I asked.

"Yes, very much so! What bakery is this from?"

"Vicky made it."

"That's right. Nonna helped me bake it yesterday."

"Wow..." Master Clark let out an adorable noise of wonder, but then realized what he'd just done and turned bright red.

"There's plenty more where that came from," I assured him. "Take your time."

"Thank you. You really can do anything, can't you, Ms. Sellars?"

"Oh, that's not true."

"But it is! Great-Uncle Bernard always brags about you. He says that on top of being able to speak four languages, you're also good at cooking and cleaning and organizing documents. Not only that, but you're very athletic, too!"

Nonna beamed proudly, as if to say, "That's right!"

"I grew up needing to be independent," I explained. "I was separated from my parents when I was eight years old, and I had to do whatever I was told. I had to learn languages, too, but I turned out to really enjoy it."

"You thought learning languages was fun?"

"That's right. I haven't traveled that much. In fact, moving to this kingdom was the first trip I ever took! So before that, I just read books about other lands. My workplace had many books, but they were all in foreign languages. At first, I didn't know what they said, so all I did was gaze at the illustrations. But eventually, I got fed up with that, so I started studying to be able to read them."

"A place with a lot of books… Did you work at a noble's house?"

"Yes, that's right."

Master Clark finished eating his second helping of cake. "I guess it was kind of selfish for me to complain about not being good at studying," he said, seeming a little glum. "I'm going to work really hard. Your lessons are very fun, so I think I'll be able to learn lot of new words."

"Goodness, that's wonderful! Let's all do our best, okay?" I said.

Nonna suddenly exclaimed, "I want to study today, too!" and looked up at me with sparkling eyes. Master Clark's eyes were sparkling, too. How could I say no to these children when they were so looking forward to it?

"All right. How about we study something today we can't learn at the estate?"

"Climbing trees!"

"Nonna, I don't think Master Clark—"

"I want to do it! Please teach me how to climb trees!"

"Ha-ha-ha. All right. Let's do that, then."

After Nonna and I changed clothes, the three of us walked for a bit over to the spot where I'd fought with the second prince. There were a lot of big trees there, so it was the perfect place to practice climbing.

"Let's use this tree. The first thing you need to do before you climb a tree is to make sure it's not dead. If you try climbing a withered tree without any leaves, its branches might break abruptly, even if they're thick, and you could get seriously injured. If worse comes to worst, you could even die from hitting your head on the ground when you fall. You can tell for sure a tree is alive if its leaves are green. In the winter, breaking off one of its branches is another way to check; the inside will be green. Avoid climbing trees if you can easily snap their branches."

"All right," said Master Clark.

"Now, I'll climb the tree first to demonstrate. Pay close attention to which branches I choose, and how I select my footing."

I took off my shoes and felt the children's respectful gazes on me as I scaled the tree in my socks.

I shimmied up quite high, then reversed the process to climb down. Unable to stand it anymore, Nonna kicked off her shoes and expertly climbed the tree. She went all the way up to the spot I'd reached, sat on a branch, and waved at us.

"Okay, now it's my turn!" Master Clark said. He kicked off his shoes just like Nonna, then struggled to climb the tree. It took him much longer than Nonna to reach the same branch, but when he sat down on it, he looked very pleased.

"Branch."

<Branch.>

I enunciated the word in both languages clearly, and the two of them repeated after me.

"Climb."

<Climb.>

"I climbed a tree."

<I climbed a tree.>

"I climbed down from a high branch."

<I climbed down from a high branch.>

Their two voices were synchronized as they repeated after me.

"I climbed a tall tree, then I climbed down."

<I climbed a tall tree, then I climbed down.>

"Wonderful job, you two! All right, Nonna. You get down first."

Climbing down a tree was more dangerous than going up. Nonna safely came back down, and then I climbed up to where Master Clark was. I tied a rope around him for support. I wrapped it under his armpits twice and fastened it securely, then held the end of it while both of us climbed down together. On the way down, I heard the captain's familiar voice exclaim, "Oh my!" from a distance. Apparently, he'd been watching us.

Once both Master Clark and I were safely on the ground, the captain came over.

"That was amazing, Clark!"

"Uncle Jeff! Hello. I just climbed a tree for the very first time!"

"Did you like it?"

"Yes!"

The captain looked at me with amusement, and I suddenly felt very awkward. I was certain he was stunned at just how much of a tomboy I was, and also at the fact that I'd made the only son and heir to House Anderson climb a tree. And to top it all off, now I was thinking about when the captain hugged me that time.

"I'm sorry for teaching your nephew something without permission."

"No, it's fine. This is the first time I've seen Clark so happy and carefree. I've always thought it wasn't good for him to be so quiet and reserved all the time. I'm sorry he came over on your day off."

"Don't be. I enjoyed myself."

As the two of us chatted, the children ran around the yard shouting, <Branch!> <Climb!> <Tall!> and so on in Randallish as they played tag. They looked like they were having so much fun. The two of them played like that for more than an hour before getting tired.

"I should probably take Clark home," the captain told me. "Would you like to go out for dinner with me later?"

"Thank you. But didn't you just take me to dinner recently?"

"I've actually been fighting the urge to ask you for a while now," he said kindly, looking away. "It's a casual place, so there's no need to dress up."

"Okay."

The bashful way the captain spoke made him seem like a big, clumsy silver bear.

Master Clark looked disappointed, but he brightened when I said, "Come back to play again soon, okay?" and he happily nodded over and over before returning home with the captain.

"Nonna, we're heading out to dinner with the captain again tonight."

"Are we going to dress up, Vicky?"

"Maybe a little bit. He said it's not a fancy place."

"There are restaurants where you don't have to dress up?"

"That's right. It'll be a good experience for you, Nonna."

"Yeah!"

I put on a bright-green dress and changed Nonna into a navy-blue dress. We tied our matching wine-colored ribbons in our hair and smiled at each other.

"I'm excited, Nonna."

"Yeah! And I had fun climbing trees with Master Clark today! I learned how to say 'I climbed a tall tree' in Randallish!"

"That's amazing. You're good at learning languages, Nonna!"

"Yay!"

Nonna ran over and threw her arms around me. I leaned over and hugged her, deeply inhaling her sweet scent. She smelled like only young children do; it was a scent that I adored and made me feel at peace.

* * *

That night, the captain took us to a restaurant that was popular with commoners called Swallow House.

I sure am spending a lot of time with the captain lately, I thought.

All the seats at Swallow House were semiprivate rooms, with walls separating each one except for the seats facing the street. I looked around and saw that most of the other patrons were couples. I wondered if it was all right that we'd brought a child along.

"This is a nice place. I bet it was difficult to get a reservation."

"I asked a subordinate of mine for a good restaurant to take a lady out to."

"Goodness, you went to all that trouble for me? Thank you."

I couldn't believe he'd asked his subordinate that. He must really not have cared what people said about him.

After a while, we were each given our orders on a large square plate. The main dish was stewed venison along with colorful vegetables. It was arranged so beautifully on the plate that it almost looked like a painting. It was even garnished with tiny flowers.

"Wow!" Nonna cried with delight. Not only was it pretty to look at, but it was delicious, too.

"It's absolutely scrumptious, Captain."

"It really is, isn't it?" The captain had a healthy appetite and cleaned his plate. He chatted in his attractive voice as we ate.

"I spoke with the prince. He insisted he broke his ribs after a fall. So I don't think you have anything to worry about. After all, he came at you with a knife. No matter how you look at the situation, he was in the wrong."

"It seems like you have your hands full with him, Captain," I said, and he gave me a sheepish chuckle.

After the meal, we drank some wine and had dessert: some sliced figs in syrup arranged to look like a flower. I decided to bring up something I'd been pondering for a while.

"Captain?"

"Yes?"

"What kind of person is the prince? You don't have to talk about him if you don't want to, of course. I'm not very strong, so it took all my strength to somehow chase him off, but if he'd gone up to someone else like that, his life could've been in danger. I just can't believe someone of his status would do such a thing."

The captain's eyes fell upon his plate.

"It's true. He could've lost his life. I should tell him he's lucky he went up against you. He didn't have any ulterior motives, though. He's the second son, and he was brought up with great care. He's trained with the sword since childhood, and I think he's quite skilled for someone of his position. He can be reckless at times, so that's always been a worry, but everyone who serves him adores him."

"I see."

The captain looked at me with concern. "Why do you ask?"

"I'm worried that the prince will change his mind. If he tells people I'm the one who injured him, it could put me in a bad position."

"He won't. He may be a little eccentric and causes trouble sometimes, but he would never do something so cowardly," the captain answered firmly.

Well, if he insisted, then I suppose there was nothing to worry about. And I knew it would be fine now even if they investigated my background, so I could relax a little.

"I see. That's a relief. Well, should we call it a night? Nonna seems tired."

Nonna had been yawning while we chatted. She'd run around playing with Master Clark for a long time today.

"Are you tired, Nonna?" the captain asked.

"A bit."

"Oh, of course. I'm sorry to say good-bye, but let's get you home early tonight."

We drove home in the Asher family's comfortable carriage.

"Dinner was delicious, wasn't it, Nonna?"

"Yes! But I like your cooking better, Vicky."

Honestly, I just love my daughter so much! The captain was smiling at Nonna, too.

Anyway, I'd asked him about the prince for a particular reason.

If the royal family had their eyes on me, it might be worth considering using the second prince as one of my cards. Playing it would be a double-edged sword, but it was better to have a risky option than none at all.

If the organization was to track me down, there was a possibility they might demand that I be extradited. I truly believed I'd worked enough to repay the amount they'd invested in me, but they might think otherwise.

If I tried getting close to the royal family before that point, however, I might be able to avoid extradition. But as I schemed, a question came to me: *What are you clinging onto so much that you'd go to such lengths?*

The captain came by our house at eight the next night. He said he was in the middle of a shift.

"You still have to work after this? That must be rough."

"There's something I need to tell you about how the first prince had you tailed, and about the incident with the second prince, too. The truth is, this all happened because I forced you to come along with me to the soiree. I put you in a terrible position, and I'm truly sorry for that. I just wanted to say that. I know showing up here unannounced is very rude, but I had to let you know this as soon as I could."

He's such a good person, I thought. And here I was hiding a mountain of things from him.

"Captain, I'm the one who agreed to come with you. And I'm the one who pointed out the thief. There's absolutely no reason for you to feel responsible for this. It was my call to make, and I'll accept the consequences of it. I don't think it's your fault, and I'm not blaming you. So please don't worry about it."

He bit his lip and stared at me.

"What's wrong?" I asked.

"You're such a strong person."

"I hear that a lot," I said with a laugh. The captain took my face in both hands, gently as if he was holding something fragile. I panicked a little, thinking, *Did I say something in this conversation to prompt that?*

I could feel the heat of his body through his touch. I couldn't help but think how nice it would be to have him around to warm me up when I got chilly in the winter.

His natural masculine scent and the faint fragrance of his woodsy cologne enveloped me. He smelled incredible. I stayed still and let him do what he wanted with me.

He held me like that for a while, then let go.

"When I'm with you...I just feel so relaxed," he murmured, as if he was talking to himself, then left abruptly without even saying a word.

Come on, at least tell me good night!

Only now did I understand why the organization had made us abandon our real names—they wanted to prevent us from becoming the way I'd been lately.

Officially, operatives needed to give up their real names to make it easier to cut ties from the people they met while undercover and forget them more easily. Even though I understood that, and even though I thought, *I should leave here and cut off all ties,* I couldn't run away from this place. If I had met these people under my real name, it would've been even more difficult.

I thought about the people I'd worked with at the organization, and those who would sign up in the future.

No one joined by force. No one was working against their will. I was certain there were some who felt conflicted about their jobs, but everyone was in the organization because they wanted to be there.

So why did I feel like I was betraying the Hagl special operations members and future candidates by obtaining mundane happiness?

"Victoria, I was shocked to hear this morning that Clark visited your house on your day off. I'm terribly sorry about that." Lady Eva frowned and apologized.

"Lady Eva, both Nonna and I were happy to see him. We'd like him to come over again sometime, so please don't scold Master Clark."

When Master Clark heard this, his face brightened.

"We had a wonderful time, didn't we?" I said.

"Yes, we did!" Master Clark replied.

"Well, if you say so," Lady Eva added. I've always been concerned that he's far too introverted for a boy. When my husband and I heard about him coming out of his shell lately, we were just so bewildered!"

"Whether Master Clark is quiet or active, he's a lovely boy."

"Goodness! Thank you." Lady Eva smiled and moved on to the next topic. I listened and nodded where appropriate. Master Clark was gazing at me adoringly, but I pretended not to notice.

That day, I decided to conduct my lessons in the format of a play.

We would be performing a play based on one of this kingdom's fairy tales, *The White Princess and the Blue Lizard*.

In the story, a princess with white hair gets lost in a forest and comes across a blue lizard trapped in a spider's web. The lizard can speak the human language and pleads for the girl's help in defeating a wicked witch. The princess rescues the lizard from the web and joins forces with it to take down the witch. This breaks the curse the witch had placed on the blue lizard when it tried to defeat her alone, and it transforms into a handsome young man. The story ends with the young man proposing to the white-haired princess.

"All right, who wants to play the blue lizard?"

"Me!"

"Okay, Master Clark will be the blue lizard. Who wants to play the princess?"

"……"

"Hmm? You don't want to do it, Nonna?"

"I want to play the witch. You play the princess, Vicky."

"But the witch dies at the end. Don't cry, okay?"

"I won't."

"Okay, I guess I have to play the princess, then. That's a shame… I *really* wanted to see Nonna play the princess."

After that, my stomach nearly split from laughing so much.

Though normally impassive, Nonna dived into her role as the wicked witch, imitating my voice perfectly.

Hmm, she's only six, but she's got a knack for acting, I thought, impressed.

Everything about Nonna's performance was adorable, from the hostility she showed to the blue lizard, to the way she terrorized the princess while saying, "I'll get you, you little brat!"

Even though the children were a bit nervous because they needed to say their lines first in Ashburian and then in Randallish, I enjoyed hearing both Nonna's adorable, high-pitched voice and Master Clark's clear, boyish voice. We repeated the lines over and over until they got the hang of them.

<Will you marry me, Princess?>

"Watch the pronunciation of your *r*'s when you say, 'marry me.' Try to make them a bit clearer, like this: 'Marry me.' Yes, yes, that's right!"

I made Master Clark practice his pronunciation of the phrase *marry me* in Randallish several times, only to realize that his face, ears, and neck were bright red.

Uh-oh, I messed up. Here I was, an older commoner and his teacher, asking my young aristocratic charge to say, "Marry me"! This might constitute harassment.

"I'm sorry, I got carried away. I shouldn't have made you ask your old teacher to marry you over and over again."

"Not at all! You're not old at all, Ms. Sellars! And you're very lovely!"

For some reason, Nonna glared at Master Clark when he said that. All of a sudden, she stepped in between us and stretched out her hands, shouting, "No! Vicky's *mine*!"

I burst out laughing. She said I was hers! Had I ever imagined hearing this adorable little girl say that about me would make me so happy? No, I certainly hadn't!

"Ms. Sellars?"

The smirk on my face probably looked suspicious, and now Master Clark seemed concerned.

"I'm sorry. I was just delighted to hear Nonna say that. All right, let's go back to when they first meet in the forest. I'm going to say all my lines in Ashburian, but I want you to say yours in Randallish!"

Our rendition of *The White Princess and the Blue Lizard* in Randallish was amazing.

As a teacher, I was pleased that things had gone so smoothly. And even though the two of them made a few mistakes, they were so adorable that it was fulfilling all the same. It was so fun, in fact, that I almost felt a little guilty that I was being paid to do this.

No one stopped by the room while we were practicing, but once we took a break, Lady Eva and some maids came inside.

"You sounded like you were having so much fun, I couldn't help but check what was going on."

"Please stop, Mother. I promise I'm studying."

"I'm sorry for the commotion, Lady Eva," I said.

"No, not at all. I just wanted to see what the lesson was like! The servants were all surprised. They've never heard Clark sound so happy!"

"Would you show us, Master Clark?"

"What? No way!"

I was torn between the two sides and at a loss for words, but just then, Nonna piped up and began saying the witch's lines in Randallish.

<You cheeky little lizard!>

"Goodness! You're so young, but your pronunciation is fantastic!

You started learning Randallish along with Clark, right? I'm so impressed!"

Nonna was thrilled to hear Lady Eva praise her, and Master Clark pouted a little.

"Nonna, say your line again. Then I'll say mine," he urged.

"Okay."

<You cheeky little lizard!>

<I'll protect the princess! I won't let you hurt her!>

Lady Eva and the three maids all leaped to their feet and started clapping.

"Clark, Nonna, that was wonderful! Your pronunciation was flawless! Say, Victoria. What do you say about continuing his lessons even after Uncle recovers? If you can get Clark to show such enthusiasm so quickly, you definitely have a knack for teaching!"

"Can we, Ms. Sellars? I want you to be my teacher forever!"

"Well, I'll have to consult with Mr. Bernard first..."

I liked tutoring Clark so much that I didn't want to quit, but I owed Mr. Bernard since he had hired me first. I couldn't say yes without his permission.

Fortunately, Mr. Bernard immediately agreed.

Once he fully recovered, I would work as his assistant six days a week, with reduced hours on the days I tutored Master Clark.

"Are you sure it won't be too much work?"

"It's no trouble at all, Lady Eva. In fact, it's a huge help to me since Nonna can participate in the classes."

I was thrilled that she was building up a good foundation for her future. And teaching them languages was very fun for me.

That night, the captain visited my house again.

We hadn't promised to meet, so I wondered what brought him here. He told me that the mystery behind the attack at the soiree was solved in a surprising way.

"We were only able to apprehend the man thanks to you alerting me, so I thought I should let you know the outcome," the captain said.

The man at the party had committed the crime out of resentment for the marquess sexually assaulting his sister. He'd used almost all his money to get a criminal organization to set him up as servant at the castle, and he spent a year plotting his revenge.

"When we informed the marquess about this, he said, 'I have no recollection of doing any such thing. Surely, the man's just angry over my firing a maid with a bad attitude.' But the man confessed everything. Until now, he'd remained silent out of concern for his sister's honor."

"Sexual assault..."

"According to the perpetrator, the marquess never showed any interest in his sister until he got wind of her engagement. That was when he attacked her, and she ended up breaking off the engagement. She was so shocked by the assault and brokenhearted from the break-up that she fell ill. Now she's housebound."

"That's terrible! Will the marquess be brought to justice?"

"The official story is that he's being held accountable for causing the commotion at the soiree. He was forced to retire and abdicate his title to his son. He also held a position in the Ministry of Finance, but His Majesty decided that his son won't be inheriting it."

Well, that's the way the cookie crumbles.

"What about the man?"

"He was found with a poisoned knife on the grounds of the royal castle and attempted to kill a marquess. That's a capital offense."

"I see. I suppose that's how it is in every country, isn't it? The life of a commoner is worth far less than the life of a noble."

The air grew solemn, and the captain bid me farewell.

That night, I spent a long time alone, deep in thought.

Chapter Seven

Nonna Home Alone

One day, while Nonna and I were holding hands on the way home from work, I asked her to stay home alone for the night. Unsurprisingly, an anxious look came to her face.

"Vicky, do I really have to stay home alone?"

"Yes. This time, I absolutely can't take you with me. I won't budge on that. But I'll come home as quickly as I can."

I'd never left Nonna home alone before. But as I'd said, I couldn't take her with me this time.

"Think of staying home a very important job you have to do, Nonna. I'm going to have to leave you home alone every evening for a while. I'll come back as soon as I possibly can. Trust me. If there's ever any trouble, you can go to the main residence for help."

She didn't answer.

"If you really don't think you can manage, I can ask someone at the main residence to watch you while I'm gone. What do you want to do?"

"...I'll wait for you at home."

"That's a huge help, Nonna. Thank you."

I inwardly apologized to her but didn't say it out loud. If I apologized, Nonna would feel like she couldn't speak up at all. And I wanted her to feel free to express her feelings, which I cared about.

Once we got home, I decided to leave right away. No matter what she asked me, I refused to go into detail about what I was doing. I just told her I had an important errand to run.

"I'll try to be home in about three hours. Worst case, it might be four. If you get hungry, have a snack from the cupboards."

"I want to eat with you."

"I know. I want to eat dinner with you, too. That's why I'll hurry home!"

I didn't want Nonna to be home alone for too long, so I rented a horse for two weeks. Now I could use it whenever I had somewhere I wanted to go. If I liked it, I could even buy it. The horse had to be returned to the rental shop every day, however. That way, I wouldn't have to explain to Lady Yolana what I was doing with it.

"Miss, do you have experience with horses?"

"Of course."

"Make sure to let it rest every now and then."

"Don't worry, I'll treat it nicely. I'm just going to visit my sick mother and come back."

Next, I disguised myself as a red-haired woman and visited a pub at the end of a twisting alley.

"Are you Hector?"

"Who wants to know?"

"My name is Kate. I've heard that you can provide certain services for a fee."

"That depends on the service, and how much you're paying."

I told him that I needed help eloping.

"I'm in love with a married man. We're considering running away together, but his wife waits for him at the exit of his workplace every day. I shudder to think what she'll do if she finds out. I want to help my lover escape during the day so his wife doesn't find out."

Hector frowned. "Just have your man say he ain't feelin' well and go home early."

"Although we're in different departments, my lover, his wife, and

I all work at the same place. She'll discover we ran away together immediately."

"Ahh, now I see your problem. Where d'ya work?"

"The castle."

"The castle? Well, that's gonna up the price a bit."

"By how much?"

I paid him the amount he requested on the spot.

"This is all the money I have. Are you sure you can do it?"

"I just gotta sneak him outta the castle, right? Piece of cake."

"We want to leave the capital, so could you take him all the way to the gates?"

"Sure. Meet me here tomorrow. No—day after tomorrow. We'll go over the details then."

"I understand. Thank you."

From there, I hurried to the castle dungeon. I showed the guard some identification papers I'd forged for "Kate" and said, "My boyfriend is the man who was caught at the soiree with a knife. I've come to visit him."

I pleaded for a visitation with tears in my eyes.

"Oh, you mean Carl? Sorry, miss, but I'm going to have to pat you down."

"I understand. Go ahead."

Even though I was prepared for it, being patted down was very unpleasant. The guard, a man in his forties, didn't just check my pockets; he slipped his hand in my undergarments to search those, too. The way the other guards smirked as they watched the process filled me with rage, but this was how all women were treated in every country when requesting a visitation with someone awaiting execution.

The guard accompanied me to the very last cell, which was constructed entirely of stone.

"Hey! Your girlfriend's here!" the guard called, and the man who lay on the simple cot sat up.

This was the first obstacle.

Compared with this, the guard's pat-down was nothing. I gave the man an intense look that said, "Just play along." *Please let it get through to him!*

The man looked at my face, then bowed his head deeply to the guard. "Thank you."

"I heard my boyfriend is getting executed soon. Guard, won't you please give us some time alone?"

"Sure. I don't see why not. Visitation is limited to one hour. I'll come get you when the time's up."

"Thank you!"

We were at the very end of the row of cells. The man's cell was made entirely of thick, sturdy stone. Its heavy iron door was secured with a huge lock. And the guard had given me a thorough search.

Perhaps for all those reasons, the guard had felt secure enough to quickly agree, and he walked off.

The moment he was gone, the man whispered, "Who are you?"

All I said was, "I want to help you, so pretend I'm your girlfriend. For now, I need you to be quiet."

I looked out the barred dungeon window and strained my ears. I could hear the soldiers' armored shoes clacking. I spent the entire hour listening, counting and memorizing the intervals at which they patrolled.

I confirmed that the lock on the grated door was easy to undo, then quickly opened and shut the door.

Seeing this, the man was stunned. I said, "Don't even think about escaping through this door. The soldiers will spot you and kill you immediately."

I thanked the guards and left the castle. I rode the horse back to the rental shop and returned it.

Now I need to hurry home. I quickly bought some bread, meat, and fruit at the market and jogged back to the cottage.

"I'm back!"

"Welcome home!"

I set the groceries on the table and immediately hugged Nonna.

"Thanks for minding the house for me while I was gone, Nonna."

"I was fine by myself. Vicky, are you sweating?"

"Yep. I was so eager to see you that I ran all the way home!"

Nonna's eyes narrowed like she was staring at something very bright.

"Vicky, you don't have to run. I'll be right here waiting for you."

"Aww, okay. Thanks. You're such a good girl, Nonna. And you're very strong."

We ate a simple but delicious dinner that night.

It was the second day of Nonna staying home alone.

That evening, I went to go visit the man in prison again. Once the guard left and we were alone, I immediately started cutting through the bars on the window. Since it was so high up, I needed to ride on his shoulders to reach it before working. I covered the saw blade with thick leather to muffle the sound while I worked. That made it more difficult, but if I didn't do that, the scraping noise would stand out and echo throughout the dungeon.

I was using a tool called a wire saw, which was designed specifically for cutting through metal. You used it by putting your fingers through the loops at both ends. I'd hidden it in a secret place to get it in here, along with my lockpicking tools.

When I considered the length of visiting hours and the frequency of the patrols outside, I realized I could only saw one bar per day at most. Realistically, I would only be able to manage cutting the top or bottom of a single bar per day. There were five bars in total. I thought about finding out the exact date and time of the execution, but that would've taken more time, and since the castle servants were usually very observant and serious about their work, it might've elicited unnecessary suspicion.

As I used the wire saw, I asked the man where his sister was.

"She's at home. I'm very worried about her managing to eat without me. She's unable to go out in public anymore. She's mentally ill."

I see. All I could do was hope that his sister was alive and well.

I wedged tiny pieces of black leather into the cut iron bars to hold them in place. At a glance, no one would ever guess they had been cut through.

"Why are you helping a complete stranger? Did my sister ask you to do this?" the man asked repeatedly. I was currently disguised, plus it had been dark outside on the night of the soiree, when I'd knocked him unconscious, so he didn't recognize me.

"I'm doing this for myself. Don't worry about it," was all I said. The less the man knew, the better.

I left the dungeon a bit early and locked the door behind me. "Thank you. I'll come again tomorrow," I called to the guards.

"Then I'll have to give you another pat-down tomorrow," the guard said. The other guards chuckled lewdly. *Go ahead and laugh all you want.*

Once I left the castle, I went to a store that sold carts.

I bought a cart and hitched my horse to it. The horse I'd rented was not only well-behaved but also intelligent. It was very obedient and pulled the cart nicely for me.

I rode the horse all the way to the outer gate in the southern quarter in search of a farmhouse.

"Excuse me! Good afternoon!" I raised my voice, and a plump woman came out to greet me. "I'll pay you for your trouble, but could you look after my cart for a few days? I'll come back with the horse later. I'll include extra to cover the cost of caring for the horse, and I can give you the money in advance."

"Why do you need to leave the cart here?" the farmer's wife asked, looking suspicious.

"My brother wants to get married, but our father doesn't approve of his fiancée. He's hoping to leave the capital to prevent our father from forcing him to come back home. They're planning to travel a long way to avoid being caught. I thought I could at least give them a cart as a wedding gift."

After I explained that through fake tears, the wife nodded. "All right, I understand. I'll take care of it. I'll make sure the horse is looked after. Don't you worry a bit."

"Thank you so much! My brother should arrive in a few days. My brother's fiancée will come first, though, so please let her wait in the barn for my brother."

"No problem. I'm sorry to hear your father's being so stubborn."

"Thank you, ma'am! I'll be indebted to you for the rest of my life!"

"Aw, shucks. It's no big deal."

I rode back into the city, returned the horse, and hurried back home.

"I'm back!"

"Welcome home, Vicky!"

"Shall we have dinner? Let's use what we have in the cupboards."

Nonna seemed relieved that I was home.

That night, I waited until Nonna was fast asleep and left the house. I ran as fast as I could. I visited the house the man had told me about and knocked on the door.

I heard the frightened voice of a young woman from inside. "Who is it? What do you want at this hour?"

"Shh. I'm here with a message from your older brother."

Thank goodness his sister's still alive.

She opened the door, and I told her his message and explained what I was here for. I asked her to repeat it to make sure she understood.

"Got it? Don't tell a soul what's written down on that piece of paper."

"Of course. But what's your name?"

"Kate."

"Kate, why are you doing all this for us? Did Maria and the others ask you to?"

"Who's that?"

"The marquess did the same thing to them before. I heard afterward that he also assaulted Maria, Luna, and Eliza. So you don't have anything to do with them?"

"No, I don't."

She looked suspicious.

"All this will be for nothing if you don't build up your stamina. I know you don't want to go out in public, but you need to get some food and eat something. Do you have money?"

"Yes," she said, her eyes darting around. That meant she didn't.

"This isn't much, but use it to go buy food somewhere. I want you to eat, sleep, and start moving your body properly. Do you understand? We can't have you holding your brother back and getting caught."

The sister nodded. I left her house and ran back to my own. I needed to quickly forge identification papers for her and her brother.

On the third day, I unlocked the door once the guard left, then I went inside and climbed up on the man's shoulders. I focused on cutting through the iron bars. I kept this up for a few more days.

When there were only two more bars left to cut, I visited Hector again.

"I'd like to confirm the day and time. I want it done on this day, at this time," I said.

"You want to decide on a day already? Well, that'll be an extra fee."

"What?! You keep jacking up the price on me! Well, whatever. But this is all the money I have left!"

"Sure, that's plenty. I'll send someone to fetch your boyfriend in three days at that time, and then they'll take him to the gate in the southern quarter, okay?"

"Yes, that's right."

I was currently sawing through the last bar.

My arms were trembling from the strain of working in such an awkward position for several days. I ignored their screams of pain and just kept cutting. The man spoke to me as I sat on his shoulders.

"Hey, Kate. Why are you helping me? Is my sister really safe?"

"Your sister is safe. Like I said, I'm helping you for myself. I won't tell you anything else. Okay, they're all cut. Now I can go home. Let me down."

I'd gotten a lot faster at sawing through the iron bars.

* * *

The only thing we had left to do was escape.

At the beginning of my next visit, I removed the pieces of leather, then took out the bars. I helped the man climb through the window, then hopped up through the window and escaped myself. The window was long horizontally but short vertically. I was glad that the man had lost weight during his imprisonment.

I took out a bag of spare clothes I'd hidden in the bushes beforehand, and we both changed. We smiled and chatted with each other as we leisurely strolled near the patrolling soldiers and boarded the merchant's cart waiting at the carriage lot.

Inside the cart were empty boxes meant for soldiers' and maids' uniforms. We each hid inside one of the boxes.

The coachman, who had been sent by Hector, seemed to think he was just assisting in an elopement. He chatted casually with the gatekeeper when we went through the city gate, as though everything was perfectly normal.

More than an hour had passed since the beginning of my visit. By now, the prison break had probably been discovered, but the merchant's cart had already reached the outer gate in the southern quarter of the capital.

We got off our ride, and I led the man to the farmhouse where my horse and cart were waiting.

"Talk to the farmer's wife over there. And don't forget to pretend that your sister is your fiancée. She should be waiting inside the barn."

"Thank you so much for everything. I'll never forget your kindness!"

"No, you should forget me. Here's some money for your lodging along the way, and for your new life. Keep it in different places in small amounts in case of theft, so it won't be stolen all at once."

"Kate..."

"Don't cry on me. Go on now. Enjoy your life. And take good care of that horse."

I pushed the man forward and watched him leave. I observed from a distance as the brother and sister, now dressed as peasants, drove the cart out of the outer gate.

Nonna's ten days of staying home alone finally concluded.

"I've grown fond of the horse, and I want to buy it," I told the rental shop owner and filled out paperwork to purchase it.

I went shopping, then hurried home.

"I'm back!"

"Vicky! I'm starving!"

"So am I! I bought some meat on the way home. How about I grill it with some butter?"

"Yay! Meat!"

I was glad everything had gone smoothly, and it was all over.

I was organizing material from some old Haglian books I'd received from Mr. Bernard.

"Vicky, I made tea!"

"Thanks. Let's go ahead and take a break."

Those siblings had new names and identities thanks to the identification papers I'd forged for them. I'd instructed them to travel via the cart during the daytime and stay at inns overnight, making their way toward the border. What happened after that was none of my business, and I had no desire to get involved any further.

I was very sleepy. I'd been staying up late making the identification papers, so I'd only slept one or two hours a night.

I listened to Nonna chattering away about something and dozed off on the chaise longue. When I woke up some time later, I had a blanket on me.

Meanwhile, the castle guards were baffled.

For the past several days, a slender woman with red hair had been coming to visit the man who was slated for execution. She would ask a guard to be alone with her boyfriend each time she came, then leave wiping away her tears after the hour she had for a visit was up.

Since the man would soon be executed, she had to visit him standing outside his locked cell, which meant the guards only saw her when she arrived and departed. Her boyfriend's cell was at a dead end, so there was no reason for them to worry about the man escaping, since he would have to pass right in front of them. Plus, there were soldiers patrolling the perimeter of the dungeon.

The day before, however, the woman didn't come back after her visitation time elapsed, so a guard went to check on them…and he discovered that she and the prisoner had gone missing. The cell door was still securely locked, but all the bars on the windows had been sawed off.

There was an uproar, and the castle gates were sealed. The guards searched every nook and cranny on the castle grounds, but they didn't find them. After that, the Second Order of the knights and the security force expanded the search to include the entire capital. So far, however, no one had spotted the escaped criminal and the red-haired woman.

One night, two weeks after the prison break, the captain showed up at my house and said, "I bought you some sweets from a popular bakery."

I made some tea, and the three of us ate the cake he'd bought. There was a generous layer of chestnuts coated in syrup on top of the icing. The cake was so decadent and delicious that I couldn't help but smile. Nonna was about to lick the icing off her plate, but I told her not to. She looked at me with surprise.

"Do that after you carry the plate into the kitchen, away from company," I said with a serious face, and the captain and Nonna burst out laughing.

"Mm, that was delicious! You look tired, Captain," said Nonna.

"It was really good, wasn't it? And I am tired. The man from the soiree escaped from jail. Apparently, he had help, too."

"What…?"

"The castle's in a complete uproar over a prisoner escaping from the castle dungeon. It's a huge scandal. The knights and I have been combing the city for him for two weeks now." Fatigue was written all over his face.

"I can see how exhausted you are. So what happened to the man?"

"He must be hiding out somewhere. We checked his sister's house, but she was gone. She left a note saying, 'I've entered a nunnery far away from here and will pray for my brother, who has been called to heaven.'"

"I see," I said, taking a sip of my tea.

Nonna wasn't remotely interested in our conversation. She finished eating her cake and brought her plate to the kitchen, then started reading a book on the sofa. And she didn't forget to lick her plate clean before setting it in the sink.

I made another pot of tea for the captain and myself.

"Most people think that the escapee will be caught eventually. We sent information by express messengers to all four gates of the capital. Even if they went straight from the jail to a gate, they wouldn't have gotten there in time."

"I see."

I took another sip of my hot tea and ate my last bite of cake.

"If he was going to hide in the capital, it would probably be in the slums, but since the man was an amateur, he'll probably get caught sooner or later by a snitch watching the bounty. I feel bad for him considering what happened to his sister, but...that's the way it is, I suppose."

"Right."

The captain grew somber, and it looked like he was about to leave. I felt so bad that I inadvertently reached out and gently placed a hand on his arm as I spoke. "Captain, could you take some time off and go with us to Cadiz? It doesn't have to be now. I heard that they float small wooden boats out to sea with candles on them during the summer solstice."

His face softened a little. "I'm surprised you know about that. Yes, it's sad that the souls of those who have passed away will return to this world while the candles burn."

"They just come for a little visit, don't they? I want the souls of my family to visit. There's so much I want to say to them."

He gently cradled my head against his chest. "Let's go someday. Let's float wooden boats out to sea at night. It's a promise. No matter what happens, I'll take off enough time for us to go do that."

The captain cheered up a bit and went home.

I checked to make sure Nonna was still reading, then stuffed my red wig, which was in a small cloth bag, into a cushion and carefully sewed it shut.

I'm sorry, I inwardly apologized to all the people who were earnestly searching for the escapee, including the captain. I wouldn't ask for forgiveness. I was sure that one day, I'd be punished for this somehow.

A brother and sister in their twenties came to a town on the southern border of Ashbury.

The two got along quite well as they worked together and lived modestly. They told the villagers that they had moved out after the death of their parents, and that they came from a town far to the east. The mayor offered them a vacant house to live in.

The brother and sister worked the abandoned farmland together. The other villagers were very friendly and treated them kindly.

One night, as they stood in the kitchen, the sister said to her older brother, "Living like this is a dream. You know, I was so broken up about you getting the death penalty for trying to avenge me that I was thinking of taking my life."

"I'm sorry I made you worry."

"It's okay. Just like Kate said, it's better to work hard at being happy than to get revenge."

The sister took their identification papers out of the drawer and set them on the table. They stared closely at them.

The documents were indistinguishable from the real thing. The touch of the paper, the intricate background pattern, the printed letters—it was all spot-on.

"These look completely authentic," the older brother said.

"I wonder if she used to work at the office where identification papers are made or something."

"I have no clue," he said.

"It pains my heart that we weren't able to thank her."

"She said it would cause trouble for her if we tried to contact her, so there's nothing we can do about that. But I wish we could've thanked her, too."

"All she said was, 'I'm doing this for myself,' but what could that mean? And then she said, 'The both of you living a happy life will be thanks enough for me.'"

Neither of the siblings had a clue as to why the red-haired woman had helped them. They still had a third of the money she'd given them to start their new life.

The sister was deeply grateful that her brother hadn't been executed, and that he had not become a murderer.

After Nonna went to bed, I carefully polished my shoes. The wire saw was neatly tucked inside the heel of one shoe. Its teeth had dulled considerably. *Should I sharpen it?* Well, I doubted I would ever need to cut through iron bars again.

After I meticulously polished the shoes, I put them away in the shoe rack by the entrance. I'd also had a small set of lockpicking tools hidden in the soles. But now the soles were sealed shut with glue. My lockpicking tools were stashed away somewhere else.

If anyone found out about what I did, they'd probably call me a hypocrite. And I was prepared to face that criticism, no matter how harsh it was.

Chapter Eight

Victoria's Scars

A so-called open market was held once a month in the plaza near the castle, where citizens who weren't registered with the Chamber of Commerce could set up small stalls and sell whatever they liked for a fee. Anyone could become a shopkeeper for the day, as long as they could afford the modest participation fee.

Open markets weren't only found in the capital, but also in larger regional cities. Ashbury encouraged participation, since it prided itself on being a kingdom of commerce.

I bought three delicious-looking pastries at the market and handed them to Master Clark and Nonna. We ate them as we walked. After a few steps, I noticed Clark nibbling nervously away at his pastry.

I wonder if this is first time doing something as improper as eating while walking. Well, I'm terribly sorry about that, but life is all about experiencing new things!

There must've been around seventy to eighty stalls, or maybe even more. The air was filled with the shouts of vendors hawking their wares, creating a lively atmosphere.

The three of us browsed the various stalls. There were bread and pastry stalls, vegetable stalls, secondhand book and clothing stalls, stalls selling handmade toys and dolls, flower shops, accessory shops, and more.

"Look at that, Vicky!"

Nonna pointed to a shop selling fabric-covered buttons. Rows of buttons of various sizes were neatly arranged on a black cloth, reminding me of a small flower garden. It was quite the charming sight.

The vendor was a woman around my age who wore a simple, sleek gray dress. There were rows of light-pink buttons, all covered in fabric, along the front of her dress. It looked very fashionable.

"Those are lovely."

"Aren't they? Please take your time and look around," the lady said.

Nonna and I both excitedly knelt down to examine the buttons.

"These buttons are really adorable when used on barrettes, too. I think these will look wonderful on you, young lady."

The lady picked up a large button covered in dark-blue silk and stuffed with cotton inside, then held it against Nonna's head. She looked at me and said, "What do you think?"

"Vicky, can we buy one?"

"Sure. What would you like?"

Nonna pointed to some light-blue covered buttons that looked like the sky on a sunny winter's day. They would be cute sewn onto a white dress.

"Can I have five of those buttons? I'd also like five of these dark-green ones."

"Sure. Thank you so much."

Nonna was so thrilled when I bought her the buttons that she began to skip down the street. She was really happy.

Master Clark browsed the secondhand bookshop and bought two books. I looked around, thinking I'd like to buy something, too.

Then I found it. Something I wanted so much, it almost felt like a miracle that I'd stumbled on it. It was hair. Long, beautiful black hair that was tied up in thin leather cords.

Black hair that beautiful, shiny, and straight was hard to come by, so I bought it right away. The children said, "Wow," and "That's creepy!" But this hair was perfect to make a black wig out of.

I went home feeling excited. I wouldn't have to worry about working late nights for a while. Open markets were the best.

That night, I awoke to Nonna shaking me.

"Vicky! Vicky!"

"Hmm? Yes?!"

I shot up in bed. Had I overslept? No, the room was still pitch-black. *Hmm?*

"Are you okay?" Nonna asked me.

"Why wouldn't I be? It's the middle of the night."

"You were screaming, Vicky."

"...What was I screaming?"

"You said, 'Stop!'"

Oh, that again.

"I'm sorry. I was just having a nightmare. I must've startled you when you heard me shouting."

"It's okay. Want me to sleep with you tonight, Vicky?"

"Would you?"

Nonna climbed into bed with me. We put the blankets over us, but now I was wide-awake. I waited until she fell back to sleep, then slipped out of bed.

I went to the kitchen, lit a lamp, and poured myself a glass of water.

I was covered in a film of cold sweat, and my nightclothes clung to my damp skin.

The organization psychiatrist had told me I had a strong mind, but even I had emotional scars from my line of work. When I screamed in my sleep, I must have been dreaming about a certain incident.

It happened when I was twenty-two and my colleague Mary was twenty-one. We were working with Hans, who was fifteen at the time, and the three of us were tasked with breaking into a noble's estate to steal a document detailing incidents of fraud committed by important figures.

"Mary, you're the leader," said Chief Lancome. "Since this'll be your first time being in charge, I want you to be very cautious."

"Yes, Chief."

The problem occurred that night. Right before the mission, Mary changed the plan.

"Hans and I will enter the mansion while you stand watch, Chloe. Hans, you follow after me."

"All right," he said.

"Wait, that wasn't the plan. Hans was supposed to be the lookout," I said, and Mary shot me a sour glare.

"I'm the leader. Do as I say."

"But this is Hans's first mission. He should be on lookout duty."

"No."

The air between Mary and I grew tense. Hans said, "I'll go. Chloe, don't worry. I'll be fine."

Mary and I had always been at odds, and I didn't want to argue anymore, so I reluctantly agreed to the change.

Shortly after the two of them broke into the house, I heard a commotion and shouting from inside the mansion. Mary jumped out the window, and Hans followed soon after.

A burly man began to chase them but seemed to decide he couldn't catch up—so he threw a heavy sword that stabbed right through Hans's chest. He fell forward, motionless, the blade still protruding from his chest.

I didn't know what happened inside the mansion. But it was undeniable that Mary had left Hans, her inexperienced partner, behind and fled first.

Mary and I ran as fast as we could, hopped on our horses, and rode them back home. Once we got back to central control, Mary suddenly spoke to me before she made the report.

"Chloe, if you've got something to say, then spit it out."

"Don't talk to me."

"You always act like you're so superior. It gets on my nerves! Lancome always gives you the big jobs! And you act like you're the best spy here just because you're his favorite! I can't stand it!"

I usually ignored her standoffishness, but this time, I rose to my feet, and everyone in the room tensed up.

"If you've got a problem with the way Lancome runs things, maybe you should take it up with him. I'm not the person you should be complaining to. And you've got some nerve taking it out on me, because I'm not the one who sucks up to Lancome—it's you. You should be ashamed of yourself."

Just then, Mary threw a punch at me.

Idiot. The person who attacks first faces the consequences.

I dodged Mary's fist and elbowed her square in the face. She would have a nasty bruise the next day, but I didn't care. Hans had been stabbed through the heart. We hadn't even been able to recover his body. And it was my and Mary's fault.

Mary clutched her face and groaned. I leaned forward and hissed into her ear, "The worst kind of leader acts self-important but abandons their colleagues to die when things get tough."

Mary let out a guttural noise and lunged at me, but the men held her back.

"You're too easily provoked. That's why you never get any big jobs. And if I was a supervisor, I would never give a crucial mission to someone who can't control their emotions like you, either. Why did you change the plan at the last minute? Why did you leave Hans and run away? Before you take your frustration at your own failure out on me, you'd better get down on your hands and knees and apologize to Hans! But no matter how much you apologize, he'll never come back!"

If Mary had gone with the original plan, Hans would still be alive. If I hadn't obeyed her and insisted Hans be lookout, he would still be alive. But death was final. No matter how much I regretted it or apologized, you couldn't bring someone back to life. His potential, his entire future, was now gone because of me and Mary.

I didn't think I'd be able to get back to sleep tonight, so I decided to do some work. I would make a wig out of that long black hair I'd bought at the open market. Some agents purchased their wigs, but I preferred to make my own.

I kept the hair bundled together as I washed and dried it. I took out small groups of several strands at once and wove them together with an ultra-fine crochet hook. I made a hairnet that fit my head perfectly, then started weaving in the pieces of hair to make the wig. It was a labor- and time-intensive task, but I didn't mind it.

As I focused on my work, I gradually calmed down. Memories I didn't usually think about floated to the forefront of my mind.

I was remembering Hans tonight. His smile, how happy he'd been when he ate meat. How he'd had a crush on a colleague his age. How he'd always boasted that his sister was such a pretty little girl. How he'd said he wanted a promotion.

Remembering Hans was my way of atoning for his life ending after only fifteen years, and it was also a way of reminding myself.

I'd been raised by the government to do illegal work, and that was how I'd made my living. But even I had things I wanted to protect. I wanted to avoid deaths if at all possible. I saw the finality of death more than the average person.

"When a mission is done, you need to forget it. Regret is a poison, and nothing more," Lancome had told me. At the time, I'd been grateful to hear it.

But not now. If I forgot Hans's death, I felt like I would lose a very important part of my humanity.

Nonna was staying with Susan at the main residence tonight, so I could take my time and enjoy a drink.

"Hey, there. Welcome."

"The usual."

"Liquor? Comin' right up." Zaharo brought me a glass of strong, amber-colored alcohol and sat down across from me.

"Unusual for you to sit with your customers."

"I've been worried about you ever since you asked me where you could find Hector."

"He doesn't know who I am. Don't worry."

"Just don't do anything reckless. I'll be sad if you stop showing up here." I could tell his dark eyes were filled with concern. I lowered my head to him.

"Thanks, Zaharo."

Tonight was the first time I stayed very long at his pub.

It just so happened that there were few customers present, so we both moved to the bar to chat and drink together freely.

Zaharo stood on the other side of the counter while I sat at the bar. He gazed at my glass and murmured softly, "Hector's looking for a woman with red hair. Red hair, brown eyes, a mole by her mouth, slender."

"Is that so?"

"Be careful."

"Whatever do you mean?"

He grinned at me and filled my glass back up.

I decided to order some food for the first time. "Do you have anything to eat?"

"I can offer you either a boiled-pork-and-cucumber sandwich or vegetable soup with cheese. Which do you want?"

"Hmm, I can't decide. I'll just have both."

"Comin' right up."

Zaharo quickly made the food, and both dishes were delicious.

"You can cook, too. Pretty impressive," I said.

"I was raised without a mother, so I had to learn to do it myself. I can make most things as long as they're simple. Cheaper than buying it."

"I see," I said, tipping my glass. I noticed the puzzled look on his face.

"That's where you tell me about your upbringing."

"I left my parents as a child to work. So there's not really much to say about my upbringing."

"...Oh."

Once I started eating, four other customers ordered the same thing. Drinking makes you hungry, especially when you see someone else with food.

At last, the other customers went home, and I was the only one left.

"Next time you need to ask Hector for a favor, you should go through me instead. He's looking for you. He said, 'If you knew a woman that capable, why didn't you tell me? I'd have asked her to join us.'"

"Huh."

The jailbreak had happened after I asked Zaharo to find Hector, so surely, he was onto the fact that I was behind it.

"You won't sell me out?" I asked.

"You came here again because you know I won't."

"That's true." To be honest, I had doubted him a little, because you could never underestimate the bond of friendship between men.

The customers who'd been at the bar earlier were clearly regular civilians, so I trusted him now. One of the reasons I stayed here longer than usual tonight was to see if Zaharo was someone I could trust—if he would sell me out to Hector.

I stayed late after midnight drinking. Just as I was about to go home, Zaharo said he'd escort me.

"All my other customers are gone, and you've had a lot to drink tonight."

"I don't want you to know where I live."

"What, you still don't trust me?"

I didn't know how to answer. I walked a few steps, and then I paused. "I trust you a lot, Zaharo. But trusting people completely never got me anywhere."

"I get that. How about I drop you off close, then?"

He maintained a proper distance from me as he followed behind.

Surely, that was fine; there were countless houses in the eastern quarter. We walked together in silence. Once we passed from the southern district into the eastern district, I turned around toward him. "Here's fine."

"Here? You live in the eastern quarter? Don't tell me you're a noble!"

"Of course not. Well, good night."

"Yeah. Be careful on your way home."

I hopped over the fence and made it to my cottage, where I lit some candles. I brought the candles close to the floor to check for footprints. The baby powder hadn't been trampled on. Nothing seemed out of the ordinary. This was a ritual I did nightly to make sure I could sleep without worries.

I locked the door, changed into my nightclothes, washed my face, and got into bed.

I wondered how the brother and sister were doing. Despite how I'd insisted that I wouldn't have anything to do with them anymore, and that whatever happened to them was none of my concern.

The prime minister visited the king's chambers.

"Your Majesty. I'm sorry to bother you so late at night. But we just received a message from our man in Randall."

"And?"

"Victoria Sellars is a real person, and her age, outward appearance, and characteristics mostly match the woman in question."

"Mostly?"

The prime minister looked at the documents that had come in the report. "She's a completely ordinary commoner. Her father is a carpenter, her mother a market vendor. She went missing at age seventeen, and her whereabouts remained unknown for ten years. She seems to have grown a bit taller during that time. Her parents divorced after she disappeared. Their locations are currently unknown. She entered our kingdom from Randall, exactly like she said she did."

"I see. Thanks for your hard work."

The prime minister excused himself. The king rang a bell, and a maid entered.

"Get me a drink."

The servant silently bowed her head and quickly went to fetch a bottle of wine. She poured it in a glass for him, then disappeared once again into the adjoining chamber.

"I see. So she *is* real. But what was she doing during those ten years?"

As far as he knew, seventeen was far too late to be trained as a spy or assassin, especially for someone who'd been raised as a commoner her whole life.

It was too difficult to train once you were fully grown, especially for women. And from a mental health perspective, both men and women had to be molded from childhood to pledge their lives to the organization and the government, or else they would become mentally unstable and unfit for duty as their careers progressed.

"So the lady Jeffrey fell for is innocent after all. That's a relief."

The next morning, the king summoned Prince Cedric.

"How are your injuries?"

"The pain is mostly gone. I'm sorry for worrying you."

"Claudia was very concerned. You shouldn't worry your mother so."

"Yes, Father. By the way, are you done checking into the woman Jeffrey brought to the soiree?"

The king studied Cedric's face, wondering how he'd heard about that.

"Why do you ask?"

"Jeffrey's in love with her, which is quite rare for him. I've been curious about what she's like."

"I had her investigated, and she's clean. Just an ordinary citizen from Randall."

"I see. All right. Well, if you'll excuse me."

"Cedric."

"Yes, Father?"

"You let Conrad worry about Jeffrey. Don't do anything unnecessary."

"Yes, Father."

Cedric quietly excused himself from his father's chambers and muttered to himself, "'An ordinary citizen,' my ass. I'd like to know what Father's investigator thinks is ordinary!"

He walked out to a secluded spot in the garden. He liked to go here when he needed to do some thinking.

Cedric was very athletic and had been praised since childhood for his aptitude in swordsmanship, horsemanship, and martial arts. Even though he was a prince, he had a hard time believing all that was merely lip service from his teachers.

Some of his teachers hadn't held back on him during their training sessions, despite his royal status. Plus, there was Jeffrey. He'd praised Cedric, too.

So he thought he was fairly strong. Yet he'd been powerless against a slender woman in her late twenties. He'd never faced someone like that in his entire life—it'd been quite the rude awakening.

He wanted to apologize to the woman and ask her to train him in martial arts.

Jeffrey would never agree. He was fuming when he found out my brother had ordered someone to tail her. Even Conrad was shocked when Jeffrey had such strong words for him. At this point, I just need to...

"Yeah, I just need to apologize. I'll tell her I was in the wrong. I was curious about her, but I underestimated her because of her gender. First, I'll tell Jeffrey about how I want to apologize to her."

But when he went to do that, Jeffrey Asher replied with eyes as cold as ice, "I know what you did, Your Highness. Victoria means a lot to me, and I would appreciate it if you left her alone. I'll relay your apology to her. Oh, and one more thing—I'll give you some thorough training in swordsmanship. There's no need to hold back. I'll take you on right now."

And so Cedric got roped into sparring with Jeffrey. No matter how many times he fell to the ground, Jeffrey would yell, "Not yet!" "Once more!" or "Is that all you've got?" and fought with him until he couldn't even stand up anymore.

In the end, Jeffrey ended up forcing Cedric back with his sword until he was on the ground of the training area.

Cedric spat out a mouthful of sand and muttered, "I knew I shouldn't have told you, Jeffrey." He rolled onto his back and closed his eyes.

I heard the clunking of a carriage pulling up outside Lady Eva's estate.

"Guests?" I said, looking out the window to find a black carriage emblazoned with the golden crest of a griffin. *Why, that's the seal of the royal family of Ashbury!*

"Master Clark, it seems like you're about to have some very important guests," I said, and the three of us headed toward the foyer.

A servant opened the door, revealing a slender young man with golden hair.

It's him.

Although the color of his hair was different now, I recognized the way he walked. He was the second prince. He sauntered over to me and said, "Oh! Hullo, Ms. Sellars. Long time no see."

Long time no see, indeed! I thought with a dry chuckle.

Prince Cedric greeted me in a voice so cheerful, you'd never think I'd broken his ribs. Neither "It's nice to meet you" or "It's nice to see you again" seemed appropriate, so I just bowed silently.

"I heard from Dowager Countess Haynes that you were here. May I have a word?"

"Of course, Your Highness."

"Oh, Lady Anderson—I only came to chat a bit. There's no need to make tea; I'll be going home right away. May I speak to you alone, Ms. Sellars?"

"Of course, Your Highness."

Lady Eva showed us to a parlor. Prince Cedric's knights inspected it briefly, then excused themselves. Master Clark peeked in through the door, but Nonna grabbed his hand and pulled him away. She *did* turn around and glare at the prince on the way out, though. Then it was Master Clark's turn to grab her hand and pull *her* away.

Why was she glaring at him?

"I came here today to apologize to you. It's no wonder you responded the way you did. When a woman is approached in that manner, she has no way of knowing what the other person will do to her."

I wasn't sure what the point of him telling me this was, so I just quietly waited for him to continue.

"The truth is, I've been curious about you ever since learning you were the person who knocked the man unconscious at the soiree."

"I'm sorry, but that wasn't me."

"Ha-ha-ha. I see. But you were quite strong when you went up against me."

"The captain of the Second Order of knights told me that you injured yourself in a fall."

Prince Cedric grinned sheepishly. "Please don't tease me like that. I came here to apologize to you sincerely. I'm truly sorry. Please accept my utmost apologies." He placed his hands on his lap and bowed deeply to me.

"Your Highness, please stop. I'm nothing but a commoner from another country. Please lift your face."

"Will you forgive me, then?"

"Yes, of course."

"Good! Jeffrey won't even let me come near you. Please don't tell him I visited you today. I just couldn't feel right without apologizing to you."

The captain was right; the prince wasn't a bad person. Thank goodness I hadn't broken his arms and legs. In fact, as long as he didn't do anything to me, I had no animosity toward him.

"I have a favor to ask of you," the prince began. "Would you train me in martial arts? I promise you'll be handsomely compensated."

"I'm sorry, but no."

"Don't you think you're a bit too eager to refuse? Why? You forgave me, right?"

Perhaps I needed to spell it out to him at this point.

"If anyone finds out I am training you in martial arts, they'll take an interest in me. And once people find out a woman in her twenties is training you, they'll say, 'I want to see what she's made of, too!' and then people will start coming out of the woodwork. Right now, I'd like to focus on my job and raising my child. I don't have time for anything else."

"I promise I'll make sure no one finds out. Just one hour a week. Please."

He's positively obsessed with training.

"Wouldn't someone in your position prefer having someone strong by their side over polishing their skills?"

"Then will you stay by my side?"

"Absolutely not. No."

"See?"

I burst out laughing. *"See" indeed!*

I kept turning the prince down until he finally said, "All right. I'll come back when I think you've changed your mind!" with a cheerful smile, and then left. *Talk about stubborn*, I thought. I'd never met someone who was so enthusiastic about training before.

Lady Eva peppered me with questions about the prince's visit, but I brushed her off vaguely and said, "Oh, he just wanted to talk about the captain," and then Nonna and I went home. It wasn't exactly a lie. I told Lady Yolana the same thing. I certainly couldn't tell them the whole truth.

There was a knock at the door after dinner. I wondered who it could be, but then I heard the captain's voice.

"It's me, Jeffrey."

"Vicky! It's Jeff!" Nonna looked thrilled. She raced to open the door. There was the captain, in uniform. I'd always thought he looked even more handsome in uniform.

"Good evening, Captain."

"Victoria, I heard from a member of the royal guard at the castle that Prince Cedric went to visit you. Did he really?"

He already found out, Your Highness, I thought with an inward laugh.

"Yes, that's right. He asked me to train him in martial arts."

"And what did you say?"

"I said no."

"I thought I'd made it clear that he shouldn't go anywhere near you! Now I'm really going drill it into him tomorrow. I've known the prince since he was three years old, and he's always been stubborn as an ox. He's twenty now; you'd think he'd learn his lesson. But he's only ever been interested in training, so I suppose everyone just put up with it."

I quietly readied a pot of tea and cut off some slices of butter cake with walnuts baked inside. I set the plates on the table. I'd just baked the cake the day before, so it was still moist and tasted even better today.

"Victoria?"

"You're one of the king's knights. I can't ask you to do that for me."

"Still..."

If the captain tried to deter the prince from coming near me any further, it would eventually cause trouble for the captain and his family. I didn't want that. What if it did and the captain distanced himself from me? Imagining that made my heart ache.

"There's only so much I can ask you to do for me, Captain. I would be devastated if things went wrong after I asked you to do me a favor and you pulled away from me. I'll continue turning down the prince, so please don't worry."

The captain rose to his feet. He walked over to me and peered into my face with concern. "I would *never* pull away from you."

"I can take care of my affairs on my own. You've already done so much to help me, but I can manage by myself. So you really don't need to worry."

"Vicky, are you mad about something?"

"I'm not mad at anyone. Don't worry, Nonna."

I tried to keep my voice down, but that just scared Nonna even more, because she had tears in her eyes.

I smiled at Nonna and patted her head reassuringly. The captain put one arm around Nonna and his other arm around me, pulling us both toward him.

"All right, I understand. So stop giving me that sad smile. Won't you tell me what you're afraid of, Victoria?"

I didn't answer him; instead, I comforted Nonna, who had started crying, then carried her to her bedroom and tucked her in. The captain waited for me until I was done.

"I can't tell you what I'm afraid of, Captain. I'm sorry."

"I see. I know you have your own things to worry about. I'm sorry I forced my feelings on you."

"No, I'm sorry. Would you like to drink some wine with me?"

"Yes, I'd love to."

Red wine went perfectly with walnut butter cake.

We sat together, quietly drinking our wine and eating the cake. I'd roasted the walnuts until they were crispy; they crunched when I chewed on them. It reminded me of the walnut cake my mother used to make when I was little. I'd only lived with her for eight years, so my memory of her face and voice was quite faint now, but I still vividly recalled the cake she would bake for me.

"A long time ago, my fiancée would never come to me for anything important," the captain said. "Perhaps my desire to protect the people I'm close to is just too strong."

"You...you have a fiancée? Are you sure you should be here?"

"She passed away. She took her own life ten years ago. I couldn't save her."

"Oh… I see… I had no idea that happened to you."

That must've been unbearable for someone so protective, who had such a strong sense of duty. Now it made sense why he hadn't gone on a date with a woman for ten years.

"I'm sorry to make you talk about something so painful."

"It's all in the past. There's no reason for you to worry about it."

I wanted to change the subject. I had to.

"Someone told me recently that I don't know how a normal conversation should go. I suppose there are a lot of things I'm clueless about," I admitted.

"Who told you that?"

"Someone you don't know. The owner of a pub I frequent."

He looked surprised. "You go to pubs?"

"Yes, only when Nonna's staying over at the main residence. This may sound silly, but I go there when I want to be alone around other people."

The lull in conversation made me feel anxious, so I just kept rattling on.

"Can I visit that pub with you sometime?" he asked.

"I only stop by there for a few drinks and then head straight home. I'd rather go somewhere else with you."

Zaharo knew too much about me, so I didn't want him to meet the captain.

"If you're up for martial arts training, you can spar with me. I'm stronger than the prince."

"No way."

"Why not?"

"When I spar, my hair gets all messed up, and I sweat. I must look awfully frightful, too. I don't want you to see me like that."

"Does that mean I'm someone you want to look good for, then?"

"……"

Answer that question yourself, Captain.

Chapter Nine

A Baby-Pink Dress

After Nonna, Master Clark, and I successfully finished the play *The White Princess and the Blue Lizard* in Randallish, I thought we'd wrap up learning languages through dramas, but then Lady Eva said, "I'd love for my husband to see the play. We want to watch it!"

That was only natural, so I agreed. Then the maids brought up something I hadn't thought of. "If His Lordship will be watching, we must have costumes!"

"It's only a play for our language class, you don't have to do all that…"

"Oh, it's no trouble at all! Our tailor is already excited about it! The maids were chatting with them, and they've already designed costumes for the three of you!"

The Anderson family had their own private tailor, of course.

I suppose for a family as wealthy as them, making their children costumes isn't a big deal, I thought.

A while later, a tailor delivered costumes for us. Master Clark wore a lizard costume made of blue fabric, along with a fancy costume fit for a prince. Nonna had a black witch's dress and a pointy hat, and they even gave her a cute little staff.

"Nonna! Oh, my tiny little witch! I've never seen a cuter witch than you. That black dress really brings out your blond hair."

"Vicky, can I keep this?"

"You like the witch costume? I'll ask Lady Eva if I can buy it for you. Leave it to me!"

"Yaaay! Thank you!"

Now, that was all well and good. However, since I played the role of the princess, I kept insisting I would wear a dress of my own, but Lady Eva wouldn't hear it. She said the tailor would make me a fluffy princess's dress sewn from pink fabric.

"Lady Eva, I'm only the tutor! This dress sounds more expensive than the other two costumes combined. I feel so guilty, I simply must insist I wear my own dress..."

"You brought such cheer to our dreary house, Victoria. It's not a problem, I promise. Making you this one dress is the absolute least we can do! Please don't worry about it. Well then, I need to leave for my charity work!" Lady Eva said with a smile and rushed off to her engagement.

"What am I going to do...?" I raised my arms in vain as Lady Eva left, then hung my head with disappointment.

One week later...

"Victoria, your princess dress is finished!" One of the maids held up a baby-pink dress that was so cutesy, I felt my face twitch.

This is something a teenage girl would wear! Well, I suppose the princess is *in her teens...*

The maids proudly handed me the dress. I was at a complete loss as to what I should say.

"Will you try it on and show it to everyone? I simply can't wait!" Lady Eva said with glee. Nonna and Master Clark looked at me with anticipation. I couldn't say no.

If I could faint on command, I would right now...

I trudged off to another room to change, wishing fervently that I would somehow fall unconscious. Once I finished, I gritted my teeth and went back out in front of everyone.

"Vicky, you're so pretty!"

"You look beautiful, Ms. Sellars!"

The children showered me with compliments. Lady Eva and the maids seemed overjoyed. I felt a cold sweat come over me, but as long as everyone else was happy, I suppose it was fine. I was clenching my teeth so tightly while I smiled that my mouth began to hurt.

"Oh, I know! I'll call Jeff over! We can have the play on his day off!"

Noooo, Lady Eva! I wanted to scream, but I somehow managed to stop myself.

I knew if I said, "Please—I don't want the captain to see me in this baby-pink dress," Lady Eva would just give me a puzzled look and say, "Whyever for?" And I wouldn't be able to answer that question.

So instead, I gritted my teeth even harder and agreed.

Lady Eva sent a servant over to the captain's to ask him when his next day off was, and we set the date and made plans. She was extremely capable as a countess. But at this moment, I despised her efficiency.

"Oh, I'm so looking forward to it! Aren't you, Victoria?"

"Yes... I can hardly wait..."

Out of the blue, I was reminded of a mission I'd had several years ago.

I'd been working undercover as a servant in a high-ranking aristocrat's house in the kingdom of Hagl. I spent five months there, exchanging communications with our informant. My collaborator was a woman who lived in the mansion and was a candidate to become the nobleman's second wife.

She was only twenty-two at the time. She had a baby face that reminded me of a doll's, and pretty features. And she looked wonderful in pink.

One day, the woman was finally able to produce evidence of the noble's wrongdoing. I decided to help her escape before the man found out. I waited impatiently for the woman at our meeting place, and she showed up in a baby-pink dress.

"How many times did I tell you not to wear anything that calls attention to you? You're going to have to wear that when we travel through the mountain pass."

"I'll go change, then."

"You can't. If he finds you, he'll kill you."

"All you ever do is tell me that I can't do this, can't do that! I'm sick of it!"

"Quiet down! If anyone finds us here, we're both done for!"

The woman wore that baby-pink dress as we escaped, complaining, crying, and cursing at me the entire way. Halfway through, I got fed up with it and bought her a plain commoner's dress, but then she said, "I'm too tired. I can't walk another step!" and refused to move. "He loves me. He won't kill me even if he finds me. I'm telling you, it's fine!"

I suppressed the urge to yell at her and gently consoled her, encouraged her, and took her hand as we continued to escape. We headed for the capital of Hagl. Once it was all over and I handed her over to my supervisor, I was shocked to discover I had four surprisingly large canker sores in my mouth from clenching my jaw the entire way.

Compared with that mission, this is nothing, I told myself in an attempt to lift my spirits.

On the day of the play, the captain showed up at the Anderson manor carrying a huge bouquet with several varieties of white and pink flowers.

"Flowers for the White Princess," he said, holding out the bouquet.

"That's incredibly sweet of you, Captain...but the play is for the children. I feel bad accepting this."

"I brought treats for them, of course."

"Well, in that case, I'll accept them. Thank you."

"Victoria, you look wonderful in your usual dresses, but you look even lovelier in pink."

"......"

I wanted to toss everything into a container labeled "endurance," slam the lid shut, and throw the whole thing into a fire to forget it as soon as the play was over. I was mortified.

I was wearing a fluffy, baby-pink dress adorned with ribbons and frills at the age of twenty-seven. How could I ever live this down?

At any rate, the children's adorable performance charmed the adults. I was particularly surprised to see Mr. Bernard, who was usually quite stoic, take off his glasses and dab at his eyes with a handkerchief. The play wasn't sad, and there was certainly nothing to warrant tears. I wondered if I would cry watching a production like this once I reached his age. I gazed at him with warmth.

Lord Michael Anderson, Master Clark's father, also seemed to be thoroughly satisfied.

"Victoria, it was truly magnificent! Your performance exceeded all my expectations. I'd be thrilled if you would continue to serve as Clark's tutor for a long time to come."

"That's right, Victoria!" Lady Eva added. "I'm beside myself with pride at having invited you to be his tutor."

"I love taking classes with Ms. Sellars!" Master Clark exclaimed.

I gratefully accepted the Anderson family's praise. I had to admit that I'd caught myself thinking up a curriculum for our classes while I cleaned Mr. Bernard's house. My job as a tutor was so enjoyable that I couldn't help it.

The captain was about to offer his thoughts on the play, but I gave him a fierce look that said, "Please don't say a word!" so he closed his mouth.

Thank you for being so considerate, Captain!

That night, my back teeth ached intensely, and it hurt so much to chew that Nonna was worried about me.

Lady Eva agreed to let Nonna keep the costume, and Nonna showed up at the main residence wearing the witch's dress and the pointy hat, sending Lady Yolana and Susan into a tizzy.

"Why didn't you invite us?!" Lady Yolana accosted me.

Since the eastern quarter was where the nobles lived, Nonna had no opportunities to interact with the neighborhood children.

Children of nobles began their education at a young age, and when they went out, they always had a servant accompanying them. They did not play with commoners.

So Nonna had no female friends her own age. This had been bothering me for some time. I wanted to let her play with other little girls, but I didn't have ordinary friendships when I was a child, so I didn't know how to go about it. I wanted to ask someone for advice, but both Lady Yolana and Lady Eva were wealthy noblewomen. I'd thought the lady's maid, Susan, might have some words of wisdom, but she told me that she'd started working for Lady Yolana when Susan was ten years old and had never had a chance to play with other girls her age, either.

"Hmm..."

"What's the matter, Vicky?"

"I wanted to help you make friends with other little girls your age, but I don't know how."

"I'd rather train. I like training."

"But you train all the time."

"More. I want to train more."

"Do you? Well, shall we do some training today, then?"

"Yaaay!"

We'd had this conversation three times already, but I was worried I wasn't doing enough for her.

I'd already taught her how to cook, sew, converse in a foreign language, and climb trees. The other skills I could teach but hadn't yet included writing and decoding ciphers, forging documents, making disguises, and lockpicking.

No, no. I can't teach her such things. If she learns those skills, she might give in to the temptation one day and get involved in something bad. Her whole life would change.

I was positively stumped, so every time, I just said, "Okay, how about we train today?"

* * *

Today, we went to the yard of a vacant house next door. I was demonstrating how to use a stick for self-defense.

"All right. I'm going to slowly come at you with the stick. You dodge it."

"Okay."

Nonna did as I said and crouched slightly, her feet apart. I slowly swung the stick down at her. I did it from top to bottom, from left to right. Each time, Nonna dodged it nimbly. I gradually increased the speed, and once she was comfortable with it, I added other moves in, like sweeping the stick horizontally, diagonally, or even a slow thrust at the end.

At some point, Nonna became excited, and a slight smile came to her face as she dodged the attacks. Just then, she smoothly executed a slow backward somersault.

"Whoa," I couldn't help but murmur. Nonna completed another flawless backward flip, then crouched back down, ready for the next attack. "You're really talented, Nonna."

"Yaaay!"

One might say, "You call that talent?" but it was true; Nonna was gifted physically compared with other children. She showed little signs of fatigue even after long training sessions. That was because she moved without any wasted effort. She was a natural.

There had been many candidates when I started training at the organization's academy, but a lot of them dropped out. There were various reasons for it, such as being too afraid or being unable to handle the rigorous training, but the undeniable truth was that some of the children simply weren't cut out for it. Those kids would find work as servants in noble households. Although those types of jobs were by no means free of difficulty, at least they allowed the children to return to a somewhat normal life.

"All right, now it's your turn to attack me with the stick."

"Got it. Here I come, Vicky!"

"Bring it on."

Nonna swung the stick at me with her full strength, and I dodged it in the nick of time. Nonna's smile had vanished. She must have found it frustrating that she couldn't touch me, no matter what she did.

Since we were already at it, I decided not to hold back. It was a good workout. We continued training until nightfall.

"That was fun!"

"Really? I'm glad you enjoyed it."

We walked home hand in hand. I felt how small and soft Nonna's hand was as we walked.

"I can teach you lots of things, Nonna."

"Yeah!"

"How about we take a bath now?"

"Let's take a bath together!"

"Okay. I'll wash your hair."

"I'll wash yours, too!"

"Thanks."

We walked home together, our hair damp with sweat. On our way, we ran into Lady Yolana, who was out by the flower beds.

"Goodness, you're both dripping! What on earth have you been doing?" she exclaimed with surprise. But Nonna just giggled and ran off toward the cottage, shouting, "It's a secret!"

I offered a wry smile and nodded before heading after her. Once I was inside, Nonna and I looked at each other and burst out laughing.

"Training was fun," I said.

"Yeah! Now let's get ready for a bath," Nonna replied.

After we took a bath and had dinner, I climbed into bed with her. I drifted off to sleep feeling grateful for this wonderful time together, silently wishing that these peaceful, happy days could last forever.

Chapter Ten

Miles

Every other morning, I would get up early to go for a run.

Since helping out at Mr. Bernard's estate wasn't physically demanding, I'd gradually felt my stamina dropping. But once I started running again, I could tell that not only had my muscles weakened, but my heart and lungs had, too, which surprised me.

I woke up before dawn, went running for about an hour, then got back home just as the sun was rising. The servants in Lady Yolana's estate woke up around that time, so I hopped over the wall before they were out and about.

Once I started going for regular runs, I noticed that there was a man in his sixties living in a small house that was right behind Lady Yolana's estate. I was a little curious about him.

He had a large horse with a black mane and tail, and I'd seen the man riding the horse several times. The way he rode was so beautiful that I couldn't help but stare; it was like he and the horse were one.

The man had short white hair and an imposing physique. I wondered if he'd been in the military.

On a run a while back, I found the man resting his horse near a stream in a glade I passed through. I slowed down just as I entered the glade, and we made eye contact. I thought it would be awkward if I turned around, so I called out to the man. "Good morning."

"Oh, morning! You out for a run?"

"That's right."

"Unusual to see a lady running around."

"I suppose you're right."

After that, we chatted a little about the weather, then I bowed and took off running again. That happened several more times. The man seemed to start to look forward to his chats with me, and I could honestly say the same.

One day, the man brought up something other than the weather. "What do you do for work?"

"Oh, nothing special. I'm a commoner, and I work to support my daughter."

"I see!" He looked interested. I walked over to his horse and spoke gently to it, then patted its nose.

"That's a beautiful horse you have there."

"He's old, just like me," the man said, then introduced himself. His name was Miles Grant, and he was a former soldier who'd worked in the military until he retired along with his beloved horse.

"You served your country for a long time, didn't you?"

"Well, I didn't do much. As you know, there aren't many wars in this kingdom. So I had a lot of time on my hands. I'm just grateful to have earned a pension that lets me live out the rest of my days in comfort," Miles said with a smile as he patted his horse. The horse neighed happily and nuzzled its nose against him.

"I love horses. I'd love to have one of my own, but I live in a cottage on my landlady's property. She's a wonderful landlady, so I want to be a good tenant to her."

Miles blinked his light-blue eyes at me as he listened. "I could take care of a horse for you. If you want a horse, I take it you know how to ride?"

"Yes, I can ride. My older brothers were in the military, and they taught me how. Are you sure? Of course I'd pay you to take care of the horse."

"I can even pick a horse I think looks good for you. I think I'm probably a little better at judging horses than you. Would you ride him for a bit so I can get an idea of your level?"

I climbed up on Miles's horse and walked, then cantered him around the glade a bit.

"I see. You're pretty good. What are you looking for in a horse?"

"One that I can ride long distances."

"Got it."

Before I knew it, we got to talking, and I was asking Miles to buy a horse for me. I agreed to pay him to keep it on his property.

A few days later, Miles was waiting for me in the glade alongside two horses.

"Miles, is that horse…?"

"Yep. This is your horse. He runs well and is really clever. He was well within your budget, too. They called him Aleg at the stables. Go ahead and try him out."

Aleg was staring at me with reservation because I was a stranger. Once I mounted him, however, he obediently followed my commands. I walked him slowly around, then took him at a light canter around the area. Yes, he was a good horse.

"I love him! Thank you."

"Then I'll take good care of him for you."

"Thank you. I'll come to ride him every other day."

"Around dawn?"

"Yes."

Although I'd promised to pay for Miles's labor in advance, he said he would mostly cover the expenses himself.

"But caring for horses is tough. Please let me pay you," I insisted.

"Nah, I've got nothing but free time on my hands. Besides, with that horse around, my horse'll think he has to keep up with the young'un. It'll raise his spirits!" He chuckled.

I wanted the horse for emergencies, in case I had to flee with Nonna. I couldn't steal Lady Yolana's horse and carriage.

I returned home and made breakfast, then went to wake up Nonna. As we ate together, I told her about the horse.

"Nonna, would you like to practice riding horses? You'll do it with me, of course."

"A horse? I want to ride with you, Vicky!"

Her eyes widened, and she leaped out of her chair, panting excitedly as she chewed her toast.

"I have to work during the day, so we'll have to ride early in the morning."

"I'll get up! I'll wake up early to ride!"

"Okay. Starting tomorrow morning, we'll ride every other day."

"Got it!"

"Oh, and another thing—don't tell anyone from the main residence about our horse yet."

"Why not?"

"Because until you get good at riding, they might say, 'Stop that, it's too dangerous!'"

"Oh, I get it. Just like when I said I liked climbing trees."

She told them about climbing trees. Of course she did...

"They might be worried until you're good at riding."

"Okay. Can I tell them once I'm good at riding?"

"Sure, once I tell you that you can."

"Got it!"

That whole day, Nonna was beside herself with excitement while we were at Mr. Bernard's. She must've really been looking forward to riding. I went to go check on her to remind her to keep it to herself and saw her whisper to Mr. Bernard, "Guess what! Guess what! I've got a secret!" and run away. She was acting quite mysteriously.

Mr. Bernard was in the middle of doing research, so I quietly closed his door and asked Nonna to do one of her favorite tasks in front of me—polishing the silverware. I sat at the kitchen table with her, doing translation work. Nonna looked up at me as she polished the spoons, forks, and knives. As soon as we made eye contact, she let out a laugh that sounded like "Mwe-hee-hee!"

"You're really looking forward to it, aren't you? Let's take a bath early tonight and get to bed early, too."

"Okay! What kind of food do horses like to eat?"

"Horses eat grass like we eat meat and bread. And for snacks, they love to eat apples and carrots."

"Whoooooaaa! Hey, Vicky. Let's buy some apples and carrots on the way home!"

"Sure. Let's do that."

I couldn't help but giggle when she said, "Whoooooaaa!"

When Nonna was sitting there quietly and not doing roundhouse kicks or somersaults, she looked like she could be the daughter of an aristocrat. She was very animated and funny. Not to mention she had a real knack for martial arts and combat.

That night after dinner, we quickly took a bath, brushed our teeth, and got into bed. I was looking forward to the following day, too.

I had the next day off work, so I took Nonna to visit Miles's house. He was in his yard.

"Oh! Is that your daughter?"

"Yes, that's right."

Nonna wasn't listening to our conversation. She was staring right at Aleg. She giggled "Mwe-hee-hee!" again under her breath. She was even walking with a lilt, so she was clearly very excited.

Miles walked over to Nonna and spoke to her. "What do you think? Horses are big, aren't they?"

"Yes! Very big! And pretty!"

"Aren't you afraid?"

"Not at all! I want to ride it!"

"That's a good answer!" Miles explained the basics of riding safety to Nonna. Don't turn around, don't startle the horse by shouting, match the horse's movements, and stay calm.

Nonna and I mounted Aleg. We were both wearing riding pants that I'd made for us. We were also wearing shoes that were very similar to riding boots.

I put Nonna in front of me and slowly walked Aleg around. Aleg was a smart horse. He moved more carefully with Nonna on him than he had when I'd ridden him alone. Miles was a wonderful judge of a horse's character.

"Mind if I ride along with you?" he asked.

"Would you? That'd be wonderful. I'd be thrilled if you showed us to your favorite spots around here."

And so the three of us rode together, with Miles on his beloved horse next to us.

"By the way, Miles. What's your horse's name?"

"Night. In the army, they called him Nightmare."

"Nightmare! Did he earn that name on the battlefield?"

"When he was young, I rode him in a race against some of my buddies and their horses. They gave that name to him then."

Miles and Night must've been quite strong with a nickname like that. I wished I could have seen them back in the day.

After that, we leisurely rode to the northern quarter of the capital. That was where the woodworking shops, sawmills, furniture shops, weaving workshops, and so on were located. After we passed through there, we rode down a gentle slope until the road turned into a forest. It was my first time coming here, and although we'd traveled slowly, we took a break.

"It should be about that time," Miles said.

I wondered what he meant. He dismounted Night near a row of chestnut trees.

Nonna and I got off Aleg, and the horses grazed freely.

There were loads of open chestnut burrs on the ground. They were even large for mountain chestnuts.

"I'm gonna gather some chestnuts. You girls can do as you please."

"I want to gather chestnuts, too!" I said.

Miles and I stomped on the chestnut burrs with our boots to crack them open and get the chestnuts from inside.

"Here!" he called out, tossing over a cloth bag. He had one for himself, too.

And so Miles and I focused on gathering chestnuts for about an hour while Nonna gazed at Aleg and Night up close. The horses reached out their necks and sniffed her.

"Don't touch the horses without permission," I warned.

"Okay!"

Finally, both our bags were so full that they were about to burst, so we mounted our horses again. We were walking them slowly, but since Aleg was still young, he looked back at me several times and whinnied.

"Looks like he wants to run. Want me to take your daughter for you?"

"Nonna, will you ride on Miles's horse with him?"

"Whaaat? But I wanna ride with you while the horse runs!"

"This is your first time on a horse. You can't ride Aleg when he runs at full speed yet. You have to get used to riding more first."

Nonna nodded reluctantly. Miles held out his arms and took her from me, then set her in front of him on the horse, holding her firmly with one arm.

I gave Aleg a kick, and he immediately burst forward as if to say, "It's about time!" I controlled Aleg as he raced forward through the breeze, adjusting my movements to match his. They say when a horse and rider become one, it's almost like they can read each other's minds. It had been a long time since I'd felt this way.

After a while, I could tell Aleg was satisfied, so I gradually decreased his speed and came to a stop next to Miles and Nonna, who had been watching.

"You're so cool, Vicky!"

"You're a great rider. I have newfound respect for you," Miles said.

"Thank you. Well, shall we go back home now?"

We took the mountain side of the northern quarter through the western quarter to avoid the crowded southern quarter, then returned to the eastern quarter, passing in front of the castle. After I gave Aleg some water and brushed him, I thanked him for a good ride and said good-bye to Miles. Then we walked around Miles's property to come back to Lady Yolana's estate.

"Vicky, couldn't we have climbed over Miles's wall to get to Lady Yolana's house? I saw the roof."

"We could have, but that's not something you should do all the time. Let's make sure to walk unless absolutely necessary, okay?"

"But we can climb over it if we have to."

"Only when your life is *really* in danger. In other words, don't jump over walls. Let's walk instead."

"Okay!"

We went back to the cottage. I sat down and used a small knife to peel the skin from the chestnuts. Nonna wanted to do it, but I told her she was too young to use the knife. I peeled the chestnuts about 80 percent of the way, then passed them to Nonna. Her job was to remove the nut from the skin. There were a lot of chestnuts, so by the time we were done, my shoulders were stiff.

I did some housework that had accumulated, then made some stew with pork belly and chestnuts. I put some of it in a dish and delivered it to Miles's house. Nonna said she would stay home alone.

"Good evening. I cooked dinner using those chestnuts we gathered today, so I wanted to share."

"Oh! This is interesting; I only know how to boil chestnuts or roast them!"

"I made a stew with them and some pork belly. It might be a little rich, but it'll taste perfect with some alcohol."

Miles slowly walked toward the foyer, then stuck his hand in his pocket. All of a sudden, he turned around and threw something at me.

I quickly dodged whatever it was and braced myself for the next attack.

"Sorry for testing you like that. It was just a wooden toy. Don't worry. You said you're an ordinary commoner, and you might be able to fool other people, but you can't get past me."

"I told you that I have a brother in the military who taught me how to ride, remember?"

I gently set down the bowl of stew on the small console table in the foyer where Miles had placed his keys.

"And here you almost ruined the treat I brought you and everything! Honestly!"

"Oh, is the food safe? Well, I figured you'd be able to dodge while still protecting it."

I quickly glanced down to see what he'd thrown at me. It was a tiny, hand-carved wooden bird.

"I'm surprised you'd play such a prank on me, Miles!"

"You think you're hiding your expertise, but you can't suppress it completely. You had no qualms about letting me hold your child today, so I can tell that you trust me. But it was careless of you to do so."

Miles gestured toward a chair and turned around to make some tea. *You say that while showing your back to me?*

"What drew my attention to you wasn't your ridership. You're pretty good at riding—don't get me wrong. But you always kept me in the corner of your eye. Every time I tried to get into your blind spot, you casually moved closer to me. Guess it's a force of habit on your part."

I see.

"So? What are you going to do to me now?" I asked.

"Nothing. But now that I've seen you with your daughter, who looks absolutely nothing like you, I was sure of it. That little girl isn't related to you, is she?"

"No, she's not. She was abandoned by her mother when I met her."

"Taking in the child was awfully reckless."

"I don't regret it one bit. Thanks to her, I'm finally living a normal life."

Miles handed me a cup of tea. "I'm sorry about before. You're just such an interesting person."

"Let me say it one more time: I'm an ordinary commoner who's simply raising her daughter."

"Of course, of course. We'll go with that. But I want to tell you something: If you ever need help, you can come to me. I can at least stall your enemies."

"But why?"

"Because you're a woman with a past raising your daughter among ordinary folks. I'm not going to ask you why you're doing it. But as an old man with nothing but time on his hands, I'd like to help you out."

I gave him the kind of carefree smile you'd see described in the organization's textbooks.

"Ordinary commoners don't have enemies," I said. "As long as you take care of my horse, that's more than enough for me."

Miles dipped his finger into the stew I'd brought and tasted it. "Mm, this is good."

"Thank you. And thank you for the tea." I was about to close the door, but then I turned around. "And thank you for your advice."

"You're much obliged. From now on, be careful when you interact with people who seem to be skilled."

Today was language-lesson day.

Nonna was bragging to Master Clark. "I know a shop that sells a super-delicious apple pie," she said. I overheard their conversation as I was checking their spelling in their notebooks.

"Is it really that good?"

"Yep. The apple pie was so yummy. The crust was crispy, and it had lots of apples inside."

"Ahh, that sounds so good! I love apple pie. I wish I could eat it every day."

"Wanna go together sometime?"

"Really? Are you sure?"

"Sure. Vicky and I can take you."

"I can't wait."

Hang on a second!

Their conversation was so adorable, my hand shook as I graded their papers because I was suppressing my laughter.

"Master Clark, would you like to go with us to eat apple pie?" I asked.

"Yes, Ms. Sellars! I'd love to!"

"All right, then. After I'm done with my work at Mr. Bernard's tomorrow afternoon, Nonna and I will come over and pick you up."

"No, I can go to Great-Uncle's house by myself. It'll be faster that way!"

Mr. Bernard had made a full recovery and was now back at his estate.

The next day, the three of us visited the bakery in the southern quarter where Zaharo had taken Nonna and me before. At the counter, Master Clark and Nonna both bought apple pie, while I purchased a thick slice of butter cake. All three of us ordered tea.

"Ms. Sellars, this apple pie really is delicious! Mother and Father don't like sweets very much, so our cook doesn't really make them."

"Really? Well, all the more reason for you to enjoy it."

Master Clark took a bite of pie with a dreamy look on his face, and for some reason, Nonna looked triumphant. The expression a beautiful girl got on her face when she was boasting was something else.

As the three of us enjoyed our snacks, I saw a woman in her fifties enter the bakery. I could tell by the way she was dressed and how she spoke that she was a noble's servant. She was arguing about something with one of the workers in the back.

"I'm sorry, ma'am. But the apple pie is sold out for the day."

"You don't even have a single slice?"

"No, I'm sorry."

"*Haah*... Now what am I going to do?"

Whoops. That was probably because I'd bought an entire apple pie to bring back to Master Clark's family. The woman seemed to be in trouble. I could get something else for the Andersons, so maybe I should let her have the pie? I turned and spoke to her.

"Excuse me, but I just bought a whole apple pie as a gift for someone. Would you like it instead?"

"Are you sure?"

"Yes, I can come back and get something else another day."

The woman thanked me profusely. She took the apple pie carefully in her arms and bowed to me again several times before leaving.

"Do you like apple pie so much that you bought a whole one, Ms. Sellars?" Master Clark asked me.

"I do love apple pie, but I bought that one for Lady Eva and the earl. If you say they don't really like sweets, though, then I'll get them something else. They sell lots of delicious things here."

And that was that.

That day, I put Master Clark, who was very satisfied, in the Andersons' carriage and sent him off back home. Then Nonna and I walked home together.

We took a bath and washed ourselves with the luxurious soap Lady Yolana had given me.

After that, Nonna and I went to sleep side by side. I loved sleeping in the same bed with her.

Even though she could sleep by herself now at six years old, I wanted to make up for all the loneliness she had experienced in her early childhood. I would wait until Nonna fell asleep, then read books, work on some translations for Mr. Bernard, or do some training.

The following week...

"Say, Victoria. I heard you know Baron Hanson's maid?" Lady Eva asked.

"Hanson...? No, I can't say that rings a bell."

"Well, I know Baron Hanson through my husband's work. Just today, his wife, the baroness, visited with some rare tea leaves, and her lady's maid recognized Clark! And she said you let her have a whole apple pie."

"Oh! Now I know who you mean. Last week, we were at a bakery in the southern quarter when I met the woman. The apple pies were sold out, and I'd just bought the last one, so I let her have it."

Lady Eva nodded enthusiastically. I thought that was the end of it, but apparently not.

Three days later, Baron and Baroness Hanson arrived at the Anderson manor with their maid. Then Lady Eva summoned Nonna and me.

"Victoria, Baron Hanson has something to say to you both."

This is certainly a lot of fuss over a single apple pie! I thought. I had a bad feeling about this.

Nonna and I went into the Andersons' parlor. A lady who was the picture of a noblewoman rose from her seat and looked at Nonna. They both had blond hair. The woman put a hand over her mouth and teared up.

What? Don't tell me they're Nonna's parents?

There was something about them that just reminded me of Nonna.

"It's nice to meet you." Nonna and I greeted them. The man also looked overcome with emotion.

"Victoria, do sit down. This is the Baron and Baroness Hanson. Baron, this is Victoria, and the girl is named Nonna."

Once we sat down, the two of them stared at Nonna.

"When our maid told us, I just couldn't believe it. But she really does look just like her!" the baron exclaimed.

"I know. Identical!" the baroness agreed.

"Excuse me, but what is this all about?" I asked.

The baroness dabbed at her eyes with her handkerchief and explained, "Our daughter died of an illness when she was three years old. Had she lived, she would've looked just like this girl here."

"And so, Victoria," said Lady Eva, "Baron and Baroness Hanson would like to adopt Nonna."

"……"

My bad feeling had been spot-on.

"I'm sorry, but I have no intention of giving up Nonna."

"Please think about this carefully, Victoria," the baron began. "I've heard you're single and that you're raising the child on your own. We have plenty of money to adopt. And when Nonna gets older, we can have a nobleman marry into our family to carry on our name. Don't you think this is the best opportunity for her?"

I see. This is all about status and money.

"Vicky, what are they talking about?"

"The baron and baroness want you to be their daughter, Nonna."

"What? No way."

The baroness immediately intervened. "A child of six doesn't understand the importance of this conversation, Victoria. Obviously, she's going to say she prefers to be with the person she's grown accustomed to. But you must consider her happiness when she grows up. Why, if anything happens to you, she'll end up on the streets!"

It was true that if I got too sick or injured to work, we would be in trouble.

I fell silent, and the baron suddenly made a bold proposal. "Nonna, how about you stay at our house for a week to try it out? I'm sure you don't know what it's like to live as a noble, so you might change your mind once you try it out for yourself!"

"That's right! I can make you a dress. And I'll buy you a lot of jewelry to match those pretty eyes of yours. We can go see plays, and we can put pretty decorations in your room and get whatever you like!"

Did she think she could bribe a child with promises of luxury? My Nonna wouldn't be swayed by such cheap promises.

Considering Lady Eva's personality and the status of both families, I expected her to firmly dismiss the matter of adoption, but for some reason, her tone of voice was soft.

"Baron Hanson, Nonna is quite an active little girl. I think it might be difficult to bring her up as a noblewoman and discipline her as such."

"No, no, Duchess Anderson. You let us worry about that. I'm sure the girl will change her mind once she stays at our house for a week."

I was the one who was raising Nonna, yet no one asking *my* opinion about this. I decided I would turn them down firmly, once and for all.

"As I said before, I—"

"How many days do I need to spend there? Seven? Or six?" Nonna interjected, leaving me speechless.

The baron and baroness's faces lit up with delight.

"Six nights. Or seven, if you'd like. You're a very bright little girl!" the baron said.

"I'm so happy, Nonna."

I was stunned to find a satisfied look on Nonna's face.

I wanted to say to her, "Why? I thought things were going well between us. We're having fun living together, aren't we?"

"Nonna, why…?"

"If I stay with you for six nights and I don't like it, then can we say no for good?"

"Of course. You can come over to our house right away and spend the night starting tonight."

"Okay."

Wait a second. Tonight?!

"Please wait a minute, Lord Hanson. Nonna doesn't have a change of clothes."

"Victoria, she doesn't need a change of clothes," said the baroness. "We can give her everything she needs. I'll buy her all the dresses she wants. You're like a dream come true, Nonna!"

"That's right. Let's go shopping on the way home," the baron added.

And so they whisked Nonna away, like they were taking her away from me forever. I was completely bewildered as I watched Nonna wave to me impassively from the carriage. Then she was gone.

"Ms. Sellars! Why did Nonna just get into that carriage?!"

"Master Clark…I honestly don't know."
"Huh? Ms. Sellars?"
"I'm sorry… I need to go home."

I felt endlessly depressed as I walked home. I passed through the gates to Lady Yolana's estate and trudged down the pathway. As I walked by Lady Yolana, who was tending the flower bed, she called out to me.

"Oh, Victoria! Where's Nonna?"

"She's staying the week at a baron's house."

Lady Yolana immediately picked up on my dejected mood, and concern came to her face. "What happened?"

I gave her an honest account about everything that had transpired.

"And so if Nonna likes the aristocratic life, they have plans to adopt her."

"And Nonna agreed to this?"

"It certainly seems that way."

"Hmm, I see. You said the baron's name was Hanson? Ah, yes… Now I remember. I think they intend to make Nonna the replacement for their daughter who died."

"It seems that way. If you'll excuse me, Lady Yolana, I'm feeling very confused right now, and I'd like to go lie down."

I did my best not to hang my head as I walked to my cottage. I heard Lady Yolana offer some kind words of encouragement from behind me. "This won't go well for them. I'm sure of it. Mark my words, Nonna will turn them down and come back home."

The evening sky gradually darkened.

I was at a complete loss and listlessly sat in my chair until it was pitch-black, but I couldn't bring myself to stand up.

I'd never imagined Nonna would so easily agree to leave me. I thought she would refuse on the spot. I'd assumed she'd stay with me forever. I almost cried when I thought of Nonna's brusque manner of speaking and the way she'd smile when she effortlessly backflipped and somersaulted through the air.

Sitting alone in this empty room made it feel cold, like the life had been sapped out of it. Come to think of it, until I left the organization, I had always been surrounded by people. And ever since I'd arrived in this kingdom, Nonna had been by my side. I'd finally gotten a taste of normal life, but now it looked like I would be living alone.

All of a sudden, there was a violent *boom, boom, boom!* Someone was pounding on the door.

"Victoria! Are you in there?"

It was the captain's voice.

Ugh, I don't want him to see me like this, I thought, so I didn't answer.

"I know you're in there, Victoria. If you don't open up, I'll break this door down!"

Please don't. That would cost a lot of money to fix.

"It's unlocked," I said.

The door swung open, and the captain came inside. He stood still in the pitch-black room for a moment, then lit the lamp I had on the little table by the door.

"It was completely dark in here, and I was concerned. Lady Yolana sent word to me. I was so worried about you that I ran all the way here. She said Nonna went to some noble's house?"

"I assumed since Nonna was a child, she'd stay with me forever. Even though I had no right to dictate her life."

"Victoria." The captain came up to me as I sat and rested a hand on my shoulder. "I think Nonna went with them because she must have a plan."

"Yes, I think so, too. She's a clever girl. But from an outside perspective, this would be the best possible scenario for her. Becoming the adopted daughter of nobility in this kingdom would ensure her status, security, and happiness, unlike being raised by a single foreigner like myself."

The hand on my shoulder moved slightly.

"Don't talk about yourself like that. You're a wonderful, strong, and independent woman. I'm sure Nonna will come back to you. That's what I truly think."

"But she'd be happier if she didn't, and that's what hurts."

"Victoria… Nonna can decide what will make her happiest. Knowing her, she'll be just fine. She'll choose you and come back home."

His gentle, deep voice resounded in my heart. His hand felt so big and warm on my shoulder, and I felt a glimmer of strength deep inside.

If only Nonna and I could live together again, I thought, imagining all the things I would do for her.

"You're right," I said. "I think I'll sew those buttons on her clothes to surprise her when she comes home."

"That's right. Moving your hands will help you keep your mind off things."

I slowly rose to my feet and bowed my head to the captain. "Thank you so much. I'm fine now. I think I'll cook dinner. Have you eaten already?"

"No. I was going to, but then I got the message from Lady Yolana."

"Well, I'll prepare something for the both of us, then."

I chopped up some vegetables I had on hand to make soup, then seasoned some pork and cooked it. Normally, I wouldn't use too many spices, but tonight, since it was just the adults, I gave it some kick. Finally, I sliced up some slightly hard day-old bread.

"This is all I have."

"It's more than enough. It looks delicious."

Will Nonna really come home?

Either way, the captain was right. Even if she was only six years old, Nonna should be able to decide what made her happy. Living an unhappy existence that was forced on you by others was unbearable, but you could get through hard times if you were leading a life you'd chosen. And Nonna was strong and clever.

"I think Nonna will come home, but if you don't like this, don't hesitate to speak up. You can go to that baron's house and get Nonna back. If you don't want to go alone, I'll go with you."

I thought about it for a bit and then shook my head.

"I want to put her feelings first, so I'll wait it out."

"All right. Well, if you change your mind, just let me know. I'll join you."

The captain seemed worried about me after dinner, but he said, "You should get to bed early tonight," then went home.

The next morning, I woke up after spending the night without Nonna.

"I suppose I should do things I can't do when Nonna's around."

I tried to change my state of mind. I cantered Aleg at top speed and ate simple meals that emphasized nutrition over taste. When I had free time, I worked on my black wig. It was almost finished.

That evening, I visited Miles's house after work. There was something I wanted to check on.

"Hmm? What brings you here?"

"I was wondering if you would spar with me, Miles."

"Sure. What's your poison?"

"I have a short sword with the edge dulled, for training purposes."

"I'll use my training sword, then."

Miles's sword looked heavy enough to break someone's bones if it connected right. We'd barely said hello, but we were already getting ready to spar. I could tell he was excited.

"Come at me any time," Miles said.

"Here I go."

I ran toward him and lunged out right in front of him as he held his practice sword at the ready. I spun around and landed a kick on the back of his left shoulder.

He regained his posture, then turned around and swung his blade at me with a *swish!* I managed to dodge at the last second and gripped my short sword. I dodged his swings again and again, then slashed at his side with my short sword. In an instant, I leaped at Miles's slightly exposed neck from behind, wrapped my left arm around it, and pressed the side of my sword firmly against his forehead.

"There, I gouged out both your eyes," I said.

"Argh, you got me! Ready for another round?"

"As many as you want."

We sparred for another five intense minutes. Despite his age, Miles still had formidable skill. I wouldn't have stood a chance against him if he was in his prime. As the two of us panted and the sweat dripped into our eyes, he broke the silence.

"What happened to the kid?"

"She's staying at another house."

He lunged at me before I finished speaking. I intercepted him with my short sword. *I messed up!* My right hand throbbed.

I deflected his blade with a push and delivered a swift kick to his right hip—his dominant side.

"Oof!" He let out a groan.

"I was actually aiming for your groin," I said, panting.

"Aiming at an old man's groin could be a critical hit!"

"Oh, so *now* you play the old-man card." It was so funny, I had to laugh. "Hang on a minute!"

"There's no waiting in battle."

"I can't stop laughing!"

"Ah, so you've finally cheered up."

"Yes."

"Then how about some tea?"

"Sure!"

Miles didn't ask me anything. Once I was finished with my tea, he said, "You can come back again anytime. I really enjoyed myself." And he sent me off with a smile.

I felt about 80 percent better. And I confirmed what I'd gone there to confirm.

After that, I immersed myself in work for several days. Master

Clark was down in the dumps, and sometimes, he would give me very troubled looks.

"Master Clark, I know what you want to say, but I'm trying to respect Nonna's wishes."

"I never would've let her go." He wouldn't accept my decision at all.

I exercised every morning, continuing my jogging and horseback riding. There were plenty of things to do; I just had to look for them.

Now that my black wig was complete, I decided to trim it to shoulder-length. I bundled the hair into sections and then snipped it. Since I'd cut it so short, I had plenty of hair leftover, so I decided to make a child's wig, too. It was only long enough for a boy's haircut, but I thought Nonna would look good disguised as a little boy with black hair if need be.

Six days had passed. The following day, Nonna would be making her decision.

That night, I was startled awake by a noise. I reached down and took out my dagger from a cloth bag I had attached to the back of the bed.

I slipped out of bed and quietly stood next to the front door.

The doorknob slowly turned from the outside, but the door was locked, of course. I strained my ears and heard the footsteps move from the front door toward the kitchen window. I thought for a moment and then raced to my bedroom and sneaked out the window. I thought I'd stab the person from behind the moment they climbed through my kitchen window, so I circled around the brick cottage, gripping my dagger.

I turned the corner twice, and there she was. Nonna was struggling to open the kitchen window, relying on the moon as her only light. She was wearing a pure-white nightgown drowning in frills, and luxurious white slippers made of silk.

"What are you doing?" I asked.

"Eek! You scared me!"

"You're the one who scared me, sneaking around at night. Come on inside."

"Yes, Vicky."

We went inside, and I turned on the lamp, then wiped off my dirty feet. Nonna took off the frilly nightgown right there in the foyer.

"This lace is so itchy and noisy. I hate it."

"I can't believe you went out walking alone at night wearing that. What if a bad person attacked you? Why ever did you do such a thing?"

Nonna said, "Hang on!" then rushed into the bedroom, returning with her favorite light-blue flannel nightgown.

"Well," she said, pulling the soft flannel nightgown over her head. She fastened her buttons and explained, "They locked me in my room today. And they called me Dolores. And they told me to call them Mother and Father. I didn't like that. I'm not Dolores, and they're not my parents."

I felt a bit sad for the baron and baroness, but I'd figured that would happen.

"So then how did you get out of the mansion if they locked you in there?"

"I hung from the windowsill of the second-story window, then let go. I rolled as soon as I landed, just like you taught me! And I did a really good job!"

I wanted to burst out laughing at the triumphant look on her face. I'd taught her to do that in emergency situations only. She was desperately trying to make excuses.

"I was locked in, so it was an emergency. They were using me to replace their dead daughter, and that was an emergency, too!"

I let out a weak laugh. I warmed up some milk and put a little honey in it, then handed it to Nonna. She blew on it to cool it down, then began to sip it.

"So you *did* know they were trying to use you as a replacement for their daughter. I do think it was cruel to lock you inside. Personally, I don't think you should've agreed in the first place, though."

"Well, Lady Eva was in trouble. When Lady Eva feels distressed, she twists her hankie really tightly. And I saw her do it then. That's why I went. They said if I went and I didn't like it, we could say no."

Hmm, so Nonna had noticed that Lady Eva was distressed, too.

"Have you ever seen her that way before?"

"I have. When I kneed Master Clark, Lady Eva came into the room and twisted her hankie."

Wait just a minute. She kneed Master Clark?!

"Back up there. You've kneed Master Clark?"

"I sure have! Because he said, 'Show me how you do it!' Don't worry, Vicky. I didn't tell him how you did that roundhouse kick and karate chop, and I didn't show him, either!"

What in the world have you been doing when you're away from me, Nonna?

The next morning, before I took Nonna over to Baron Hanson's estate, we stopped by the Andersons' on the way there to apologize to Lady Eva.

"Late last night, Nonna slipped out of the baron's house and came back home. I'm sure they're worried about her, so I'm going to take her to the baron's house to apologize. I just wanted to come let you know first." I bowed, and Nonna followed suit. But Lady Eva shook her head.

"No, I don't think you should go there. I'll contact them myself. I caused a lot of trouble for both you and Nonna because I couldn't bring myself to refuse on your behalf," she said, then whispered something into her maid's ear. The maid nodded and rushed out of the room.

"Four years ago, there was a flu epidemic that went through the capital, and everyone who fell ill got very high fevers," Lady Eva said.

"Clark caught the flu and was burning up for five days straight. Thankfully, he made it through, but many children and elderly people died during that time."

Every few years or so, there was a bad epidemic. Surviving was a matter of stamina, so weaker people losing their lives was an unavoidable consequence.

"As I told you before, my husband is the minister of foreign affairs. For some reason, rumors spread that we had access to a medicine from another country that was effective against the flu. It was true that we had come across some very good medicine that worked well for burns some time ago, and we gave it out to those in need. That must have given rise to the misunderstanding. No matter how much we denied having medicine for the flu, the rumors persisted. While this was going on, Baron Hanson showed up at our house. He'd taken the rumors as truth and begged us through tears for the medicine to save his daughter's life. He said he would give us all the money he had. I tried to explain we'd never used medicine to help Clark recover, but he just wouldn't listen."

Ah, I see.

The Hansons were still holding a grudge against the Andersons over that incident, and Lady Eva still felt guilty over it. That was why she'd found it difficult to flatly refuse their suggestion of adopting Nonna.

"Lady Eva, you and your family aren't responsible for what happened at all."

"Rationally speaking, I agree. But those two are not rational. That's the tricky part of the whole situation. Perhaps they know deep down that we didn't have the medicine. At any rate, that story has nothing to do with either of you. I'm sorry for dragging you into matters involving my family and the Hansons. I apologize."

In the end, we simply went straight to Mr. Bernard's.

"Eva treated me kindly, but it sure is good to be back home," he said.

"I'm just happy you're looking well, Mr. Bernard."

Nonna handed him a tiny yellow flower she'd found blooming along the roadside. "Here you go, Mr. Bernard!"

"Ooh! This is the first time I've ever gotten flowers from such a beautiful girl!"

I was thinking about the baron and the baroness.

Even though Nonna and I had lived together for just a few months, the thought of losing her was agonizing. I couldn't even imagine the grief the Hansons had felt when they lost their three-year-old daughter. I'd only experienced a bit of that pain.

Once we got home, I cooked some meat on the stove and did some dusting, then polished the windows. Imagining Nonna no longer being in this world brought me close to tears. I got a message from Lady Eva that said, *I've taken care of everything, so there's no need to worry any longer.*

The next day, we received a letter and a bunch of packages from the Hansons.

We've decided to return to the barony and focus on governing things there. Thank you for making us feel like we'd gotten Dolores back, even if for a short time.

—William Hanson

Inside the various boxes were expensive dresses, shoes, accessories, undergarments, nightgowns, slippers, and purses. Nonna didn't show much interest in them, but I felt a lump in my heart as I looked at them all.

The Hansons had crossed a line by locking Nonna in her room, but how had they felt once they learned she had run away with no intention of returning, and when they had let go of all these things? Perhaps they finally realized there was no replacement for their daughter and that she was never coming back.

Then a thought crossed my mind: Had my parents been sad after they'd let me go when I was eight? I could no longer ask them, of course, but I wished I could. If they were still alive, would they say, "Of course we were sad"? After all this time, I wished they would, even though I knew it was pointless.

I informed Lady Yolana and the captain that Nonna had returned and that the baron and his family had gone back to their domain. And with that, the incident came to a close.

That night, Nonna and I had a leisurely dinner.

Suddenly, there was a knock at the door. The captain had come to see us.

"Oh, Victoria. I have news for you."

"What is it?"

"Lady Eva went to my older brother for advice about the incident with Nonna. He went to Baron Hanson and gave him a warning, saying, 'Until both parties have agreed and the paperwork is officially completed, Nonna's legal guardian is Victoria.' He also added that I am your guarantor."

"Earl Asher spoke to them on my behalf?"

"Yes, my brother is familiar with the baron."

I would wager that Baron Hanson was very surprised when the earl showed up.

"I've heard that the baroness was mentally unstable for some time after the death of their daughter. Once, she forced a blond commoner girl all the way to back their estate and said, 'I found our long-lost daughter.'"

"Oh dear..."

"Apparently, they kept the child's family and the servants quiet about the matter because it could affect the baron's reputation. I'm not sure where my brother heard this, but he's the one who told me. I wasn't aware of it before, and neither was Lady Eva."

I had noticed that the baroness seemed rather emotional, but I never would've guessed that had happened.

"My brother was worried and said, 'If Nonna really does resemble their child that much, the baroness might've refused to let her go even if she wanted to return home.'"

"Captain, I'd like to go thank Earl Asher in person sometime soon."

"You don't have to do that. My brother's grateful for everything you've done for Uncle Bernard. But if you'd really like to thank him, he loves a good snack to eat with alcohol. I can deliver it to him."

That night, the captain went home with a smile on his face.

"Nonna, did the Hansons do anything scary to you when you were staying with them?"

"No. But I didn't like it when I was alone with the wife. Because she kept calling me Dolores. And it was scary when she kept saying, 'Finally, our family's back together again,' and started sobbing."

What a tragic story.

"But it doesn't bother me anymore."

"You're such a strong little girl. And very kind."

"Vicky."

"Yes?"

"Can we live with Jeff?"

Did she come up with that idea because she almost became part of someone else's family? I wasn't sure how to answer, so I just patted her head.

I wish we could. But we can't, I thought.

Chapter Eleven

Preparing to Leave the Kingdom

As Victoria, Nonna, and Jeffrey walked down the main street of the capital, Victoria thought back to the day she came to Ashbury.

When she first left Hagl, she'd thought she would only stay in one place for about six months, moving or going to another country after that. She'd been planning on constantly changing locations for about three years or so.

The Hagl Special Operations Force was always training new members, and she believed they wouldn't spend more money searching for her than they had training her.

A few days ago, something transpired that made Victoria decide to move.

Namely, her training session with Miles had convinced her that he wasn't the real owner of that house. The real owner had lived there for a long time and had been left-handed. They'd also been much shorter.

The first thing that tipped her off to this was the discoloration on the brass doorknob of his front door, which suggested that someone had turned it using their left hand for years.

She thought that could be explained by Miles being ambidextrous, so she'd asked him to spar with her to be certain. That was when she learned that Miles was not ambidextrous, but right-handed.

There were more clues inside Miles's house suggesting he wasn't the original owner; there were some old socks set aside as rags next to the cleaning tools by the front door that weren't Miles's size. There were hooks hung up to organize things around the house, but they were right at his eye level. There was no way he would install the hooks there.

A skilled ex-military man lives directly behind a former operative, but he is not the true owner of the house. And a few days after I began jogging every other morning, he happened to be resting right along my route.

Victoria was convinced that wasn't a coincidence. Someone had sent Miles to that house to investigate her.

Even if this turned out to be a huge misunderstanding on her part, she was fine with that. But her instincts were telling her, *You need to leave right now.*

Her heart ached at the thought of having to suddenly cut ties. So she decided to at least write letters of thanks and an apology for moving so abruptly to the people who had helped her. There were eight letters in total. Victoria resolved to ignore her heartache.

Shortly before sparring with Miles, I'd just finished giving the children a language lesson when Master Clark asked me a question.

"Ms. Sellars, do you think the kingdom of Hagl is cold?"

"That's what I've heard. And I've read it starts snowing there in November."

"The next time Father goes to Hagl for business, he said he's going to take me with him. I wish you and Nonna could come along."

"We're looking forward to hearing all about your travels, Master Clark."

"Vicky, is Hagl far away?"

"Yes, it is. It takes three weeks by carriage one way to get there."

"Oh, then I'll pass. I'm not going to Hagl. Susan's teaching me how to make lace."

Indeed, every time Nonna went to spend the night with Susan, the maid would teach her how to make bobbin lace. It was a labor-intensive process that involved braiding threads and winding them around a bobbin without using any needles or crochet hooks. Susan was very good at it; she'd shown me her work once, and it was intricate and beautiful.

Nonna loved physical activity, but she was also very fond of detailed work. She always diligently polished the silverware. She was a little like me in that regard, which made me happy.

I had no intention of going back to Hagl, no matter what. And I certainly couldn't take Nonna with me. If anyone from the organization saw her, she'd be sent to the academy immediately.

Jeffrey and his mother were having a conversation at his family estate.

"Jeff, I appreciate you being concerned about my health, but you're so busy. Shouldn't you put yourself first?"

"I'm a carefree bachelor, Mother. I don't have that much going on."

Dowager Countess Courtney Asher's golden hair swayed as she tipped her head to the side with a smile.

"Edward told me you have a close lady friend. When will you introduce her to me?"

"Would you wait a bit longer, Mother? Nothing's been settled yet."

"Oh dear. I thought the captain of the Second Order of the knights was supposed to be brave! How cautious of you. If you're concerned about the lady's social standing, we can do something about that, you know."

That wasn't the problem.

It was clear Victoria didn't outright hate him, but every time he took a step forward, it was like he was also taking a step back. Perhaps that was because...

Jeffrey stopped himself and let out a sigh. Even though night hadn't fallen yet, he bid his mother good night and withdrew to his room, where he let out another sigh in earnest.

The night of the soiree, Victoria had noticed the man was suspicious before anyone else in the venue. Now he was almost certain that she had knocked him out in the garden. After all, she'd taken on Prince Cedric, who was quite skilled, and broken his ribs in the process while coming out unscathed.

She could speak four languages, could cook and clean, was better than Prince Cedric in martial arts and swordsmanship, and could climb trees. He couldn't think of anyone else with all those talents.

These facts led to one answer: She was a covert agent who had left her organization.

Since special forces operatives were brainwashed from a young age to pledge their loyalty to the organization and were given high salaries, he'd never heard of anyone defecting. But there were always exceptions.

"There's no benefit in getting close to me or Uncle. It was the Andersons who asked her to be Clark's tutor, not the other way around. And she's too young to have retired. So..."

The only conclusion he could come to was that she'd left the organization. That explained why she didn't want to talk about her past, and why it seemed like she was afraid of something but refused to say what it was. *Victoria Sellars* was probably a pseudonym.

At this point, his thoughts always went in circles.

If he wanted to live with her, the best choice would be to renounce his title and become a commoner so as to not inconvenience his brother and his family. And he would resign as captain of the knights as well.

"What if the three of us—Victoria, Nonna, and I—went to another country together?"

He'd thought about this scenario many times. Luckily, he was healthy and could manage speaking the languages of the neighboring countries, so it would be possible to find some kind of work to sustain them.

But Victoria always seemed to be telling him to stay out of her life. He feared that the moment he confessed his feelings to her and suggested they live together, she would disappear with Nonna. And if she was serious about disappearing, he knew he'd never be able to track her down again.

Jeffrey raked a hand through his shiny silver hair and looked up at the ceiling.

At Victoria's house, Nonna set the book she was reading down on the counter. "Vicky! When is Jeff coming again?"

"I don't know. The captain is very busy."

"I hope he comes soon."

"So do I."

Just then, there was a knock at the door.

"That must be Jeff!" Nonna said, racing over to the door, but then she froze. One of the very few house rules was that she must always ask who was there before opening the door.

"Good evening. I brought over some delicious roasted chestnuts."

Once Nonna heard the familiar voice, she quickly unlocked the door and opened it. "Jeff! Hello! Yaaay, chestnuts!"

"Good evening, Captain. Thank you for always being so considerate."

Jeffrey, Victoria, and Nonna all ate the roasted chestnuts together and made small talk.

He knew that Victoria could disappear if he pried too deeply into her affairs, so he settled for savoring the time he got to spend with her and Nonna.

Once Jeffrey left, Victoria began using the fireplace to burn things that she couldn't let anyone else see.

"What are you doing, Vicky?"

"Hmm? Just tidying up. Nonna, will you put the items that are the most important to you in your shoulder bag?"

"I only have one thing that's important to me. It's this!" Nonna showed her the first present Victoria had ever given her—the blue ribbon.

"I see. Well, could you at least put one day's worth of clothes and underthings into your bag?"

"Sure."

Victoria decided she wouldn't tell Nonna they were moving until the last minute. She didn't want to run the risk of her leaking it to anyone. And what if the captain tried to stop Victoria? What if Master Clark looked devastated? What if Mr. Bernard and Lady Yolana were disappointed in her?

No. This is the right time. This is what I decided from the very beginning.

She looked over at Nonna. She wouldn't be able to give her a quiet, peaceful life again for a while, but she hadn't forgotten the promise she'd made to never let her go.

That was when she realized that Nonna's face was strangely red. Her eyes were moist. She immediately went over to her and placed a hand on her forehead.

"Oh, no. You're burning up!"

Victoria carefully put the bag containing her new identification papers in the corner of the room and quickly put Nonna to bed.

Several days had passed since then.

Victoria continued to nurse Nonna from her bedside.

It looked like Nonna had caught the flu. Her fever was high, and she had a terrible cough. She didn't have an appetite, and she would only drink tiny sips of water or diluted fruit water. Victoria recalled the story Lady Eva had told her about the last flu epidemic, and she felt her mind wander to dark places.

Don't worry. Nonna's a strong girl.

She kept telling herself that, but this was the first time she was caring for a sick child. She had no idea if Nonna would get worse or recover. All she could do was put a cold washcloth on Nonna's hot forehead and change her clothes when they got soaked with sweat. She was frustrated that she couldn't do more to help.

"I'm sorry, Vicky…"

"Why are you apologizing? Kids often get sick. Just get lots of rest so you recover soon, okay?"

"Okay."

Her fever and cough were persistent.

But around the fourth day, the fever finally broke, and Nonna began showing signs of an appetite. Her wet cough lingered, but it had improved.

"Nonna, you beat the flu!"

"It doesn't hurt anymore."

"Really? I'm so glad to hear that. Now you need to eat and sleep to make a full recovery!"

"I want apple pie."

"It might be a little soon for that. It'll startle your tummy!"

After around ten days had passed since her fever began, Nonna had made a complete recovery.

She still isn't healthy enough to travel by horseback, Victoria decided.

Interlude

The Chef from Hagl

Earl Norman Highland from Hagl had come to Ashbury for a visit. The Highland territory specialized in woodworking, importing premium timber from Ashbury to craft luxury furniture. When Earl Highland traveled abroad, his chef, Dave, always accompanied him; that way, every time they had a delicious meal, Dave could sample it to re-create it for him back home.

After they secured the timber and enjoyed some seafood, they were getting ready to return home when a noble from Ashbury placed a large furniture order, saying they wanted to completely refurnish their house with pieces from Earl Highland's company.

And so the earl and Chef Dave decided to delay their return and headed to Ashbury's capital. As the carriage traversed its bustling streets, Dave spotted someone familiar in the crowd and brought his face close to the window. It was a female cook named Carol, who had been an apprentice at Dave's previous job working for a marquess's family. The nobleman who'd introduced her to the family said she was the daughter of a friend.

Carol had good instincts when it came to cooking, and it seemed like she was destined to become a wonderful chef. She'd gained favor with the young prospective second wife of the noble and often kept her company.

But then one day, the noble fell from grace. The young bride-to-be hastily fled with her jewels, and Carol inexplicably disappeared with her. Dave had written to the person who'd introduced Carol to the family, but the reply he received was dismissive and vague: *Carol is no concern of yours.*

She was walking with a muscular, silver-haired man who appeared to be an aristocrat. There was a pretty little girl with blond hair with them, and the three of them had smiles on their faces as they walked together.

I wonder if Carol married an aristocrat. Come to think of it, I wonder what happened to that prospective bride, too. I remember she loved the color pink and had several dresses all in slightly different shades, he recalled, but then his employer spoke to him, pulling him out of his reveries.

Afterward, Dave and Earl Highland returned to Hagl.

One day, Dave was on the way home from shopping at the market when he noticed a man standing there. It was his benefactor, who had introduced him to the position where he'd worked for the marquess before the noble fell from grace. Before the man could climb into his carriage to leave, Dave called out to him.

"Earl Ixley! It's so nice to see you again. I'm Dave, the chef you introduced to the marquess some time ago."

"Oh, yes. I trust you're doing well?"

"Yes. I'm currently in Earl Highland's employment."

"I see, I see. Well, good luck to you, then!" Earl Ixley got into his carriage and was about to speak to the driver as if to say he was done with this conversation, but then he heard what Dave said next.

"I'm sorry I couldn't help Carol more. I know you were the one who arranged her employment. I saw her in Ashbury, and she seemed to be doing well."

"Carol? You saw her? Are you positive it was Carol?"

"Yes. She's as beautiful as ever, and she looked very happy."

After that, Earl Ixley began to grill Dave about Carol. He wanted to know where he saw her, whom she'd been with, what she'd been wearing, and how she'd styled her hair. He finally let Dave go once he answered all those questions, leaving him standing there, speechless.

Hagl Special Operations Force, central control.

"Is that true, Earl Ixley?"

"Yes. A chef who worked with her for five whole months spotted her, so it has to be correct."

Lancome peppered Earl Ixley with questions and took notes. After the earl left, Lancome made an announcement to the operatives.

"Chloe's been found."

All the operatives gathered around, looking stunned.

"It seems she's in Ashbury's capital."

"Does that mean…Chloe's defected?"

"So it seems."

The operatives exchanged surprised glances.

"Ashbury? And why would our top agent defect?"

"I'm going to retrieve Chloe. Dan, Jacob. You're coming with me."

"Yes, Chief. But we can go ourselves. There's no need for you to come with us…"

"Can you promise you'll be able to convince Chloe to return and bring her back unharmed? We don't want a silent corpse. Our goal is to recover Chloe's expertise and abilities."

Dan's face tensed up; his remark earned him a piercing gaze from Lancome.

Lancome immediately tried to seek permission to depart, but the prime minister kept Lancome waiting for some time before coming into the room.

"There's no need for you to go yourself. It's a shame we lost Chloe, but you should give up on bringing her back."

I knew he'd say that, Lancome mused dejectedly. He thought it was a shame to let Chloe disappear like this. She could contribute much to the organization if she continued gaining experience and eventually became an instructor at the academy.

"I'm going to convince Chloe to return and bring her back no matter what, so that she can serve this kingdom again. Please give me permission." Lancome bowed deeply.

A thin, wry smile crossed the prime minister's face as he watched him. "This is Chloe we're talking about, Lancome. There's no way you can bring her back home alive. But more importantly, this is going against His Majesty's wishes. He says, 'A dog who can't swear loyalty to his master should be eliminated.'"

"……"

"We need to get rid of her before those Ashburians realize her worth. Make it look like she was the victim of a crime. This matter is no longer in your hands."

That meant it was now in the hands of the assassination squad.

"Go ahead and submit all the information you have regarding the sighting of Chloe."

"…Yes, sir."

Mary's breakfast was brought into a cramped, dreary room on the third floor of the building used by Hagl's Special Operations Force. A young man carried it in; Lancome hadn't been coming around lately.

"Where's Lancome?"

"He's busy helping out at the academy."

"Is there a new chief?"

The man didn't answer. He carelessly set down the tray of food on the table and left.

Mary decided to eat. She couldn't let her stamina dwindle. Her chains clanked heavily on the floor as she stood up to go over to the table. There were iron shackles around her ankles, connected by a long chain. The windows were barred.

It had already been two months since she'd been imprisoned here, and no one had come to save her.

I've been abandoned. They're going to kill me.

They must have thought they could still get some use out of her; that was the only reason why she wasn't dead.

Right before she was captured, she'd sneaked out to meet someone, and when she came back, they shackled her.

"We finally have evidence of your betrayal. Did you think you weren't being watched?" Lancome spat.

Mary had been twenty when she became a double agent.

The underclassmen were getting better grades than her, and she began to panic after she only received small missions. It was then that a person from the kingdom of Randall approached her.

"I want you to give us information about the Special Operations Force. Randall is looking for someone exceptional like you. If the worst happens, we'll make sure to rescue you. You're very important to us."

She was a fool to have taken the offer at face value.

Both Randall and Hagl had used her. Lancome had probably never even filled out the paperwork to make their marriage legal. In all likelihood, their union was nothing more than a way for Lancome to keep a close eye on Mary after he grew suspicious of her.

Time was running out. She needed to do something before the new chief wrote her off as useless and had her killed.

"Hey! Mary! What's wrong?"

The man who brought her dinner saw Mary lying on the floor with blood dribbling from her mouth and raced over to her. "Hey! Mary!"

The moment he stood up to go call someone, she grabbed his ankle, yanked as hard as she could to topple him to the floor, and wrapped the chain from her shackles around his neck.

Once she was sure he'd lost consciousness, she used the rope she'd made from her ripped sheets to bind and gag him. She stood up and ran her tongue along the inside of her mouth. The cut she'd made inside the tender flesh there with her nails was quite deep. She grimaced at the pain and the metallic taste of blood. She patted down the man and found the key to the room.

He didn't have the key to her shackles, so she used the silver toothpick on his person to pick the lock. At last, she heard a clicking sound as the shackles opened. She looked down at the man, blood still smeared around her mouth.

The man groaned. "You're going to kill me eventually, aren't you?" he said when he regained consciousness. Mary kicked him in the head and laughed.

"I'm not going to kill you. You're too lowly. You're not even worth doing in." She took the last scrap of the sheets and moistened it with water from the cup, then carefully wiped the blood off her mouth. She left the room and locked the door. She didn't know where to go, but she knew if she stayed here, she would be killed.

I'll never trust anyone again.

Mary went down to the second floor, jumped out the window, ran through the dark, and hopped over the wall.

Chapter Twelve

The Third Order of the Knights

The northern wing of Ashbury Castle.

"You. Come here a moment."

The administrative director handed over documents to his subordinate detailing the behavior of the marquess and his son.

"We can end this matter now. The marquess and his son have behaved abhorrently."

"We were fortunate that the incident at the soiree brought his actions to light."

The administrative director looked reluctant.

"The marquess just doesn't seem to understand that doing these things breeds anger and resentment toward nobility among the commoners. I know it's hard to believe, considering how capable he was."

"His son has quite a lot of problems as well. Not only has he been seen frequenting underground gambling operations, but he's also borrowed a staggering amount of money from some shady characters. If the son inherited his peerage, he would only abuse it to his advantage."

The administrative director spoke as he twirled a glass pen with his fingertips. "That's probably why he engaged in gambling in the first place. The marquess must have rigged things in favor of his son.

I'm honestly baffled things turned out this way; they were both such capable individuals."

It was the height of foolishness for nobles to incur the wrath of the commoners. He couldn't help but think of the countless royal families throughout history who had been brought to ruin due to public outcry and rebellion.

"So the redheaded woman still hasn't been found?"

"No, and after investigating the man, it seems he only tried to assault the marquess out of spite, so her motive in helping him escape is unclear. We couldn't narrow down the search area, making it difficult to find her."

"I see."

"The whereabouts of his sister remain unknown as well. According to testimonies from her neighbors, she was mentally unwell, so she might not even be alive anymore. It's possible she's with her brother, but there have been no leads."

"Hmm. The man had extenuating circumstances, but since he committed his offense at the royal castle, the king's hands were tied."

The administrative departments were located in the dimly lit north wing of the castle. It was a far cry from the more glamorous departments, like Finance and Foreign Affairs.

Three departments were situated in the north wing; the Department of Repairs occupied the second floor, Document Management was on the third floor, and the Department of Institutional Maintenance had the fourth floor.

However, those three departments were actually a single entity, rumored to be called "the Third Order of the knights," or simply, "the Third Order."

The true nature of the Third Order was highly confidential, known only to a handful of individuals. Even some of the ministers were in the dark about its specifics; they were only aware of the existence of the organization.

The chief of the Third Order was the prime minister, but the one who actually ran the show was the head of the Department of Institutional Maintenance.

The heads of the other departments were referred to as ministers, but the head of this department was known as the administrative director, which was perceived by the general public as an expression of disdain.

The current administrative director was a former civil servant who'd been selected for his role thanks to his sharp intellect, high ethical standards, keen insight, and ability to avoid conflict.

Once, the crown prince had said, *"If you want to get to the bottom of people's gossip, asking the administrative director is the quickest way."* And he wasn't joking; he meant it sincerely.

His insights were so accurate that it made the prime minister feel unsettled at times.

Despite the administrative director saying his department was burdened with all the tedious tasks of the kingdom, he worked diligently and enthusiastically.

Now alone, the director retrieved an envelope labeled PENDING from a locked drawer and took out three documents from within.

One was a report on Victoria Sellars, whom he'd investigated at His Majesty's command. Another was a report on the mysterious woman from the soiree incident, and the last document was a report on the prison break.

"They were all young girls. And Victoria Sellars just entered the kingdom recently."

The man brushed back his glossy silver hair, which was tinged with strands of white, and let out a sigh. If he believed the report from Randall, Victoria Sellars was clean. But it conflicted with things he personally knew to be true.

For instance, the report said her parents' whereabouts and status were unknown. But he'd heard that both her parents had died in a fire. It was highly unlikely that people perishing in a fire could be misconstrued as them going missing.

And when it came to horses, apparently, she'd said she had an older brother in the military who had taught her how to ride, but the *real* Victoria Sellars didn't have an older brother.

"You let your guard down, Victoria," the director muttered with a troubled look on his face as he gazed at the documents.

There was one more thing. His instincts were telling him Victoria was the red-haired woman who had helped that man escape from jail, although he didn't have a lick of evidence to prove it.

If Victoria was behind all three of these incidents, then why had she come to this kingdom? Why had she helped a man slated to be executed escape when she got nothing out of it? He wished he could ask her himself.

The director had made a suggestion to his cousin's husband, Earl Anderson. *"I know you've been worried about Clark's language education, so why not hire Victoria to tutor him? It'll help her out, too, since she'll be making less money now that Uncle's injured."* He'd done this to keep her as close as possible to watch her.

Personally, he was fond of Victoria. He owed her a great deal for finally freeing his younger brother's heart from the prison it had been locked up in for a decade. He wanted to foster Jeffrey and Victoria's relationship as much as possible. But there were just too many things that remained uncertain.

Perhaps she was running away from something. Depending on the reason, he wanted to offer her protection, but at the same time, that reason might compel him to hand her over to another country's government.

And if she had committed some kind of crime, he couldn't put Ashbury's international relations at risk for the sake of a single foreign woman.

"Ugh," Edward Asher groaned to himself. *I won't tell the prime minister my theory yet*, he decided. Up until this point, he'd just broadly encouraged the king and the prime minister to keep these possibilities in mind.

"The prime minister is hasty, so I know he'll say, 'Come up with some reason to deport her.'"

He raked his hand through his hair again, a tic of his when he was pondering something.

Edward put the three documents back in their original envelope, returned it to the drawer, and locked it. He knew a cheap lock like that wouldn't keep out someone who was really interested, but when there was a lock, he tended to use it. That was just a function of his personality.

This time, he called over a separate subordinate.

"Where's the report from Miles? Oh, I see. It's going smoothly? Tell him to continue as is."

Surely, his brother had finally realized Victoria was no ordinary commoner.

I hope Jeff doesn't do anything rash, he thought. For a moment, he forgot his position and went into big-brother mode, worrying about his younger brother, who was sometimes too kind and devoted.

"Miles, I'm going to take Aleg out now."

"Gotcha. Your daughter isn't here with you today?"

"No, she's just getting over an illness, so she's at home."

"I see. I hope she feels better soon."

"Thank you."

And that was the last time Miles saw Victoria. Normally, she took Aleg out early in the morning and returned a half hour to an hour later, but that day, she was still out by evening.

She said her daughter was staying home alone. Did something happen to her?

Worried, Miles went to see Lady Yolana. At the old woman's house, he saw a horse with the knight's emblem on its saddle.

* * *

"Good evening. I wanted to ask about Victoria. My name is Miles, and I live behind this estate."

"Please wait just a moment. I'll be right back."

The servant came back a short while later and showed him to a parlor where a muscular man with silver hair, whom he assumed was the owner of that horse outside, was sitting.

"Pardon me, I didn't know you had company. My name is Miles, and I live behind your estate. I'm here because I needed to ask about Victoria."

The moment the man with the silver hair heard him say "Victoria," he turned and stared at Miles. Maybe something *had* happened to her.

"I'm Yolana Haynes. What's this about Victoria?"

"I take care of her horse for her, and she came to retrieve it earlier. But she hasn't returned. I'm worried something happened to her while she was out."

Lady Haynes and the silver-haired man exchanged glances for a moment, then both looked at Miles.

"You kept a horse for Victoria?" the man asked sharply.

"Yes. She paid me to take care of it for her."

Suddenly, he noticed several letters on the table near the old woman.

"You said your name was Miles? But the man who lives behind me is named Peter. He used to be a government official."

"Yes, I moved in a while ago. Peter moved away to live with his daughter."

"I see. Well, Victoria's not here anymore. Apparently, she departed early this morning. She left a letter for you, too. I was wondering who 'Miles' was, but I suppose that's you."

She slid an envelope over to him, and he quickly opened it and read the letter inside.

Thank you for taking such good care of Aleg. I had a wonderful time gathering chestnuts with you.

That was all it said. The silver-haired gentleman asked to see it, so he showed it to him.

"I'm relieved to hear nothing bad happened to Victoria. Well, if you'll excuse me." Miles smiled and left the estate, then returned to his temporary home. He fetched his horse and rode straight to the castle.

Jeffrey rose to his feet. "Lady Yolana, I'll go deliver the rest of the messages."

He picked up the letters, which were addressed to Lady Eva, Clark, Bernard, and Edward, then put them in his pocket.

"I'm sorry for calling you all the way here and putting you through so much trouble. But may I ask you something, Captain?"

"Go ahead."

"Are you sure Victoria didn't tell you about all this?" Lady Yolana regretted her words the moment they left her lips. Normally, the captain had a serene smile on his face, but for a moment, it twisted with pain, then disappeared completely.

"No. Unfortunately, she didn't say a word to me." He smiled faintly again, bowed, and excused himself.

"Susan! Susan?"

"Yes, Your Ladyship?"

"I'm sure Victoria and Nonna will come back. Stop crying now." Despite her scolding, Lady Yolana looked awfully sad herself.

The letter addressed to her had been filled with apologies and thanks. *I cleaned up as much as I could, but please dispose of the remaining items*, it said. It was clear Victoria didn't intend on coming back. She'd left so few things behind.

Please be safe. And please come back home one day, Lady Yolana prayed.

Even though they'd only known each other for six months, she was distraught. She wondered why Victoria was living like this, but no matter how much she thought about it, she could only come to the conclusion that Victoria had done something terrible and was running away from it.

She thought fondly of the time when Victoria had freed her hat from a tree.

Jeffrey rode his horse quickly to deliver the letters. Once the recipients read them, each grew shocked and saddened.

Clark insisted that he wanted to know what happened, but Jeffrey told him he didn't know. He rushed back to the knights' dormitory and went to his office, where he opened the letter addressed to him.

Victoria's handwriting was neat and unhurried.

Dear Jeffrey Asher,

I'm so sorry for disappearing out of the blue. Something has come up, and I can no longer stay in that house. Thank you so much for encouraging me, being kind to me, and laughing with me.

Living here was the happiest I've ever been in my whole life.

To be honest, I'd intended on leaving sooner, but I was having so much fun that I kept putting it off.

You took me on my first picnic, and I had the most wonderful time. I loved eating roasted chestnuts and chatting with you.

It's all thanks to you that I made so many lovely memories.

Thank you for everything. I'm sorry.

—Victoria

* * *

"Don't thank me for taking you on a picnic and eating roasted chestnuts with you. How many times did I beg you not to up and disappear on me?"

Three days after Victoria had disappeared.

"Captain, a lady I met at the pub told me, 'A silver-haired knight helped me, so I want to express my thanks,' and paid for my drink! She asked me all kinds of questions about you. Did you help someone?"

"No, not that I can recall... Wait a minute. What did she look like?"

Jeffrey's young subordinate thought for a moment and said, "She looked like she was in her thirties. She was a really friendly lady. She had a round face, dark eyes, and black hair. She was beautiful."

A woman asking after him two days after Victoria disappeared... He didn't recall helping anyone. He thought it was too suspicious to be a coincidence, so he gathered together all the other knights and asked them if anything similar had happened to them.

"A young woman in her twenties asked me if you had a girlfriend, Captain. She'd fallen for you at first sight!"

"I ran into a woman with a child who said your girlfriend helped her, and she wanted to thank her for it!"

"There was a man at the pub who was praising the knights and bought my drink for me! He might've asked about you, Captain, but I was too drunk to remember..."

Something was amiss here.

"Listen up, if anyone asks you if I'm dating anyone, just be honest. I don't have any memory of helping anyone out. It's widely known that Victoria stayed on Lady Yolana Haynes's property. I'm going to assign the Second Order to focus on protecting Lady Yolana's estate for a while, especially at night. Understood?"

"Yes, sir!"

After that, he stationed four people at the guest cottage and five at the main residence overnight. *Did I go overboard?* he wondered. Late on the third night, however, he was surprised to find members of the Third Order present there as well.

The knights from the Second Order were also shocked by the men, who wore all-black uniforms with knit caps low over their eyes.

"I never heard you were coming."

"Second Order Captain Asher, we received our information from a separate source. According to the reports, an assassination squad from Hagl will launch an imminent attack on this residence."

"An assassination squad from Hagl?"

When Jeffrey heard those words, he had no choice but to yield. The Second Order's duty was to maintain security in the city. From that point on, the Third Order was in charge of dealing with the assassins, and the Second Order focused on protecting the perimeter of the estate. But Jeffrey was adamant about assisting the Third Order with the assassins.

"That puts us in a difficult position. Don't come crying to us if you get hurt or die."

"I promise."

The next day, with the decision made for the Second and Third Orders of the knights to jointly keep watch, assassins appeared before Jeffrey and the others, who were hiding in the darkness of the guest cottage.

The four members of the Hagl assassination squad rode their horses for ten days until they reached the capital of Ashbury.

The "muscular man with the silver hair who appeared to be an aristocrat" from the reports was almost certainly Jeffrey Asher, captain of the Second Order of the knights.

They made contact with their operatives living in Ashbury to find out where Jeffrey Asher's girlfriend lived. They also hired citizens from Ashbury, paying them handsomely for their time.

In just a few days, they were able to uncover Chloe's pseudonym and where she lived.

"That's it. Chloe's probably living in that cottage."

They staked out the house during the day and marked the cottage as their target.

When night fell, the four of them approached Yolana Haynes's residence. There were lights on in the main house and the guest cottage.

"Let's wait an hour after the lights are off. Three people go in, one person stands guard," the leader said, and the other three nodded.

At last, the lights went out. They waited for an hour and then crept up to the guest cottage. One of them expertly picked the lock on the front door. They entered the cottage and split up.

Two of the intruders quietly opened the door to what seemed to be the primary bedroom and sneaked inside. The leader and his partner approached the lump in the bed. The moment they readied their knives, there was a whooshing sound.

They whirled around just in time to block a knife with their own. No—it wasn't a knife; it was a sword, wielded by a large man. The leader had keen night vision, and in the darkness, the assassins saw the man's silver hair gleam and wondered, *What's he doing here?*

There was no time to counterattack. The large man completely overwhelmed them with the brute force and speed of his strikes, leaving them scrambling to defend themselves.

Meanwhile, the leader's partner was fighting another man, but the partner was quickly subdued by a group of black-clothed men who'd rushed in, pinning him to the floor and swiftly rendering him unconscious by targeting the pressure points on his neck with their hands.

The leader of the assassins struggled to fight on, hoping for a chance to escape. But as he parried the silver-haired man's sword, the men in black tripped him with some kind of ropelike instrument. He tumbled to the ground before being quickly apprehended.

The last of the three assassins invaded the child's room and paused when he heard a commotion coming from the adjacent room. *Did the other two get caught?*

Just as he got ready to rush to the other room, he was abruptly struck in the solar plexus and hit in the head with a rod. He groaned and froze as another person approached from behind, wrapping an arm around his neck to choke him.

The lookout assassin was stationed outside. Suddenly, he felt a knife press against his throat just as he saw his comrades enter the cottage. Another man with a knife was right in front of him.

"Move, and you're dead. Make a sound, and you're dead."

The man spoke in fluent Haglian. Although the lookout contemplated fighting back as he nodded cautiously, he suddenly found himself surrounded by men wearing all black. *When did they even get here?* he wondered.

After a while, many lamps were lit to illuminate the garden of the mansion.

The men in black removed the shoes and belts of the four unconscious assassins, stripped them half naked, tied them up, threw them over their shoulders, and carried them away. It all happened in the blink of an eye. The assassins had been hiding several small lethal weapons in their clothes.

One man from the Third Order approached Jeffrey and said, "Nice work," then disappeared.

Lady Yolana and her servants had all sneaked out during the day.

As Jeffrey left the now-empty Haynes residence, he glanced at the cottage, but then quickly looked away and headed to the castle.

The assassins were taken straight to the castle dungeon. Despite the late hour, there were many people going in and out of it.

Some time later, a man in a black outfit that covered everything but his eyes visited the prison.

The assassins were all kept in separate cells to prevent them from seeing one another.

"Are you the leader? Oh, right. You can't answer because you're gagged. We surprised you, didn't we? You didn't think anyone would be waiting. Ashbury has its own Special Operations Force, though it's not as fancy as yours. We knew you were coming." He spoke in fluent Haglian. Then he called out, "Come on!" and beckoned someone inside the jail.

"Are you nervous that you'll be tortured? Don't worry. Unlike you all, we don't resort to such barbaric methods. We just give you an injection."

The leader of the assassins was bound to a chair and gagged. He bit down on his gag and began to flail around.

"Relax. It stings a little, but it won't kill you. It'll only make you feel very relaxed. Unlike in your country, we don't rip off people's fingernails or waterboard them here. At least, we haven't for many years. I don't like watching such things anyway."

The man in black held down the assassin as he flailed, while another man who was dressed like a doctor gave him a quick injection. The doctor counted for a while, then glanced at the assassin.

"I think it's taken effect," he whispered to the interrogator.

The kingdom of Ashbury purchased medicines from a country far across the sea. It was said that the people there had black eyes and black hair. The medicines were quite expensive, but incredibly effective.

In addition to medicines for burns, cuts, and pain relief, they'd also imported this truth serum. In exchange for the medicine, Ashbury sold the country high-quality ebony and red sandalwood.

The interrogator pulled up a chair to sit down in front of the assassin. The door to the cell was locked for safety, but the interrogator didn't mind. He proceeded to ask him questions in Haglian.

"Now. Who were you targeting? Tell me your target's name."

The assassin's expression was calm now, and his pupils were small, as if he was relaxed. The man who was positioned behind him removed his gag.

"Chloe. We came to kill Chloe."

"And who is Chloe?"

"The top agent of the Special Operations Force. She has brown hair, brown eyes, average build, and average height. She's twenty-seven."

"Oh, she's the top agent? Very interesting. And why do you want to kill her?"

"She defected."

"Did she make some kind of mistake?"

"No. She just disappeared one day. His Majesty says dogs that are no longer loyal to their master need to be put down."

The interrogator nodded several times.

"I've heard it's not possible to quit the organization even if you want to. Is that true?"

"Quit? Quit the organization?"

"That's right. Can you quit if you want to or not?"

"No one's ever quit. We work as long as we're able to."

The assassin acted like the man had asked him a very odd question.

"There are many jobs to do. Teaching, office work, cleaning. We never leave the organization."

The interrogator made eye contact with the man standing behind the assassin, who shrugged with exasperation.

"You know, here in Ashbury, we call that 'slavery.' Slaves who receive a salary anyway. I understand the situation now. At any rate, you entered our kingdom with forged identification papers and illegally trespassed onto an aristocrat's property with weapons. You broke into a house and tried to kill its residents. That's a very serious crime. All right. Next, you're going to tell me the names of every one of your comrades who live in this kingdom."

The interrogation continued for some time, and then the interrogator left the dungeon. His subordinate followed behind him. He called out to the guard, "The medicine's going to wear off soon, so keep a close eye on him. I'll station some members of the security force here, but these guys are skilled, so don't let your guard down under any circumstances. If there's another escape, it'll be your head on the chopping block next."

As the interrogator climbed the stairs, he removed his head covering, revealing silky silver hair. He turned to his subordinate beside him. "The communication network I created is a huge success. It's quite impressive we were able to receive the information before the assassins, if I do say so myself."

"You're absolutely correct, sir."

Edward Asher's communication network consisted of a series of horseback messengers who constantly swapped routes, continuing the flow of information even overnight.

"The prime minister says it costs too much to maintain and operate, but we should use the people's taxes to ensure their safety. Personally, I think the operation and maintenance costs are pretty cheap if they can save us from going to war. And this incident only proved my point."

"Exactly, sir."

"We need to go arrest all their friends tonight. Nip this in the bud before they run away."

"Yes, sir!"

A satisfied look came to Edward Asher's face as he climbed the stairs.

Chapter Thirteen

Life on the Farm

As soon as Nonna's fever subsided, I bought the smallest wagon available.

Once she was fully recovered, I bundled her up and placed her in the wagon, traveling as much as I could while it was light outside. As we passed through the border checkpoint toward Randall, Nonna leisurely nibbled on fruit and snacks on the loading platform.

Currently, I was posing as a black-haired woman named Maria. Nonna was my black-haired son named Lyle.

I got the name *Maria* from my research into the real Victoria's situation. Maria was also a missing person. She'd entered Ashbury from Randall eight years ago and never returned. She'd been two years older than me at the time, with no children.

Since Maria had black hair, I didn't originally think that information would be useful, so when I found that long black hair at the open market, I'd been thrilled.

As we traveled through Randall, I tried to explain my situation as honestly as I could to Nonna.

"So you ran away, Vicky?"

"Yes. My old job didn't let anyone quit. That's why I needed the wig and had to change my name. And that's why we had to move. I ran away from my old job, so my former colleagues might be mad and come after me. I'm sorry I can't give you a peaceful, stable life, Nonna."

"It's okay. Now we can go to all sorts of places together."

"...Thank you. Also, will you call me Maria from now on instead of Vicky?"

Nonna pondered this and then answered, "Can I call you Mom? If I call you some other name, I might forget and accidentally call you Vicky."

I was so shocked and thrilled to hear her say that, I took her in my arms and nodded over and over again. Before this, I just hadn't been able to bring myself to ask if she would call me Mom.

"Yes. Yes, of course you can call me Mom! Thank you so much."

"Huh? Why are you crying?"

"Just because."

Right now, we were living in Randall on a sheep farm. We'd started staying there in autumn, the perfect weather for roasted chestnuts. Three months had passed since then, and now a cold wind blew in through the north as winter settled in.

Our rent wasn't too high, and it was very convenient to be able to live and work on the same property. The servant's room we stayed in was plenty warm and quite clean. We were often given mutton to eat.

Our room had a large woodburning stove that had a chimney and could be used for cooking. The bed was stuffed with straw and smelled like the sun. The comforter was luxurious, made from wool, and was warm and snug.

The farmer's wife taught me how to take care of the sheep and how to spin and dye the wool. "You're a quick learner, and you work hard," she said, praising me.

"Thank you," I said. "I like work that uses my hands."

Nonna helped me during the day by giving the sheep fresh water and cleaning out the barn. When she got tired, she played with the lambs. Every night, she would use yarn made from wool to knit a woolen version of bobbin lace. She strung together the many patterns she made to create doilies for the sofa and a bedcover.

"Do you think we could sell these, Mom?"

"You want to sell them?"

"Yes. I want to earn money."

"I can earn our money for us."

"But I want to sell them."

"Do you? I hope it sells for a high price, then."

Mina, the farmer's wife, was in her late fifties. She'd sensed we were going through a hard time and offered us a job and a place to live. Sometimes, she'd say, "It's a shame some men are violent to their wives." It seemed like she thought we were running away from my abusive husband. "Once spring comes, I'll show you how to shear the sheep."

"Thank you, Mina. But we're planning on moving again in the springtime. I'm sorry we have to leave so soon, after everything you've taught us."

"Oh? I'm sorry to hear that. It'll be lonesome around here."

I loved detailed work, so I bought some wool from Mina and spun it into yarn. I used plant juices to dye the yarn and knit sweaters. I hadn't knit since I was in the academy, when a roommate of mine taught me how. Even though that was over a decade ago, my fingers remembered.

"Mom, that pattern is so beautiful!"

"Thank you."

"That's all you ever say, Mom."

"I guess it is. Because I really mean it."

The sweater was dark blue with a white snowflake pattern around the collar and cuffs. I thought it was quite cute.

Before I knew it, I'd knit ten sweaters in three months.

The bedcover Nonna made was also finished. She'd used the wool to weave the bobbin lace, and although it had a lot of gaps air could pass through, it was strangely soft and warm when you wore it around your shoulders or on your lap.

"Shall we go to a big town to sell it? I'm sure your cover will fetch a high price," I said.

"Can we really do that?"

"Besides the wig, we can wear hats, and I'll cover my mouth with a scarf, so it'll be okay. I'm the only one you talk to every day. It's important for you to interact with other children once in a while."

And so I took Nonna to a large town about two hours away by carriage. We did lots of shopping, and then I searched for a shop that might take my sweaters. I entered a shop that stocked everyday items such as sweaters and bought Nonna several new outfits. After I paid the clerk, I said, "Do you sell hand-knit sweaters here?"

The woman nodded with a cheerful smile. "It depends on the sweater, I suppose. Do you have one with you?"

"Yes. Would you like to take a look?"

"Of course."

I laid out the ten sweaters on the counter, and the clerk bought them all at a good price.

"These will definitely sell. If you plan on knitting more, would you bring them here so I can put them up in the shop? And would you give me that bedcover for eight small silver coins?"

"Yes! I will!" Nonna exclaimed before I could answer.

"Hmm? Wait, did you weave this?"

"Yes, she made all the patterns," I said. "We pieced them together."

"You used bobbin lace, didn't you? That's impressive that you made such a large bedcover."

"I worked really hard!" Nonna's Randallish was just as good as her Ashburian.

All in all, we sold the ten sweaters for twenty-four small silvers and five large copper coins. I was surprised that Nonna was able to earn eight small silvers for her bedcover. It seemed Nonna had gained another card to play, which delighted me.

Afterward, the two of us went to a fancy-looking bakery. Nonna beamed as she told me what she wanted.

"I want a piece of cake with a ton of whipped cream!"

The two of us ate our cake, and she asked, "Where are we going next?"

I knew she was aware I felt guilty about having to move around so much. She was a clever girl. Sometimes, I wished she would complain.

Jeffrey was talking to the prime minister in his study.

"It seems Victoria was a top spy for Hagl. She defected, and that's why they sent the assassins after her."

"A top spy..."

"Yes. As far as His Majesty is concerned, Victoria was a citizen from Randall who was killed by Hagl for unknown reasons."

Why? Jeffrey asked the prime minister silently.

"If the people from Hagl find out Victoria is still alive, they'll just keep sending assassins to our kingdom. We don't want that kind of trouble. So we're telling Hagl in a roundabout way that we know they were sending assassins here, to give them a warning."

"......"

"I've spoken with the Third Order just to be sure, but they said if they need any information about Hagl, they have the four assassins, so they're not interested in the missing woman."

The prime minister pushed his glasses up the bridge of his nose.

"Officially, our kingdom doesn't know her true identity. A woman from Randall was killed by men from Hagl, and that's all."

After clearing his throat, the prime minister said to Jeffrey in a strangely dramatic tone of voice, "So? Did you know her true identity or not?"

"I had a vague idea. I'm sorry I didn't tell you about it."

"Must be my age, but I didn't quite hear you. What was that? You had no idea about her true identity?"

"No, I didn't have any proof, but I did have a vague idea."

The prime minister let out a deep sigh. "Just say you were unaware. There is such thing as being *too* honest sometimes, you know."

Despite that, Jeffrey would not retract his statement.

"Honestly. Very well, then. You must be punished. Await your sentence at home. And you're forbidden from ever speaking about the case of Victoria again."

"Yes, sir."

Jeffrey went to his office to gather his things, his head full of thoughts.

Victoria had disappeared right before the assassins showed up. She might not be aware that her location had been discovered by Hagl and the assassination squad was after her. She wouldn't have left Lady Yolana there in possible danger if so. She must still be in hiding, without knowing the official story was that she had died. He just couldn't make peace with that.

The next day, Jeffrey was relieved of his position as captain and was transferred to an entirely different role. He became the security administrator of the duchy where a large port city named Haydn was located. Haydn was the point that managed timber-export operations. The young members of the Second Order bid him farewell with sad faces.

"I want you all to keep working hard."

Some of them shed a tear when Jeffrey said that to them.

The reassignment meant disappearing from the public eye in the capital, so it could be seen as a demotion. But Jeffrey thought of it as a lenient punishment. There was nothing to be done about the reassignment, and in fact, perhaps he should've resigned on his own. After all, his initial intention had been to resign so he could live with Victoria. And now that Victoria was gone, those plans had changed.

At the Asher estate, Jeffrey bowed his head deeply to his older brother.

"I'm sorry for everything that happ—"

"Oh, don't worry about that. I just take care of miscellaneous chores at the castle anyway, so what happened with you won't affect me negatively. Don't worry about that and just do your best at your new job with a clear conscience. More importantly, are you all right? You've lost a little weight."

"I'm fine."

"I see. Well, the weather is temperate there. You should take the opportunity to relax a little."

"Thank you."

Edward watched his younger brother depart, feeling very thoughtful.

The official statement regarding this incident was: "A traveler from Randall was killed by a band of Haglian thieves within our borders. The thieves were dealt with by a noble's guard. It was extremely troublesome for our kingdom." It was good that they could protest and indicate that Hagl owed them for this one.

But since Victoria hasn't been found, there's no way to tell her about the details of the arrangement.

Edward didn't know what to do, but he convinced himself it would all work out and stopped thinking about it for now. He had a lot of things to do, after all.

One of the captured assassins was an informant. There was only one person among the Third Order besides himself who knew that information. The assassin was the one who had served as lookout and was seeking asylum in this kingdom. He needed to consider his fate and find the next informant.

Jeffrey rode his favorite horse to the office in the duchy where he would be employed.

"Welcome to our domain, Director. My name is Hamms, and I've been managing the territory so far. It's a pleasure to meet you."

Hamms was a man in his early fifties. He had short brown hair and a toned body. His smile was gentle, but he seemed like the type of man you didn't want to anger.

"The duke is waiting for you, Director."

"What?"

Haydn was a very important port, and the territory had been earmarked to be taken over one day by the second prince when he became a duke. However, Cedric was still a prince. *So who's the duke?* Jeffrey wondered.

"Hey, Jeffrey! My brother's really disappointed he lost you," he heard a cheerful voice say.

"Prince Cedric!"

A handsome, muscular man with blond hair and blue eyes slowly walked out of the administration office.

"I'm a prince no longer. I decided to finally get serious, so I'll be working on managing this territory from now on."

"Ah, I see…"

"That didn't sound very enthusiastic! Oh, I almost forgot; let me introduce you to my fiancée! Hey, Beatrice!"

Jeffrey squinted at the woman, thinking, *Is he engaged to a different woman who has the same name as his last fiancée?*

He remembered Beatrice being thin as a twig, but now her body was plump, and her cheeks glowed as she jogged toward them.

"Mr. Asher! It's been a long time."

"Aren't you surprised, Jeffrey? When she heard I was moving to the duchy, she said, 'I still don't have a fiancée, so make me your wife!' She's gotten so much stronger now; I almost didn't recognize her."

Hearing that, Beatrice beamed and continued, "He broke off our engagement because I was so weak and sickly. I was devastated and told myself, 'I'm going to get strong and healthy so I can show him!' I worked very hard so I could rival Cedric's future wife. But when I heard he wasn't engaged and had chosen to relinquish his title, I knew I just had to do something! So I decided to propose to *him*! Tee-hee!"

Cedric gazed at Beatrice with adoration.

"I knew it would be foolish of me to dismiss a woman with such determination!" He truly looked happy. "This territory sees a lot of people coming and going. Including the Cadiz summer festival, there are plenty of things to keep an eye on. Until now, Hamms has done a wonderful job managing things, but from now, I'll be working hard for the prosperity and peace of the domain."

"I will support you to the best of my abilities, Your Majesty."

Cedric and Hamms nodded as Jeffrey bowed to them.

Managing a territory with a high influx of foreigners won't be easy. We can't let down our guard, or illegal goods may start circulating. I'd like to begin getting acquainted with things starting today, under Hamms's guidance.

Jeffrey gazed at the young couple in love as he stood straighter, determined to focus on his job.

Sheep gave birth in the early spring. Sheep you wouldn't even know were pregnant at the beginning of winter would suddenly get big bellies as spring approached.

Nonna and I were busy making sure the mother sheep got plenty of exercise.

In the cold winter, the pregnant sheep wouldn't willingly come out of the barn. The lambs inside them got too big, the mama sheep's muscles grew weak, and that made birth more dangerous.

"Over here! Come over here!" Nonna stood at the far end of the farm and called to the sheep. I walked behind them with a large stick and slowly swung it to guide them away toward Nonna. Basically, I was the bad guy in this situation.

The mama sheep turned back and glared at me as they slowly walked.

"You can do it! Go on, get lots of walking in!"

Nonna jumped and somersaulted so much, I thought she was probably getting more exercise than the sheep.

We exercised the pregnant sheep for about an hour and then put them back into the barn. Nonna spread both of her arms and shooed the mama sheep, but they were thrilled to go back inside, so they didn't need much coaxing.

The farmer's wife came over and went to check each one. "This one looks like she'll give birth tonight," she said.

When a sheep was going to give birth, everyone from the farm waited in the barn. For difficult births, they would take turns to make sure the mama and the baby survived.

"Mom, I want to see the baby sheep being born."

"Hmm, there will be a lot of blood, though. Won't you get scared?"

"I don't think so."

"All right, we'll ask Mina. You have to promise you won't get in anyone's way."

"Okay!"

Mina gave us permission, so Nonna and I were put on watch duty after dinner.

The barn had a coal stove and a chimney, so it wasn't that cold inside. We set our chairs next to the stove. I knit by the light of the oil lamp, while Nonna read books.

I checked on the mama sheep every now and again as I knit. At one point, the mama began to get up and pace around.

"Nonna, I think she's about to have the baby sheep. Go on and get Mina."

"Okay."

Nonna put on her coat and ran out of the barn, then returned with Mina and her husband. After a long period of painful bleating, standing, and sitting, the sheep finally gave birth to a lamb. Mina wiped down the baby, which had fallen onto the straw, and her husband rubbed it with a dry cloth to massage it.

Nonna had watched the sheep's painful labor closely. Her eyes had widened, and I'd seen tension gather in her shoulders. Once the lamb finally bleated, it took more than half an hour to stand up, then Nonna clapped her little hands.

The baby lamb pressed its nose against its mama's belly, searching for milk. As soon as it found it, it began gulping it down.

The moment a new life comes into this world is very precious. I felt a little overwhelmed, and I silently said to the mama, "Thank you for your hard work. You did a wonderful job." Nonna watched the baby lamb suckle at its mother with sparkling eyes.

Now that the sheep family was safe and settled, we went back to our room.

"The mama sheep worked really hard, didn't she? But we should go to bed now. It's not long until morning," I said.

"I'm tired."

"Let's sleep together tonight."

"Okay!"

We got into the straw-stuffed bed and covered up with our woolen comforter.

"The baby sheep was so cute."

"It was bigger than I thought it would be."

"The mommy looked like she was in so much pain."

"Yeah, she did," I said.

Nonna fell silent then, and I thought she'd fallen asleep, but she was actually still awake. "I wonder if my mom who disappeared was in pain, too."

"When she gave birth to you? I'm sure she was. No birth is pain-free."

"Do you think she worked that hard to give birth to me?"

"Human labor can take even longer."

"Wow."

I wasn't sure what to say to her, so I decided to keep it simple. "Your mother worked very hard to bring you into this world, Nonna."

"Yeah."

"And you worked very hard to be born."

She didn't answer. This time, she really was asleep. I stroked her soft golden hair and pulled her tiny body next to mine. She was so warm.

"Thank you for being born, Nonna. I'm so very glad I met you," I whispered.

I still didn't think very highly of Nonna's mother, who'd abandoned her. I didn't even know what the woman looked like, but for the first time, I thought, *Thank you for giving birth to Nonna.*

The sheep looked so happy as they ate the soft spring grass. *One day, I want to have sheep of my own*, I thought dreamily.

I would settle in one place and raise sheep, shear them, spin their wool into yarn, dye it, and knit things to sell. Would I ever be able to have a life like that?

At the end of the spring, Nonna and I learned how to shear the sheep. We used huge shears to carefully cut off their wool without injuring their skin. They looked so much smaller without their wool. Once they were sheared, we put on the cloth vests Mina had made for them so they wouldn't get too cold. After we'd helped with that much, we bid farewell to the farm after living there for several months.

"Good-bye! Good-bye!" Nonna smiled broadly as she waved to Mina. I waved, too, bowing my head and thanking her repeatedly.

This time, we moved to the southern edge of Randall, to a fishing village close to Ashbury. I was currently working at a restaurant and inn in the lively town. It was a large workplace with many employees, and it was my job to clean the place, but I helped out in any way that I could when there was a shortage of staff.

"Having someone as energetic as you is such a big help."

"Thank you, ma'am. And thank you for giving us a room to stay in as well."

"Of course. By the way, Maria. About that sweater you gave me before. If I pay you, would you knit one for my husband, too?"

"Yes, I'd love to."

"It's so fashionable, and you sell them for cheaper than you can buy at the shops. I might ask for another one as well."

"So you want two sweaters? I'll knit them up as soon as I can."

"Oh, there's no rush! I'd just like to be able to wear it this winter."

"Do you have any preference regarding the pattern?"

"I'll leave that to you."

I was glad to have the opportunity to earn a little more money. Come to think of it, the Andersons, Mr. Bernard, and Lady Yolana had been very generous with their payments. At the moment, it was all I could do to make enough for us to eat. One day, I'd like to thank them and apologize to them. But for right now, I had to keep working hard to survive.

Up until now, Nonna hadn't cared for fish, but after we moved to Alde, she told me that the fish here were yummy and happily ate it. That was a good thing.

Nonna and I were cleaning the outside of the restaurant one day when the woman who ran the bakery next door called out to us. "Maria, are you two going to the summer festival in Cadiz?"

"What? Cadiz? That's in another kingdom, isn't it?"

"Yes, but only on that day, boats set off from here to Cadiz. A ton of people go to the festival, and there are so many shops and fun things to do. And thanks to the temporary ferry service, we can get to Ashbury easily without having to pass through a border checkpoint. You do have to show identification papers when you board and when you arrive, though."

"I see."

"I wanna go! Mom, please! I want to go see the festival!"

"Hmm...," I answered vaguely, so Nonna didn't press me any further on the matter in front of the woman.

I tried to avoid discussing future plans when talking to others. However, this was the summer festival the captain and I had planned to visit together.

But I'd disappeared on him without a word. It would be too selfish of me to wonder if he remembered our promise. After all, he'd been exhausted from trying to find that escaped prisoner I'd helped go free at the time. He probably didn't even remember it.

I thought that was the end of the conversation, but that night, once we were alone and in bed, Nonna asked me again.

"Mom, I really want to go to the festival."

"Okay. Let's go, then."

"Are you sure? You won't be mad?"

"Of course not. It'll be my first time at a festival."

"Really? Even though you're a grown-up?"

"Yes. Now let's get to bed. We have to wake up early tomorrow."

"Okay."

That night, I had a hard time sleeping.

There were three weeks until the summer festival. It lasted from afternoon until nighttime, and if there were as many people as she said, surely, no one would notice us if we wore our wigs.

I didn't want anyone to discover us, but at the same time, I prayed, *Please remember the promise we made that day and come find us*, even though we wouldn't be able to return to our old life if we reunited with the captain now.

Since when had I become someone who thought about such unreasonable things?

I'm probably just tired. I've been working so much, my brain won't function right, I thought and closed my eyes.

When I was in the organization, I'd been given orders, worked, and been praised, and I'd been content with that life.

But now that I was free, it was a very lonely and difficult life. Ever since we left the capital of Ashbury, there was a part of me inside that kept saying, *I'm lonely, I'm lonely!* over and over again like a petulant child.

I wonder if this feeling would go away if I went back to the Special Operations Force.

But I'd never heard of anyone defecting from the organization, and more importantly, I'd never heard of anyone returning. Yet lately, I'd been having foolish thoughts like *Maybe I can just go back and accept whatever punishment they have. I'll even be a janitor at this point.* If

I didn't have Nonna with me, I probably would have ended up wandering back to Hagl with my tail between my legs. I knew now that my life then hadn't been a happy one. But I'd thought several times it might be easier than being this sad and lonely all the time.

I must never let Nonna get near that place.

My brain hadn't been thinking too clearly lately, but at least I knew that much.

Nonna was what kept me going.

"Mom, wake up. Mom!"

"Hmm? Mm? Did I oversleep? I'm sorry, I'll get breakfast ready right away."

"What's the matter?"

"Huh?

"Your eyes are red."

I rushed over to the cloudy old mirror that stood in the corner of the room and saw my eyes were puffy and red from crying and lack of sleep.

"I couldn't sleep much last night."

"Huh."

I quickly whipped up some fried eggs and warmed up some leftover vegetable soup from the night before. I sliced up some day-old bread, and Nonna warmed it on the stove for me, saying, "Hot! Hot!"

"Now, let's have a good day at work today!"

"Yeah!"

I gave Nonna a kiss on her soft cheek, which faintly smelled of sweet milk, and then we headed to the restaurant to clean the inn.

We worked during the day, and at night, I knit. I stayed up late until I fell into bed from exhaustion, slept, and then woke up to do it all over again. Time flew by, and before I knew it, it was the day of the summer festival in Cadiz.

My shift at the restaurant ended early today.

"No one's going to show up even if we keep the place open," the manager said. "Everyone's boarding the ferry to go to Cadiz. If you two don't hurry up and go, you won't be able to get a good seat to see the pretty views."

"You're right."

Nonna listened to the woman with a serious face.

"A few hundred—no, maybe a few thousand?—little boats will be lit up with candles and float down into the sea. You have to see it at least one time in your life. It's just beautiful. I'm sure you'll be getting back late, so you can have the day off tomorrow. You haven't had one day off since you got here, Maria."

"Thank you, I'll take you up on that offer."

That evening, the two of us wore our black wigs and boarded the fishing boat. The summer sun hadn't set yet, and it was still light outside. I paid our fare, and we got on the boat. The local fishermen wanted to make money, so they pulled their boats up to the pier, picked up people from Randall, and then left. The boat was small, with four people rowing and eight passengers.

Everyone was excited, but I was nervous.

Will the captain come? Will he remember that promise we made?

No. I disappeared without telling him. I shouldn't have unreasonable expectations. I shook my head, trying to push those thoughts out of it. I wanted to focus on Nonna enjoying herself tonight. I turned to her with a smile.

"Are you looking forward to the festival?"

"Yes! Are you, Mom?"

"Yes, very much so."

It took less time to get to the Cadiz port than I'd anticipated. Several large boats passed us on the way, and we could already see the lights from countless candles swaying in the distance.

The rowers paddled our little boat to shore. Finally, we reached the port, and Nonna and I disembarked in Cadiz, Ashbury.

The port in Cadiz was a rocky place, and there were countless people here already. Everyone was holding a small boat. They would light a tiny candle, then send off their boat. Some smiled as they sent them off; some cried. Some prayed with their eyes closed.

But everyone seemed to be having a conversation with the souls of their departed loved ones, who only visited here when the candles were burning.

The area beyond the port was sandy and grassy. There were rows of plain stalls selling grilled meat, fruit, sweet baked goods, fruit water, accessories, and simple toys. All sorts of things were for sale.

Nonna was so excited about browsing the stalls that she would've gotten lost in the crowd if I wasn't holding her hand.

I found myself feeling strangely relieved, thinking, *Yes, there's no way anyone would spot us in this crowd*, but at the same time, I thought, *What's the point in consoling myself with that?*

The small space was packed with people. After much deliberation, Nonna chose a fried, round kind of bread sprinkled with plenty of beet sugar.

"Mom, this is so sweet and yummy!" she said, holding it out toward me.

I took a little bite. "Mm, it is!"

Nonna smiled happily. Lately, she'd lost her two front teeth, which made her look a little silly when she smiled, but it was proof that she was growing up. Plus, her toothless smile was pretty cute.

"Look!" Nonna pointed, and I saw that a large group of people were sending their boats off to sea now, probably because the low tide was about to reach its peak.

"Wow…"

Nonna gazed out at the sea with beet sugar stuck to her mouth. There were probably close to a thousand candles in the little boats bobbing on the waves, heading out to sea.

"Let's send a boat out, Nonna."

"Can we?"

"Sure."

We bought two of the tiny wooden boats and had them light the candles for us. We shielded the candles with our hands so they wouldn't go out, and then we made our way to the rocky shore.

"Watch your step. You'll get hurt if you fall here."

"Okay!"

The waves lapped at our shoes as we stood with the other people. We set the tiny boats in the water and then watched as they drifted out to the sea.

I spoke silently to my boat as it moved.

Dad, Mom, Emily. I miss you. I miss you so much. I've been working so hard for so long, but I'm a little tired now.

I felt a hot lump deep in my throat, and then tears started streaming down my face. Even though there were so many people around, I knelt by the shore and wept as I watched my boat leave.

"Sniff... Waaah..."

A surprising number of people were crying.

Nonna gently patted my back with her tiny hand.

"I'm sorry, Nonna. I'll stop crying now."

"You don't have to. It's okay for you to cry, too, Mom."

I wiped my face and took several deep breaths. "Well, shall we buy some souvenirs and then go home?" I said with a smile, but then I noticed Nonna was staring at something over my shoulder with a stunned look on her face.

I whirled around and saw the captain standing there.

"Jeff!" Nonna ran over and threw her arms around him. "Jeff! Jeff!" She clung to him, and he lifted her up in his left arm, then slipped his right arm around my shoulders to help me up.

"I told myself I would come here every year until I found you, but I certainly didn't expect it to happen the first time!" His voice was music to my ears, as usual.

I knew I should say something—that I should apologize, but all I could do was weep like a child.

The captain turned to a large man nearby and said, "Excuse me, but I need to go home for the day."

"Of course. Thank you for your hard work. It was so much easier with you helping out this year, Director. Good night." The man saw us off with a tender look on his face.

The captain took us to a small house.

"This is my house."

"This is your house, Captain?"

"I'm not a captain anymore. I'm the security director for this duchy," he said and invited us to have a seat on the sofa. A middle-aged housekeeper smiled at us, and he told her, "I can take it from here. You may go home for the day."

Nonna sat on the couch, nodding off. She'd had so much excitement today; she must've tired herself out. I took off her wig, and the captain easily picked her up, then placed her on the nearby chaise, putting a thin summer blanket over her.

He sat down right next to me and then pulled me against his broad chest, holding me tightly in his embrace.

"I'm so glad you're safe. I was worried sick something had happened to you."

"I'm so sorry…"

"You don't need to apologize. I don't want you to. I don't even know where to start. There are so many things I need to tell you."

He held me in his arms as he explained. He told me how the assassination squad from Hagl had come, and that the official story was that I'd died in the attack. All the elite members of the Ashbury government knew my true identity. Lady Yolana and the others were completely safe.

"Once I heard you were their top spy, it all made sense to me."

I couldn't even look him in the face.

"But you don't have to run anymore. Victoria Sellars is dead. You can live a peaceful life from now on. And if you're worried about bumping into anyone you know, you can live here in Cadiz. Many foreigners come and go through the port, but no one will come looking for you here. This is a farming and fishing town. Only locals are here except during the summer festival. Live here with me. I head to work from my house here."

I decided to ask him something that'd been bothering me.

"Captain..."

"Please call me Jeff."

"Jeff, why did you quit the knights and come here? It's my fault, isn't it?"

"No, it's not your fault. To be honest, I'd had a vague idea that you'd left the organization, so it'd been my plan all along to leave the knights so I could be with you. But then you disappeared, so I came here to work. I would've quit whether you left or not."

I wasn't sure about that. *If he'd never met me...* My thoughts went that far, and then I realized something. *Oh no! The boat!*

"Wait! We're going to miss the boat home!"

"I can send a message to anywhere you'd like to contact," the captain said. I mean, Jeff. He wouldn't let me go. "I don't want to have any more regrets. After I read that letter, I was angry at myself for not telling you sooner. If you're worried staying here in Cadiz, we can live up in the mountains somewhere. I can hunt for our food."

"......"

"Victoria, where have you been, and what have you been doing this whole time? Were you in danger?"

"Jeff, before I tell you that, I need to say something else first." I sat up straighter and looked him right in the eyes. My body was trembling with anxiety in preparation of what I was about to say.

"I entered the academy at age eight and was forced to give up my real name. Instead, they assigned me the name Chloe, which I used during my entire time at the organization. Although no one has called me it even once in twenty years, my real name is Anna. Anna Dale. That name is precious to me, because my mother and father gave it to me."

Then I told him all about what happened. I told him how we lived on a farm in Randall and then moved to the fishing village.

Jeffrey quietly listened the whole time, occasionally rubbing my back or caressing my hair gently.

Once I was done, he let out a sigh. Something seemed to be weighing on him.

"What's wrong? Is there a problem with what I've said?" I asked.

"No. Actually, I have a secret, too. I figure I should tell you it because I intend to live with you forever."

That made me very curious, since he'd already told me about his late fiancée.

"It's not about my fiancée. It's a secret my brother and I share. The reason he's always worried about me is because of our unique upbringing."

"It's okay. I don't have to know your entire past."

"No, one day, you're going to wonder why he worries about me so much."

Then Jeff divulged his secret to me. Afterward, each time I thought about it, it pained my heart so much, I thought it might rip in two.

"For as long as I can remember, our father lived separately with another family. It's not unusual for aristocrats to have mistresses on the side. But once my father's mistress bore him a child, he started abusing us. He would punch me over and over, even though I was very young."

Jeff's mother suffered from a mental breakdown very early on and had been in a state of drifting between reality and hallucination.

His father would come once or twice a week to abuse them for the pettiest of reasons. It was different each time. They never knew why they would get hit. At times, Edward would take the beating instead of his mother or Jeff to try to protect them.

"I think my brother chose the path of a civil servant because of the terrible scars left by the whip. The wounds are all over his back.

Knights change into uniform together after training, so there was no way for my brother to hide his scars. And we couldn't escape because of our mother, who was having mental problems. My brother was just a lowly civil servant then, and our mother was in terrible shape, so he didn't think he could take us away somewhere."

I recalled something I'd learned in the organization. Eventually, someone who had been beaten continuously became unable to fight back or flee. The violence dominated them both mentally and physically. Perhaps that had been the case for his brother and his mother.

Edward immersed himself in his studies to escape from his harsh reality, while Jeffrey focused on his swordsmanship. After many years passed, young Jeffrey thought, *Maybe I'm strong enough to defeat my father now.*

One day, his father was about to strip Edward's shirt and whip him as usual, but Jeffrey charged at him.

"The determination someone has when fighting for their life is different from just suffering. I was bigger than him by then. I quickly knocked down my father, grabbed a nearby candlestick, and told my shocked brother, 'I'm the second son. I'll do it. Then you can remove me from the family registry. Thank you for everything you've done for me.'"

"Oh, Jeff…"

He continued talking with a distant look in his eyes.

"When I was young, all the resentment I felt when he beat me—all the times I was terrified thinking, *He might kill me this time*—just exploded. I was deadly serious. But my brother stopped me and calmly told our father, 'As of today, I will assume the position of head of the Asher family. I will provide you and your family with enough to live on without disgrace. It's your decision. Will you hand over the position of head of house to me, or will you let us kill you? Do you think we've endured all these beatings without a plan? I've already secured a doctor who will verify that your cause of death was a heart attack, no matter what the condition of your body is.'"

At the time, Edward was twenty, and Jeffrey was twelve.

"After our father left, I cried to my brother and said, 'Because I didn't have enough resolve, I put you and Mother in the worst position. I should've done this earlier. Please forgive me for being such a coward!' Ever since then, my brother's been my guardian and protected me and my mother. It's become such a force of habit that he can't stop himself now, which can be a bit troublesome, but the two of us lived protecting each other. Our father abused us so severely, he really could've killed us."

I wrapped my arms around Jeffrey and hugged him tightly. He was so large that I could barely get my arms around him, but I hugged him with all my might.

"I don't know why my father didn't just get divorced until I started working at the castle. Apparently, the prime minister was the matchmaker between my parents, so my father was hesitant to divorce in fear of offending him. It was a completely ridiculous reason. He used us to vent his anger."

Jeffrey gave me a pained smile and then said, "My father died two years ago."

"……"

Even though it was only for eight years, I'd been raised in a warm and loving environment. But Jeffrey didn't even have that.

Just as I thought when I was in the organization, all happy families had the same things in common. It didn't matter if they were rich or poor; all happy families were loving environments.

But Lord Edward and Jeffrey had lived through hell.

"Jeff, I'm going to protect you and Nonna with my life. Let's make a happy family together."

Jeffrey smiled tenderly at me and said, "That's usually something the man says. At least let me show off a little."

Then he got down on knee in front of me. "Anna. Please marry me."

It was a simple yet poignant proposal.

Chapter Fourteen

Setting Sail

Edward Asher was reading an urgent letter sent by Hamms from the duchy. It had been a few months since he'd told Hamms to let him know if he ever saw his younger brother with a woman.

"I see. So he finally found her. First, we need to make sure she'll be safe."

His Majesty and the crown prince probably wanted to keep Jeffrey on as an aid to Lord Cedric, but both as the administrative director and his brother, he didn't want to keep Victoria and Jeff near Haydn yet. He wanted to eliminate any chances of another incident occurring.

I think that's the best place for them, he thought as he left the room and headed to the medical office in the west wing.

"Hey there, Director. What's going on?"

A short man with dark eyes and black hair greeted him. He was the son of an Ashburian woman and a merchant from a far-off land. He'd grown up in his father's country, but just before he turned thirty, he'd decided he wanted to see the world, so he took his knowledge of medicine and came to Ashbury. Thanks to him, Ashbury was able to procure important medicines other kingdoms could not.

"There's a favor I'd like to ask you," Edward said.

"Sure. What's the reward?"

"Please don't be so uncouth. I thought we were friends? But hmm...

I'll negotiate with the prime minister to give you permission to use that medicine you've been asking about."

The man's eyes widened, and his mouth curved up into a smile.

"The anesthetic used in surgery? It's ridiculously expensive, though!"

"Leave it to me. In exchange, I'd like you to help my younger brother and his wife find a place to live for around five years in your country. Oh, and they have a child. I'll pay their living expenses, of course."

That's all? the doctor thought. "My family estate is a big mansion. There's a guest cottage there, large enough for the three of them. And there are tons of servants."

"Wonderful. It's decided, then. Will you write a letter to your father? A ship from your country will be in port next month, won't it? I want you take them on that ship."

"Make sure to keep your promise to me, in that case."

"Have I ever broken a promise to you? If there are any other drugs you want besides the anesthetics, make a list. I'll negotiate to get approval for them as much as I possibly can."

It was true the director had never broken a promise, and for some reason, both His Majesty and the prime minister readily agreed to his requests. The doctor quickly jotted off a note to his father, then listed a number of medicines he wanted on a piece of paper.

Edward Asher returned to his dimly lit office with a letter to the captain of a foreign vessel in his pocket.

I returned to the restaurant and told the owner I was going to quit. "I'm sorry that this is so sudden. Here's the sweaters I promised you. I don't need any money. Please take them."

"Thank you. Did something good happen there? You look so much more cheerful now. It's a shame you have to quit, but the most important thing is for you to be happy. Here's a farewell gift for you," the woman said and gave me a little more money than the price of the sweaters. "The gods are kind to those who are faithful workers. I wish you all the best."

"Thank you for everything you've done for us."

Nonna was gathering seashells along the shore.

"Mom! Look at this pretty shell I found!"

"Sorry I took so long. Wow, it really is pretty! You'll have to treasure it."

Nonna and I began living with Jeffrey in Cadiz. It seemed like Jeff hadn't told his brother or Lord Cedric, who was now the duke of this domain.

"If Lord Cedric says something about you and word gets back to the castle, it'll be troublesome. We can just focus on raising sheep like you wanted to," Jeff said, but I doubted things would go that smoothly. I had a feeling Jeffrey had been sent here to Lord Cedric's domain because of his abilities and personality. If they found out I was involved with him again...

But all that was out of my control. I thought and thought but couldn't come up with a solution.

Ten days later, a man visited our small house. He came with an urgent message from the castle and told Jeff his name was Mike. Nonna and I eavesdropped from the kitchen.

Once Jeff heard Mike's message, his voice became tense. "But I just got here eight months ago on orders from the prime minister!"

"The prime minister agreed with my boss's suggestion. You know how wonderful Shen's medicine is, don't you? Our kingdom only buys what comes over on the ships, and it's hard to get everything we need."

I wondered if that foreign medication for burns that Lady Eva had told me about that time was from Shen. And I wondered who Mike's boss was.

"But why me? There are a ton of people who are better suited for that kind of civil service."

"Hmm, fine. I'll just be frank. This is for your own good, Lord Asher, and for the good of Victoria."

My breath caught in my throat as Nonna and I listened from the kitchen.

"We can't be sure nothing will happen if you two stay here. My boss thinks it would be safer if Victoria completely disappears until things have cooled off."

Jeffrey's voice dropped. "I'm being watched, aren't I?"

"Only to ensure your safety. If you want to live together with Victoria, the best and safest way to do that right now is to go to Shen. Head there and negotiate to establish a system for shipping and securing medicines. That will make the kingdom of Ashbury, Victoria, you, and everyone else happy. Don't you agree?" Mike raised his voice a little as if directing his last sentence toward the kitchen.

I said, "Excuse me," and went into the living room.

"Victoria," said Mike. "I'm sorry this is so sudden. The boat to Shen will arrive soon, and I want to make sure you have enough time to prepare, because the next boat won't come for another whole year. The official records in Ashbury state that Victoria Sellars has died. If, by some chance, anyone from Hagl finds you here in the duchy, you'll be in trouble again."

"I understand."

"That's why we want you to go to Shen and for Lord Asher to arrange a system for exporting medicine."

"What do you think, Anna?" Jeffrey asked.

"I think it sounds wonderful. Mike, we can take Nonna along with us, can't we?"

"Of course. The travel and living expenses abroad for the three of you will be fully paid by the government."

"For all three of us?"

"Yes. The Asher household said they would cover all living expenses associated with Lord Jeffrey, but when the minister of the interior heard that, he was concerned and said, 'We can't have the Asher family be the only one privy to such valuable knowledge and connections to Shen!'"

Jeffrey wasn't thrilled that he was being watched, but he agreed reluctantly, saying, "As long as it's all right with Anna." Mike smiled and took out a bunch of documents from his bag.

"Victoria—or rather, Anna. Here are your new identification papers, here is your marriage license, and here are the documents for the child. It's necessary for you to adopt her before you leave the country. Victoria, I didn't know your real name, so I left that column blank. Please fill that out yourself. You'll do it, right? I don't have time to go back to the capital now, so please make sure you fill it out."

They really know everything about me, I thought. The names were supposed to be printed, but he was basically saying, "I know you can fake it yourself, so go ahead."

"Yes, I understand. Should I write my name as *Anna Dale*?"

"No, you're heading there as part of Lord Asher's family, so please write *Anna Asher*. A ship going to Shen will be arriving at the port in around two or three weeks. Please make sure to board that ship. You'll come back to Ashbury in five years. I'll pick up all the documents at ten o'clock tomorrow morning," Mike said, then went home.

"Are you sure about this, Anna?"

"This is a wonderful opportunity. We get to go to a country we'd never have the chance to otherwise, and now you and Nonna won't be in danger because of me. Don't you think that's great?"

I looked up at Jeff, and he started laughing.

"When I saw you there on the shore the other day, you looked utterly depressed. I was so worried because you seemed physically and emotionally exhausted, but now I think you'll be perfectly fine."

"Actually, I was just so sad and lonely every day, I even started thinking maybe I should go back to Hagl and join the organization again. But I know I can't let Nonna anywhere near them. That's the only thing that stopped me."

Jeff let out a deep sigh.

"I'm so glad you didn't go. They're really intent on assassinating you."

"I think I was just in a bad place mentally. If I'd simply thought about it more carefully, that would've been obvious."

"Nonna saved your life."

"That's right."

Nonna crept into the living room from the kitchen. Jeff walked over to her and whisked her up into the air, tossing her up high. Nonna pretended she wasn't impressed, but after a while, she couldn't take it anymore and started laughing wildly.

"Nonna, what do you think about being my daughter?"

"You'd be my dad, Jeff?"

"That's right. Anna will be my wife, and you'll be my daughter."

"Sure!" Nonna answered immediately.

I carefully read the documents Mike gave us. According to this, it said I was a commoner born and raised in Cadiz, was adopted by a baron, then married Jeff. I wondered how many people knew that Anna was Victoria. I'd have to ask Mike the next day.

That night, I stayed up putting mine and Nonna's names on the official documents. Jeff was so curious that he kept peeking over my shoulder, but it was distracting so I shooed him away.

It took a lot of concentration to produce writing that looked exactly like it was printed.

The next day, Mike came to collect the documents. Jeffrey was at work.

Mike had no characteristics that stood out too much, just like me. That meant it was easy for him to blend into a crowd; he had the type of face and body type one would forget easily. And his movements were skilled and effortless.

"Since Lord Asher was here yesterday, we couldn't talk in depth.

But you used to be Hagl's top agent, didn't you?" Mike asked, brimming with curiosity. "I have a lot of questions for you."

He wanted to know why I defected, and how I did it.

Since he was part of the group of people working to ensure my family's safety, I decided to be honest with him in order to show him my gratitude.

"I see, I see," Mike said, nodding. "Anna, were you the one who helped that prisoner who was about to be executed escape? My boss keeps saying it was you. Of course, I won't share your answer with anyone else but him."

"Yes, that was me," I said firmly.

Mike said, "Hmm," and then muttered, "She's really impressive..." Then he asked why I did it and how. I gave him an honest answer, but I kept the details about the man's sister and where I'd helped them escape to a secret.

"I gave the man enough money for living expenses right outside the castle, so I don't know what happened to him afterward."

"I see. You smuggled in a wire saw in the heel of your shoe, huh? Hmm, a wire saw...," he muttered, then asked me more questions.

"Were you the one who knocked the man unconscious at the soiree?"

"Yes."

"Why?"

I answered him honestly.

"You wanted to prevent a murder! So there are spies who think like that? Ah, pardon me." Mike apologized when he realized he'd muttered that out loud, then turned to look at me.

"That's all the questions I have for you. Thank you for your cooperation. If you're curious about the medicines, it's possible for you to learn all about them along with Lord Asher in Shen."

"Yes, I'd love to find out more!"

"I knew you would. I'm looking forward to your activities in Shen."

"Um, do you mean you want me to steal information for you? Because if so, I'm done with that…"

Mike laughed out loud.

"No, I just want you to learn. Interact with the people of Shen and absorb everything you can while you're there. Oh, that's right; I forgot to tell you something very important. Once you return in five years, you can reunite with all your acquaintances again. When Lord Asher comes back, he will be a baron. Not even Hagl's stupid enough to try to kill the wife of an Ashburian noble. It's not worth it."

When I asked Mike why he would go to such lengths to help an ex-spy, he replied, "If I told you that, I'd lose my job. That's all I can say," and refused to elaborate.

The paperwork for my marriage with Jeffrey was complete. I had a new history, new identification papers, and a new name. We also received a letter from the prime minister to give to the captain, as well as to the family who would host us upon our arrival.

"Mike, I once went to a soiree at the castle and said I was from Randall." That had been bothering me for a while now.

"Please forgive me for saying this, but you're the kind of person who doesn't leave a lasting impression. Even if you've only met someone once, if you just insist, 'I think you must have mistaken me for someone else?' it'll work. The only ones who know that Anna is Victoria are me and my boss. His Majesty, the prime minister, and the crown prince only caught a glimpse of you from a distance at the party."

It seemed like Mike's boss would keep my true identity a secret from His Majesty and the prime minister, but why?

I was about to say, "Lord Cedric knows about me, too," but then I stopped when I realized this would implicate me in breaking his ribs.

"Despite appearances, Jeffrey's good at paperwork. I'm looking forward to your return. Best of luck. Oh, and one more thing, Anna."

"Yes?"

"Congratulations."

I didn't know whether he meant congratulations for defecting or for getting married. Either way, I smiled and bowed my head.

The day before our departure, Jeffrey quit his post as security manager, which he hadn't even held for a full year, and returned home. He said Lord Cedric had been depressed and sad the whole time.

The time for departure had arrived. The boat slowly changed direction to head back out to sea.

"Mom! Look!"

"Hmm?"

Nonna ran toward me across the deck, her golden hair streaming behind her. On the way, she leaped into the air in a beautiful front somersault and made a clean landing.

"Ha-ha. Very good!" I clapped, and then Jeffrey walked up from behind Nonna.

The little girl I'd met on my first day in Ashbury was now my legally adopted daughter, and my guarantor was now my husband.

Ever since we got married, Jeffrey was still a worrier and always wanted to be by my side. He protected me and spoiled me constantly.

"Mom!" Nonna hugged me tightly.

"You look like you're having so much fun, Nonna."

"I'm so excited to go to Shen and to ride on a boat!"

The captain of the boat came up on the deck and spoke to us. His Ashburian was very good. "Mrs. Asher, would you like to see a menu?"

"We'll eat whatever you're having. Please order us the same."

"The traditional food of Shen is very delicious. I hope you'll enjoy it."

"Thank you!"

The ship would sail along the coastline, replenishing food and water along the journey. It would take us more than two months to arrive in Shen.

I hoped there were books on board so I could start studying Shenese. Learning a new language was always exciting.

"Anna, the wind is getting chilly."

"Oh, Jeff. It's still summer. Plus, it feels nice."

"Right. Well, don't stay out in the sun too much, or you might get burnt."

"You're such a worrywart, Daddy!" Ever since Jeff asked Nonna if she wanted him to be her father, she'd been affectionally calling him "Daddy."

She told me, "Jeffrey becoming my daddy made me just as happy as the day you bought me the blue ribbon." Even when we told her she'd be living in a foreign country for five years, she didn't seem to mind.

"I'll be fine as long as I have you, Mom. And I'll be even better now that I have you, Daddy!" she said with a smile.

She seemed so carefree about it that I worried whether it was the truth or not.

"Once we get home, I'll teach Master Clark Shenese!"

"I'm sure he'll want to learn it."

The journey was going smoothly. There were no signs of a storm.

"Jeff, I'm really free, aren't I?"

"Yes, you are."

He hugged me tightly from behind as the two of us quietly gazed out at the sea together.

Nonna suddenly wriggled her way in between us and hugged me, then the three of us laughed.

About ten days had passed since the start of our journey.

Nonna and I were on the deck, watching the sun sink into the sea. She gazed at the ocean and said, "A long time ago, I sat by myself in the plaza. To be honest, I knew that I had been abandoned. That day, you stayed in the plaza with me until the sun set."

She turned to look at me. "I never told you thank you for that. Back then, I didn't know a lot of words. You were on the run, but you saved me, Mom. Thank you for making me the yummy roast lamb. Thank you for buying me that blue ribbon. And thank you for becoming my mother."

I cradled Nonna's head against my chest. All I could say was "You're welcome, you're welcome."

Only a sliver of the orange sun was visible above the horizon. Nighttime was about to begin.

If it weren't for Nonna, I wouldn't be alive today. I wouldn't have known about the assassins, and I would've returned to Hagl and been killed; I'm sure of it.

"Hey, there you two are. Let's get inside. It's time for dinner."

"Okay."

"Yes, Daddy!"

I vowed to cherish my family, build meaningful, lasting relationships with others, be a helpful person...and there were so many other things. I wanted to make up for all the time I'd lost before and live a fulfilling life.

I headed into the ship hand in hand with Nonna, with Jeff following protectively from behind.

I was prepared to protect my family, no matter what happened in the future.

I wasn't worried. Because I had many cards to play.